God help us all

Red. Dark—almost black—red.

There was nothing left of Donald's brother but the blood. The smell clung to the air, the smell of his nightmare, that sharp, coppery smell that would stay with him forever.

Donald pressed his palm to the sticky, damp sheet, pressed it until the mattress gave slightly beneath it. His eyes closed and his head tilted back, way back, his mouth opening, a low groan flowing from it. His knees buckled, clumped to the floor. He leaned his forehead against the edge of the bed.

"Nuh-no," he grunted, his eyes, hiding behind locked lids, *seeing . . . seeing . . .* "No, no. God . . . help . . . me."

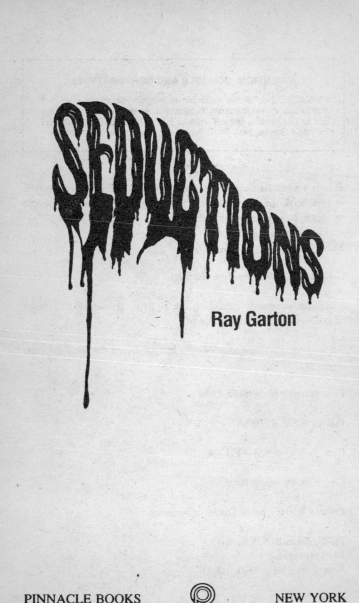

SEDUCTIONS

Ray Garton

PINNACLE BOOKS NEW YORK

SEDUCTIONS

Copyright © 1984 by Ray Garton

An original Pinnacle Books edition, published for the first time anywhere.

First printing/November 1984

ISBN: 0-523-42309-8

Can. ISBN: 0-523-43317-4

Cover art by Steve Kropp

Printed in the United States of America

PINNACLE BOOKS, INC.
1430 Broadway
New York, New York 10018

9 8 7 6 5 4 3 2 1

This book is dedicated to

Scott Sandin,
the best friend and sounding board
anyone could ever hope to find.

I would like to express my appreciation to the following people for the invaluable help they gave in writing this novel: Lynda Longhofer, for her technical assistance; Barbara Youngblood, for the information; Ron and Carolee Bingham, for their inspiration; my agent, Ashley Grayson, for *everything*; my loving parents, Ray and Pat Garton, for their encouragement and understanding.

SEDUCTIONS

Prologue

The nightmare always began like no other he'd had before: with total darkness. Then there was a feeling of rapid movement, smooth sailing through nothingness, of total freedom, touching nothing, feeling nothing, not even air, not even his own body, just the blind movement at a speed he could not even begin to fathom.

There was a tiny spot of light far ahead of him that quickly began to grow and grow until suddenly, without warning, without sound, he was surrounded by clouds, dark and puffy. He eased out of them, downward, and there appeared beneath him houses and cars and people sliding away as he silently glided over them. The street below was familiar. The houses were familiar and so were the cars parked in front of them, and the people were familiar, too. They were all hurrying toward something, all of them going in the same direction. There was a mother carrying a child, a man quickly putting on his coat, two childern together, advancing toward whatever lay ahead. There were old people and young people, vaguely familiar, yet strangers, all hurrying forward.

Then he looked ahead to see where they were going. He saw something red, far in the distance. As he neared it, he saw that it was nearing him as well, flowing rapidly on the ground like a flash flood pouring down a hill. It spilled down the center of the street, branching off and sloshing against the curb, running over the sidewalk, washing over the feet of the hurried pedestrians, into the yards, up the front walks, climbing the porch steps like a film running backward, seeping under the doors and into the houses. Its smell rose into the atmosphere and he picked it up easily. Harsh, a coppery smell that seemed to stick to the air and make it moist and pungent. The tide swept the people off their feet, knocking them down; they struggled in the strengthening current, but to no avail. It continued up the front steps of houses, over children's toys on porches and in yards, picking them up and tossing them over its undulating surface like the wind tossing autumn leaves. It made no sound as it filled the houses and began to gush out of the windows, breaking through the panes of those that were closed securely. And as he floated forward, he knew he would soon see whatever it was that had drawn the others. He wasn't sure he wanted to.

Then he began to rise, to gain altitude, to leave the ugly picture and fade into the darkness above him.

It was very cold and empty, very big, hollow. There were sounds now: voices, whispers, breathing. He was not alone, but he was blind and couldn't see the others. He could feel them, though, could feel their presence, could almost feel their shape. And he did not like it. In the soft, resonant, breathy sound, he began to make out isolated words:

". . . fuck . . ."

". . . want you . . ."

". . . us . . ."

He tried to control his speed, his direction, tried to go back, but he could not.

"do it let's do it together"

"hot and wet"

"sweeeet sex together touching and licking"

He felt a pull, a suction, and his fear began to take over completely; panic set in.

"sucking and fucking please let's do it let's do it together"

Then ahead of him in the blackness it was as if someone, somewhere, was slowly turning up the lights. A picture began to appear amidst the stirring sounds and floating words.

"we can make you beg and plead and want it"

"fuck me fuck"

"can make you"

"me do it to me let's do it rubbing and sweating"

"beg and plead for it"

The smell came again, and there was more of it below him. The street, while still there, was covered; only the rooftops of a few of the taller houses remained above what he now knew was blood. There was a lake of it, a whole *ocean* of it, churning slowly, for as far as he could see, on and on and on.

And there were things in it. Floating. Things. (oh god) (*"fuck me"*) Arms (*"we can make you"*) and legs (*"let's do it"*) and heads (*"we can suck and lick each other and I'll eat you if you like"*) and glistening, jiggling lumps floating in it, twisting in the whirlpools and bobbing in the small waves, and (*"I'll eat you if you like"*) others were coming to the surface, bobbing, lolling, and (*"eat you I'll eat you if you like"*) (oh dear god dear god) he began dropping, falling, almost as if he were being pushed down toward the mess of human bodies and parts, and (*"we can suck and lick and I'll eat you if you like I'll eat you eat you eat you"*) he screamed at the top of his lungs as he fell into the wet, thick darkness and sat up in bed, still screaming, his chest heaving . . .

And then he was silent. Rivulets of sweat trickled down his back and sides, over his forehead, into his eyes. His breath came thick and heavy in long, desperate drags and his mind raced frantically for the relief of total consciousness, wakefulness.

The nightmare had started three weeks ago and returned every night without fail, becoming more detailed, more realistic each time. As usual, he did not go back to sleep. He sat up in his kitchen nursing a glass of Scotch, thinking that something strong and horrible was happening. Something that could be very, very final.

He trembled until dawn.

one

FEARS

So on his nightmare, through the evening fog,
Flits the squat fiend o'er fen, lake and bog;
Seeks some love-wildered maid with sleep oppressed,
Alights, and grinning sits upon her breast . . .
Back o'er her pillow sinks her blushing head,
Her snow-white limbs hang helpless from the bed;
While with quick sighs and suffocative breath,
Her interrupted heart pulse swims in death.

—Erasmus Darwin

1

The classroom door opened a few seconds after the bell sounded, and students began to file in and take their seats. Donald Ellis sat behind his desk at the front of the classroom checking over the test he was about to hand out, looking one final time for any mistakes he might have missed. The side of his face rested in the palm of one large hand and he sucked in on his lower lip as he scanned the three-page English exam, his eyelids heavy.

"Hey, Mr. Ellis," one of the boys greeted him.

Donald looked up and gave a slight, heavy smile. He glanced over the quickly growing group, then looked back down at the test. His already crinkled brow tightened some more and he slowly raised his head again, his tired eyes going from student to student.

An attentive audience of four girls huddled around Leslie Newell, who spoke quietly and slowly, with confidence, her eyebrows bobbing slyly, her hands moving animatedly. Her sweater was tight and the neckline was cut low: cleavage on display.

Randy Stone, considerably overweight and unbathed, had his wide eyes glued to a comic book—Iron Man, Donald saw with dismay.

Mark Shewer and Brigitt Landis were quizzing each other with determination.

Donald blinked a few times, then scanned the room again, positive that something wasn't right.

Students were still coming in; a couple had their heads down on their desks.

Donald's brow relaxed when his eyes came to rest on Barry Sereno. He sighed quietly and rubbed one eye with three fingers. He started to get up but decided he was too tired.

"Barry," he said softly, with a smile.

The boy looked up from the Destroyer paperback he was reading, a bit of his dark, kinky hair hanging down over his forehead. He had chubby, rosy cheeks, but his body was lean and hard.

"Yeah?" he replied.

"Could you come here a second please?" Donald gestured to him with one hand.

Sereno stood and walked to Donald's desk, a little cautiously. The other students continued to buzz and study, hardly noticing.

"Yeah?" he said again, leaning forward over Donald's desk.

"I know you're probably worried about the test," Donald began, "but it's not really *that* hard. It's pretty straightforward. I think that, if you put your mind to it, you could do quite well on your own. I mean, without the, uh . . ." Donald sucked his lower lip in and sniffed once. "Do you have crib notes, Barry?"

Sereno's mouth became a tight little Cheerio and a bit of the color left his face. "Crib notes?"

Donald raised a reassuring palm and one side of his mouth

turned up in a smile. "I'm not accusing you, Barry. I mean, I'm not going to dock you or anything. I just . . ." This was always a problem, Donald realized as he groped for the right words. He tried to imagine the frantic thoughts going through the poor boy's mind as he tried to figure out how the hell his crib notes had become so obvious all of a sudden. "I'm just trying to say that I don't think you need them, Barry. That's all. Okay?"

The look of shock on the boy's face began to relax a little. "Okay. Whatever you say, Mr. Ellis." His head bobbed up and down agreeably. He backed away from Donald's desk, then turned and walked to his seat without ever acknowledging Donald's smile.

Donald sighed as he stood up to hand out the tests.

The coffee in the teachers' lounge was no better than usual, and his first swallow made Donald grimace. He plopped his large but firm body down in a chair and put the stack of exams on his lap, skimming some of them briefly. One hand swiped at his short, rusty-brown hair, then trailed down the side of his weary face.

"That stuff's a slow poison, Donald."

Donald didn't look up from the papers. He didn't even blink. He just said, "It must be, Charlie. I've been drinking it for thirty years and I'm not dead yet." He took another sip from the Styrofoam cup.

"Well," Charlie Montoya grunted as he dropped into the chair next to Donald, "all I've got to say is, you'd think that with the piddly-squat little salary they expect us to live on, they could at least supply us with coffee that doesn't burn a hole right through the seat of your pants, know what I mean, Donald?"

Donald made a noncommittal sound without opening his mouth.

9

Charlie stared at Donald a bit from the side. "You growing a beard, Donald?"

This made him look up. He ran his palm over his chin and felt the prickly stubble that he had somehow overlooked. He shrugged. "Guess I just forgot to shave."

"Forgot?" Charlie leaned toward Donald. "Look at me, Don."

Donald turned to face the short, bullet-shaped man next to him.

"God, are you all right? You look like you dropped outta the back end of a sick dog. You lost weight?"

"I don't know."

"Your eyes are bloodshot and you got rings under them. You okay?"

Donald shrugged again. "Guess I haven't been sleeping very well at night."

"You're even slurring your speech, for crying out loud. You know what I think you need?"

Donald turned his attention back to the tests on his lap.

"I think you need some exercise. Why don't you come over to the weight room with me and pump a few? Usually nobody's over there at this time. Ah, hell," he grunted, swatting a hand through the air, "that wouldn't matter anyway. These damned kids love to see their teachers get down and do something like that. 'Specially you, Donald; they love you, anyway." He paused thoughtfully, but only for a couple of seconds. "I don't really understand why, though. I mean, they're *supposed* to love *me*. I'm the goddamned P.E. teacher, know what I mean? I'm fun. You teach *English*, for crying out loud. What kinda kid likes *English?* I don't know, Donald, they're all screwed up. It's those goddamned video games. It keeps 'em out of the fresh air and the sunshine, know what I mean?"

Donald nodded slightly, not really knowing what it was he was nodding to. He'd learned to tune Charlie out.

"Well, whatta you say, Donald, you want to hit the iron?" The long pause that followed startled Donald and his head shot up. "Hm? Oh, no thanks, Charlie. I just don't feel up to it. And I've got another class in a while." He smiled at his colleague and nodded once gratefully.

"Whatever you say, Donald, but I sure think it would do you a world of good."

Charlie rattled on for a while longer, then bid Donald goodbye. Once he'd left, Donald swallowed the last of his coffee and tossed the cup into a nearby wastebasket. He leaned his head back against the wall, wincing at the stiffness in his neck. His arms felt like lead pipes, and at times his legs seemed to be water balloons, incapable of holding him up. He felt sticky and dirty, even though he had showered that morning. Whenever he moved, it was like being trapped in a movie dream sequence: slow and labored. Even sucking air into his lungs had become a somewhat burdensome task.

He closed his eyes and tried to relax the tension across his shoulders, hoping to doze a little. Just a little.

If only he could get a few nights of solid, uninterrupted sleep, he *knew* he would feel better. Sleep had become something that Donald longed for in much the same way most men long for beautiful women. He ached for it! But, night after night, it came only long enough to whet his appetite. He'd sleep two or three hours at the most before the nightmare took over. All that blood and those haunting voices . . .

"fuck me"

"What?" Donald snapped, jerking in his seat so suddenly that the exams on his lap slipped to the floor and scattered in a heap.

"I said, could you jump me?"

Donald blinked his watery eyes as he looked up at Anne Cramer, feeling disoriented.

"Donald, is anything wrong?" she asked, taking a step toward him.

He breathed in deeply and stood up, trying to smile convincingly. "No, no, I'm fine. I was just nodding off. Now, *what* did you say?"

"I was wondering if I could get a jump from you. My car won't start and I have a dental appointment. I'm parked right next to you." She squinted up at him, tilting her head with concern. Her voice became a whisper: "God, Donald, you look sick."

"So I hear." He bent down and gathered the exams together.

"Anything I can do?"

"Nah, I'm fine." He put the tests down on a small coffee table covered with issues of *Time* and *Psychology Today*, reached into his pocket for his car keys, and headed for the door of the lounge. "I don't know if I even *have* a jumper cable in my car," he muttered through a yawn.

Anne fell into step beside him. "Sure you're okay, Donald?"

"Positive." He smiled. "Want to run a race?" He went through the doorway into the corridor, car keys jangling in his hand.

They walked in silence for a few moments, Anne glancing occasionally at Donald's profile. Finally she said, "I have an idea, Donald. Why don't we have dinner tonight? We could drive up to St. Helena, go to St. George. Or we could just go to my place. I've got a roast, and I could pick up some wine. You look as if you could use a good meal. How does that sound?"

Donald slowed his pace a little and lifted one hand to massage a temple. "Oh, I don't know, Anne. I've got a truckload of book reports to read and I . . . well, I'm very tired."

They'd reached the glass doors that led to the parking lot, and Donald was already reaching out to push the door open when Anne lightly touched his elbow and stopped walking. He half turned to her. When she spoke, her voice was barely audible, even though there were only a few other people walking quietly about them.

"Donald . . . please?"

He looked down at her sharply angled face, her narrow nose, the fine crinkles around brown eyes that looked out through large, tinted glasses. The glasses had a very sexy, intelligent effect on her face. She had some gray hairs among the shiny black ones, but he thought they added dignity rather than age.

"Please, because I think we should talk. I really do. And I'd . . . well, I'd just *like* you to, you know? We haven't gotten together for . . . Have I done anything, Donald?" She was moving her head back and forth nervously, something she did unconsciously, but something with which Donald had become familiar.

"No, Anne, you've done nothing. It's just me. I'm very tired. I haven't been—" He froze, glanced at his wrist, and scowled angrily when he saw that he'd left his watch at home. "God, what time is it?"

"Quarter after one."

"Shit, I've got a class." He quickly handed her his keys. "Here, take my car. I'll be in my office when you get back. Bring the keys by."

"Dinner?" she asked hopefully as he hurried down the hall.

"We'll talk later," he said over his shoulder, then disappeared around the corner.

As she went out to the parking lot, Anne thought that, even when rushed, Donald moved very slowly these days.

*   *   *

> "This kindness will I show—
> Go with me to a notary, seal me there
> Your single bond; and, in a merry sport
> If you pay me not on such a day,
> In such a place, such sum or sums as are
> Express'd in the condition, let the forfeit
> Be nominated for an equal pound
> Of your fair flesh, to be cut off and taken
> In what part of your body pleaseth me."

Teddy Jacobs read the part of Shylock with as much evil as he could muster, but he sounded flat and bored, just like all the other students who had been assigned parts.

Donald sat behind his desk, staring down at his own copy of *The Merchant of Venice* as if following along with the students. But he never turned the pages. Normally, Donald would stop every few minutes to discuss the play, to make sure the students knew what was going on, to try to instill some enthusiasm in them. Today, though, he hardly heard the droning voices as they read their lines, barely even saw the words on the pages before him: they kept blurring, fading in and out of focus. He reached up and rubbed one of his watery eyes hard, wondering if perhaps he *should* go over to Anne's. Things hadn't been great between them, and he doubted they would ever be great again, but maybe just being with her, with *someone* . . . Maybe if he didn't sleep alone, he might sleep better. Then again, he thought, he might just keep her awake with his nightmare.

Donald considered telling Anne about the nightmare, describing it in detail, just to get it out. But there was a possibility there that he feared: the possibility that she would think he was suffering some sort of breakdown, however minor. Knowing her, she would probably assume that what had happened between them had hit Donald hard and he was just sort of giving up. Letting everything "go to pot," as his brother Bill would say. He wouldn't want her to flatter herself by thinking such a ridiculous thing. But still, he felt he needed to talk with someone about that nightmare, and she was his closest friend.

If it was just a nightmare, it might not be so bad. But there was that feeling that came with it. That goddamned feeling . . .

Donald's eyelids were slowly beginning to descend when the bell pealed loudly, almost startling him to his feet with his watery, bloodshot eyes wide open. The students stood in unison, like one organism, and fled out the door. Only one stayed behind and walked over to Donald's desk: Kyle Hubbley.

"TGIF, huh, Mr. Ellis?" Kyle said with a smirk. He held two books and a bulging notebook under his left arm. He slapped them on Donald's desk heavily.

"More like TGVMIF, Kyle."

"Vee em?"

"For Very Much. Thank God Very Much . . ."

Kyle chuckled, looking Donald's face over carefully. One eye squinted just a bit, characteristically. "Are you sick, Mr. Ellis?"

Donald stood up behind his desk, a folder in one hand, the other hand pushing a knuckle into an aching spot in the small of his back. "That seems to be the popular opinion today," he said, walking around the desk and past Kyle.

Kyle picked up his books, as well as the copy of *The Merchant of Venice* that Donald had left on the desk, then turned to follow his teacher out of the room. "No offense," he said apologetically. He pushed his black-rimmed glasses up on his crooked nose with his free hand.

Donald glanced at the boy, whose smile had collapsed some. He waved a hand casually and said, "No offense taken, Kyle, none taken. Actually, I *don't* feel well, I just wish it wasn't so obvious."

"Flu?"

"Yeah, probably a touch of the flu." He spotted his book in Kyle's hand and chuckled as he reached out and took it. "Thanks," he said, muttering something under his breath about forgetting his head if it weren't screwed on tightly. "So, what have you got planned for the weekend, Kyle?" Donald asked, stopping a moment at a water fountain for a drink. When he stood again, two drops of water clung shakily to the end of his stubbly chin. He clumsily wiped them away with the back of his hand.

"Nothing." The boy stuffed one hand into the pocket of his jeans. "My parents are going to be gone again this weekend."

"Another business trip of your dad's?"

"Nah, I think this one is more of a pleasure trip. *Most* of them are, in fact. They're going to Denver this time."

They went around a corner and into Donald's office. Donald sat down at his desk with a sigh, as if he had just exerted himself. He tossed the folder and book on the desktop. "So, it's just you and the tube, huh?"

"Yeah." Kyle sat down in the chair facing Donald's desk, making air whoosh out of the green vinyl-covered cushion. "I was wondering."

Donald sat back in his chair and laced his fingers together over his stomach, lazily rubbing his fingertips over the softness of the blue sweater he was wearing. Kyle always started questions that way: "I was wondering." Then there would be a pause and he would tell you *what* he was wondering.

"I was wondering if you were gonna be busy tonight. I thought maybe I'd rent a couple of movies maybe and bring them over and watch them on your VCR if you didn't mind."

Whether or not Donald minded was not an issue; of course he didn't mind. The two of them frequently got together and watched movies on Donald's VCR. With all their money,

Kyle's parents would not buy a VCR because they thought movies were a waste of time and mind-power. Donald, who really couldn't afford the damned thing, had purchased one anyway a little over a year ago in an attempt to escape the boredom and predictability of television. ("And to see a little skin, too, huh, Don?" Charlie Montoya had once suggested.)

"Well, Kyle, let me see . . ." Donald rubbed hard at the burning ache in his neck with the fingers of his right hand as he thought about Anne and her dinner invitation. He could use a good meal, something he hadn't been getting regularly lately. He didn't feel like going out, and he didn't feel like cooking for himself. "Tell you what, Kyle, why don't we make that another evening. I have a dinner appointment tonight, and I don't think I'll be getting back at a decent hour."

Kyle shrugged and said, "Sure, that's fine." He had his half-smile on when he said it, but Donald could hear the disappointment in his voice.

"I'm really sorry about that," Donald assured him.

"Oh, that's okay, no problem at all, Mr. Ellis." Kyle stood and stepped over to the desk, setting his books down. "There are a couple of good old movies on tonight—*The Thing* and *Key Largo*."

"Ah, that sounds pretty good." Donald leaned forward and put his palms flat on the desktop, his eyes scanning the books and papers scattered in front of him.

"Hey, Mr. Ellis, I hear you nailed Barry Sereno for crib notes today," Kyle said curiously, that left eye squinting a bit, his head tilting back slightly.

Donald chuckled, his eyes still searching the desk. "Oh, I didn't really *nail* him." His forehead wrinkled and he looked under a stack of typed papers, then under some books. He wasn't exactly sure what he was looking for, but he knew *something* was missing. He'd left something important behind somewhere today.

"No? You didn't?"

Donald scratched the side of his head, his face tense. "Hm? No, no, I didn't. In fact, I really wasn't, uh . . . well, I wasn't even sure he had any."

"You must have known *some*thing, because he *did* have them. That's not the first time you've done that. You must be able to *smell* those—" Kyle started a bit when Donald suddenly snapped his fingers sharply and stood to his feet. "Lose something?"

"I hope not," Donald breathed and hurried out of the office, leaving Kyle by the desk, staring at the doorway.

Donald ran down to the teachers' lounge and froze in his tracks to avoid colliding with Ruth Falsey, the principal of Eberhardt High School, who was just coming *out* of the lounge, holding Donald's stack of exams in one hand.

The woman looked up at him sharply. A lock of her silver hair had fallen down over one brown-penciled eyebrow, and her flat, red lips were pursed together tightly.

"I believe these are yours, Donald," she said steadily in her icy but quiet voice. She handed them to him.

"Uh, yes, as a matter of fact they are." He could have kicked himself when he reached out to take them only to see his hand shaking. But he smiled confidently at the short, older woman anyway.

"You know, Donald, it's not a very good habit to leave tests lying around like that." She nodded toward the lounge where Donald had left them on the coffee table.

"Yes, I know. It was an accident. Something else came up and I completely forgot them." He shrugged and smiled again. "A lot on my mind."

She blinked and her face relaxed, a gesture on a par with smiling for Ruth Falsey. "I'm glad I found them for you."

"Thanks." Donald started to walk away, but Ruth stopped him.

"Donald," she called softly. He turned to her. "Are you all right?" she asked him, one brow shooting downward toward her nose with her own brand of concern.

Son of a bitch, Donald thought angrily, I must look like absolute shit! "Sure, Ruth, I'm fine. Just in a little hurry." He smiled a third time, then went back to his office to wait for Anne to return with his car keys. He'd completely forgotten that Kyle had been there just moments before.

I *do* look like absolute shit, Donald decided upon seeing himself in his bathroom mirror at home. He scraped a hand over the stubble that covered his chin and cheeks and rubbed his eyes, pressing hard and making slow circles, clenching his brow tightly; then he relaxed and stared at his drawn reflection some more.

His cheekbones were more prominent than they had ever been before. His blue eyes seemed dull and glassy. He squinted and leaned toward the mirror, wondering if the wrinkles he was seeing around his throat were new, or if he just hadn't noticed them before.

He pulled his sweater over his head and was unbuttoning his shirt when the telephone rang.

"Hello?"

"Hi, Donald?" It was his brother Bill.

"Hey, Bill, how are you?" Donald sat down at the small table that occupied the little phone nook in his living room.

"Not bad. Yourself?"

"Oh, fine. I'm just fine." Donald chewed his lip lightly. This was odd. Bill *never* called him. He would call Bill once in a while. Not out of any bond that existed between them—just because they were brothers and the only surviving members of their immediate family, as cold as that sounded. Oh, they cared for one another, sure, but there was little or no closeness between them, despite the fact that they lived near one another. Bill, being the youngest, had taken the most care of their parents, particularly their father, before they died, giving up an education in the process. Donald and his sister Julie, in the meantime, had gone to school, Donald becoming an English teacher, Julie a school psychologist.

That had been the strongest bond in the Ellis family: the one between Donald and Julie. She had died four years earlier at the age of thirty-eight, while buying a loaf of bread on a warm spring evening. She'd gone into a 7–11 store and was waiting in line to make her purchase when the place was held up by two nervous teenagers, the more nervous one being armed. In a panic, he'd fired the gun, wounding the clerk and killing Julie.

"Are you still keeping the world safe for Smokey the Bear?" Donald asked. Bill was a fireman and was always complaining about the inevitable Smokey jokes that came his way, so Donald never failed to bring the bear up whenever they spoke, simply in jest, not to needle his brother.

"I'm sure trying. You still keeping it safe for Emily Dickinson?"

"I'm working on it. Remember, I'm competing with Pat Benatar and Donkey Kong. I have to keep on my toes." Donald thought about how the amenities seemed to go on forever when he and Bill spoke. "What are you up these days?"

"Well, I've got the weekend off."

He expected Bill to continue, but when he didn't, Donald tried to fill the gap of silence: "Sounds good. Going to stay in bed and sleep?"

Bill chuckled. "Part of the time, yeah. But I was wondering if . . . well, I was wondering if you'd mind dropping by sometime tomorrow. Maybe for lunch?"

Donald's back straightened a bit and he blinked with surprise. "Sure, Bill. Something on your mind?"

"Well, uh, yeah . . . sort of. There's something kind of, uh . . ." He sighed uncertainly. "Something kinda weird has happened, Donald, something kinda weird. I need to talk about it, and you . . . well, I think you have an open mind, Donald. More open than any of my friends. Hell, *you* may not even believe me." As he spoke the last sentence, his voice quivered the tiniest bit. That worried Donald. It didn't sound right, not coming from Bill. "Think you could come over for lunch tomorrow, Donald? I . . . I'd really appreciate it."

Donald nodded to himself, then said, "Sure, Bill, I'll be there. I'm looking forward to it." But he *wasn't* looking forward to it. In fact, Donald had a very bad feeling . . .

Anne sat at her dressing table, watching her reflection in the mirror, carefully pinning her hair up. Donald liked it that way, and she wanted to make him feel good this evening, make him happy.

She wore a slinky magenta and black rugby-striped pull-over and black pants. A shiny black bracelet encircled her wrist and caught the light now and then as her hand played with her dark hair. She swept a glance over her selection of lipsticks and chose Very Cherry. She felt its smoothness glide across her lips and the sensation brought with it the thin shade of a memory, the same memory that always came with the application of any makeup. Usually she let the thought pass without notice, but this evening she allowed the pictures to form in her mind more vividly than usual . . .

That chilly winter day in South Lancaster, Massachusetts, when, walking home from school, her friend Lila Peterson had handed Anne her own lipstick and insisted that she take it as a gift and use it, grow used to it, because it would do *so* much for Anne's looks.

"But my *father* . . ." Anne had breathed, frightened by the mere thought of what would happen if her father found her with lipstick, or any *other* makeup, for that matter.

"So, don't use it around him," Lila had replied. "Keep it a secret from him. *Believe* me, it'll improve your looks enormously!"

Anne realized, and was ashamed of the fact, that she was the only girl in her freshman class who came to school day after day without a trace of makeup on her face, and she knew that her looks, which had potential, suffered from it. She had taken the lipstick that day, and when Lila reached into her purse to retrieve some eye shadow, insisting she take that, too, she did.

At the dinner table that night, Anne's father had asked her to give the blessing. She had, nervously, and she'd tried to eat quickly, eager to escape from the table, and her father's perpetually icy expression. As usual, his glass of milk was laced with some sort of strong-smelling liquor, but the family— Anne, her sister Lenora, her brother Thomas, and her mother— ignored it, *also* as usual. After dinner, Anne had gone to her room quietly and alone. She'd planned not to wear the makeup anywhere near her father, but only after she'd left the house and always being sure to remove it before returning. But she simply could not resist trying it on. Surely it would be safe to just put it on and quickly wash it off before anyone saw. She'd never worn makeup before.

The sensation of applying the makeup had been entirely foreign to her, and Anne remembered savoring it like an exotic new food in her mouth. She'd put it on slowly, paying close attention to the definite change in her appearance that emerged in the small, round mirror over her dresser. What could her father possibly have against it? What could God have against it? That's what her father was always telling her: it was an insult to God, trying to improve upon something with which He was already quite satisfied. But what could be wrong with a little decoration, a little—

Anne's bedroom door had swung open then and her father stood in the doorway, tall and broad, his graying hair scraggly and wild, his eyes, a little blurry from the drinking that had pushed him from the pulpit years before, flamed with anger.

"Sneaking into your room to smear your face with that heathen paint?" he belched. "You don't think I noticed your sneaky attitude at the table?" He stepped into the room and Anne stood up, dropped the lipstick to the floor. "A heathen's way of offending God, that's what that is."

"But it makes me look—"

"It makes you look like a cheap little slut; it will make all the shifty young men look at you like you were in a big-city store window. Slut. Yes." He walked over to her and pulled a handkerchief from his back pocket. "Wipe it off."

"No," she said, trying to keep her voice steady. "I want to wear it, Daddy. Please."

His big hand had sailed through the air and cracked against her cheek and she'd fallen back against her cluttered little dresser, holding her face with her hands. He held the handkerchief, stained and crusty, out to her again. "Wipe it *off.* If you wear that stuff, you'll wear it after you turn eighteen and after you leave this God-fearing house."

Tears had tumbled down her cheeks as she nodded, wiping the lipstick off as best she could.

When she turned eighteen, Anne had left. She'd come to California and met Rick. She'd known Rick only a little more than a month when he asked her to marry him. Seeing him as a security blanket, a way to escape her loneliness, she'd accepted. It wasn't long, however, before her security blanket became a straitjacket: living with Rick was worse than living alone. But the marriage went on for fifteen years—a cold, mercifully childless life together that ended with anger and bitterness.

It was then that she'd gone into therapy, something she'd been wanting to do for some time, but hadn't for fear of enraging Rick. Unlike many others she knew, Anne was helped immeasurably during her time in therapy. She learned that there was absolutely nothing wrong with being happy, being comfortable, having fun. She learned that there was nothing wrong with feeling good and looking good, being proud of the fact that she was very attractive and using that attractiveness to find friends. And, probably most important of all, she learned that there was nothing wrong with sex. Her father had made her think all those things were, in one way or another, evil. And Rick had made her feel that they were all too much to ask of life.

A year ago she'd met Donald, and their relationship had grown quickly but solidly. A little too solidly. She'd broken one of her rules with Donald. She had closed the distance between them that, in other relationships, despite the great changes that had taken place in her way of looking at things, she'd preferred to keep. They had become a little too close.

Anne dabbed a bit of perfume here and there before getting up and crossing the bedroom to open her window. The whisper of falling rain flowed in, closely followed by its sweet fragrance. She left her bedroom and went into the kitchen to take a peek at the roast in the oven. Then she went into the small dining room, took a box of matches from the window-sill, and lit the two candles on the table. She made a quick check of all the things on the table to be sure everything was there.

At the risk of pushing things a little too far in light of the ugly argument they'd had a while back, Anne wanted to make

Donald feel good, feel special. She wanted him to relax. He'd been looking so tense lately. God, he'd been looking like hell, *period!* Anne was beginning to suspect that she might be to blame for Donald's apparent ill health. Perhaps bringing an end to the exclusivity of their relationship so suddenly had been a mistake. Perhaps she hadn't done it suddenly *enough.* In any case, something had been on his mind lately. She sighed, thinking that Donald was simply too sensitive.

The doorbell rang, followed by a quick knock. Anne quickly turned, smoothing her hands over her hips and thighs, then patting her hair, and hurried through the kitchen and into the living room.

When Anne opened the door of her apartment, she embraced Donald like a fresh, clean breeze on a cool morning. After kissing him gently on the lips, she led him inside. Donald breathed in her rich, warm perfume and admired the way her hair was pinned up—very dignified—as she glided across the living room with relaxed, comfortable ease.

"Make yourself homey, hon," she said, tossing a look over her shoulder as she disappeared into the kitchen.

Donald leaned his dripping umbrella against the wall by the door, then removed his coat and hung it in the small closet to his right. The welcoming smell of the roast hovered in the room; clattering sounds of meal preparations came from the kitchen. The living room was dimly lit and the sound of rain falling outside added a faint touch of comfort to the already cozy, personal atmosphere. Donald sat down on the cream-colored sofa and took a cigarette from the shiny silver box on the coffee table, lit it with a wooden match, and inhaled the smoke deeply, his hollow cheeks pulling inward. He held the smoke inside for a while, then slowly let it out through his mouth and nose. It was the first cigarette he'd had in nearly two months.

"Ah-ah-ah," Anne chided, coming back into the living room and curling up beside Donald on the sofa, one arm around his shoulders. "I thought you'd quit those things."

Donald half coughed. "I guess I had." He smiled at her and took another long drag on the cigarette.

"How are you?"

"Hungry, tired, and skinnier than I've been since I had my appendix out. How about you?"

She laughed and squeezed his neck, laying her head on his shoulder briefly. "Glad to have you here."

October rain whispered outside and Donald lightly brushed his cheek against Anne's hair, then kissed the top of her head.

"Dinner will be ready soon," she said softly. "We've got a pot roast . . ."

"Mmm."

". . . some of the sweetest corn you'll ever taste, a big salad with *everything*, some nice rosé wine, and chocolate-fudge ice cream for dessert."

Donald started to speak, but Anne held up a long, graceful finger, stopping him.

"After dinner, you have a choice. We can listen to music and talk. We can watch *Key Largo* at ten. Or . . . whatever." She smiled at him slyly for a few moments, both of them silent, until a buzzer went off in the kitchen and Anne popped off the sofa. A few seconds later she called from the other room, "Come and get it, kids!"

Donald bent forward and put out his cigarette in the ashtray, then went through the kitchen and into the glowing little dining room on the other side. Anne stood at the table smiling proudly. Two candles flickered, their light glinting on the wineglasses. "Have a sit." Donald sat down and they began filling their plates. Anne disappeared again to put some Earl Klugh on the stereo, and quickly returned.

The meal was eaten silently at first, with the two of them

26

exchanging smiles, then Donald commenting on the food. As she poured Donald's second glass of wine, Anne asked, "Do you like Lancer's?"

Donald sipped the wine. "Despite the fact that it's sold in shampoo bottles"—he gestured to the burnt-orange bottle, squat and ungraceful—"yes, I do."

She laughed and took the last bite of her corn.

"You gave an exam today, didn't you?" she asked.

"Mm-hm."

"Go all right?"

"Sure."

She sipped her wine. "I understand you accused Barry Sereno of having crib notes." She glanced down at her plate, took a bite of roast.

Donald was bringing his fork to his mouth, but he froze, holding it in front of him.

"Accused?" he asked, a little surprised. "You heard I *accused* him?"

She nodded.

"No, no I didn't." He stuffed a couple of inadequately cut lettuce leaves into his mouth and chewed. "I knew he had them and I told him that I didn't think he needed any. But I didn't *accuse* him."

"I guess Barry isn't exactly subtle about his cheating, then, hm?" she said, a little too pointedly.

"No, he's actually a pretty sly guy. And smart enough to keep from flashing them in front of my face." Another sip of wine.

"Then how did you know?" Anne leaned forward, her face curious.

Donald shrugged. "I don't know. I just . . . it was . . ." He closed his eyes momentarily, ran his tongue across his front teeth. "Okay, so it was a suspicion. I didn't really *know,"* he lied. His eyes narrowed. "Jesus, what is this, 'Dragnet'?"

Anne sat back and laughed. "No, no, I was just interested. I've heard that you're good at spotting things like that, and I just wondered how you do it. I could use a few pointers."

"You heard that, huh?"

"You're notorious, love."

Donald sighed and finished off his glass of wine, hoping he wouldn't have to work his way over an explanation of his ability to know things like which students have crib notes. He smiled. "I'm just sharp, that's all." He held up his empty glass.

"Ah, with pleasure," Anne said as she filled it for him. Her smooth, moist lips curled upward in a smile, but her eyes were hidden by the reflection of the candles in her glasses. "Ready for your ice cream?"

Donald nodded and she brought from the kitchen two bowls filled with chocolate-fudge ice cream. She also brought a container of chocolate topping.

"Isn't this decadent?" she asked as she spooned some topping onto her ice cream. "Chocolate on chocolate. If I keep this up I'll look like one of the Great Lakes in no time."

"That would be unfortunate," Donald muttered with a chuckle. "Then you'd only be able to date tugboat captains." He took a bite of ice cream.

Anne set the topping container down and leaned forward on the table. "You know, Donald, you're usually very witty. Usually, you're tossing remarks like that all over the place. But that's your first one tonight, which makes me think that perhaps it's more than just wit. Something on your mind?"

He shook his head, a hint of a smile on his lips. "No. Just wit, that's all."

Anne took her glasses off, put them down, then propped her elbow on the tabletop and her chin on her palm. "Donald, are you still angry with me?"

As if to get into the spirit of the discussion that was obviously on its way, Donald put his spoon down. "I never was angry with you, Anne. Not the way you make it sound. It's just . . . I was just hurt. And disappointed."

Anne sighed. "Am I supposed to feel bad? To feel guilty?"

"No, no, you didn't do anything . . . well, anything intentional."

"I didn't do *any*thing, dammit! *You*, Donald, you were the one who had a honeymoon going on in your head. I *told* you I didn't want—"

"Anne, I wish you'd stop talking like I *proposed* to you, or something. I wasn't that serious."

"Not *yet*."

"Well, no, but Christ, Anne, you can't act as if I've—"

"Look, Donald." Her voice was very quiet but firm. She sat up straight and placed her palms flat on the table at either side of her bowl. "I saw it coming, okay? I just. Saw it. Coming. And I tried to cut it off at the pass, know what I mean? But you already had us married in your mind. You were too confident, Donald. I'm not ready for that. I spent some of the worst years of my life in a marriage—nearly fifteen to be exact—and I'll be damned if I'm going to let it happen again. I just want to be free, okay? I'm forty-one years old. I want to do some of the things that I *should* have done as a teenager but *didn't* because I was so busy being so goddamned serious then, okay? I'm old enough already. I want to do them before it's *really* too late." She looked down at the table, then reached up and ran her index finger back and forth over her upper lip.

Donald began eating his ice cream again, silently.

"Donald . . ." She looked at him again; the candlelight whipped over his face, deepening the hollow cheeks and eyes. "Donald, I told you before, and I still mean it: that doesn't mean—none of that means—that you are any less important to me. I wish I could make you believe that. Can't we . . . can't we just have fun? You know, like a couple of teenagers?"

He looked at her for a while, his jaw working. He swallowed the ice cream in his mouth. "That's where we're different, Anne. I've already done all those things—the dating, the teenage stuff. I'm finished with it. I want some commitment, some devotion. That's what I want to give and it's what I want to get." He took in another spoonful of ice cream.

Anne clicked her tongue. "Well, can't we just . . . just be together, then? Without any . . . Dammit, Donald, I don't want to lose you completely. Why won't you just enjoy me while you can?"

Donald almost spit ice cream laughing. "What the hell are you saying? That is the most arrogant—" He laughed again. "What do you have, an expiration date or something?"

She sighed with frustration. "It's just not coming out right."

"It didn't come out right the *last* time we had this talk either."

Anne carefully reached over and took his hand, squeezing it gently. "I *do* care for you, Donald. Very much."

He looked as though he were about to speak, but thought better of it and remained silent. He simply squeezed her hand in return.

"I'll help you clear the table," he said suddenly, standing, scooping up his dish and bowl. He was heading into the kitchen when the room did a complete turnabout and tossed him flat on his face. The dish shattered when it hit the kitchen floor, pieces skidding clear across the room. The bowl did a little hulalike spin, spattering drops of chocolate around itself, like little machine-gun bullets.

"Donald!" Anne shrieked, immediately at his side, on her knees. "Donald, are you all right?"

He quickly held up a reassuring hand. "Fine, Anne, I'm fine. I just stood up a little too fast. Nothing wrong. Just a little dizzy." He slowly sat up, rubbing one eye.

"God, Donald, do you do that often?"

"Only when I stand up . . . too quickly." He saw that her face was dripping with worry and he patted her hand. "No problem."

"Well, that's not good. Something must be wrong."

"Nothing's wrong," he said, standing. She held his arm.

"Then why do you *do* that?" she insisted. "I don't have to be a doctor to know that *something* must be wrong."

"You're *not* a doctor. You're a math teacher. Quit playing Marcus Welby and—"

"Donald, you're not well. You haven't been for days, and everybody is starting to notice. I saw Charlie Montoya today and he—"

Donald stepped forward and put his arms around Anne's waist. "I don't want to hear about Charlie Montoya. Know what I *do* want?"

She shook her head.

"I want to go to bed."

The worry in her face chipped away and a smile grew. She pushed herself closer to him. "Sounds good to me," she purred.

"But . . . but just to sleep." He sniffed. "Just to sleep, Anne. I haven't slept well in weeks. I keep . . . I just don't sleep. I'd like to sleep here with you so . . . so I won't be alone. I'd rather not be alone. If you don't, uh, think that's crazy."

As Donald spoke, Anne's look of pleasure faded and her shoulders sagged. She leaned her cheek against his chest and gently shook her head. "No, I don't think that's crazy. Be kind of nice."

But he could tell by her voice—its tired monotone, its

31

almost *bored* sound—that she wasn't too crazy about the idea. He didn't care, though. He did want to be with someone, and this was the only someone he had at the moment.

When they got into bed a little later, he fell asleep immediately with her head resting on his chest.

Kyle Martin Hubbley despised the house in which he lived, the house that his father, a successful architect, had designed and helped build. It had four bedrooms, two bathrooms, a den, a huge living room and kitchen, an indoor sauna, a broad sun deck in the back, beautiful redwood double doors in front that opened into a hall so ridiculously long that it rivaled the endless, winding road that led up the hill to the house. Yet it was inhabited only by himself and his parents. It seemed senseless to him to have such a spacious house for such a small family. His parents had house guests occasionally, but not often enough to warrant living in such a huge place.

Whenever he had this little mental discussion with himself, he never failed to come to the conclusion that the house was just another way for his father to measure his own success, another way to tell his friends and colleagues that he was indeed very, very comfortable.

Kyle, however, was *not* comfortable when he had to spend a weekend alone in the large house. He wasn't afraid, really, No . . . just uncomfortable. Just—

Bullshit, he thought, as he stared at the flickering black and white images on the television screen; you're afraid and you know it.

Scientists were slamming a door on the horned hand of the alien that was terrorizing them in their Arctic station. The monster, played by James Arness, roared with pain and anger and pulled his hand from the doorway.

And if you're afraid of being here alone, Kyle thought some more, than why the hell are you watching *this?*

He pushed a handful of popcorn into his mouth, a few of the white puffs rolling and bouncing down over his chest and stomach. He was slouched in a fat, furry brown beanbag chair in front of the television in the den, which, especially when he knew he was alone in the house, seemed cavernous. He reached over and picked up the can of Dr. Pepper on the floor next to him and drank from it.

The film cut away and was replaced by the image of a woman: tall and lanky, wearing a clinging black dress with a low neckline that revealed a shadowy valley of cleavage—deep, but not *too* deep. The dress's neckline was surrounded by a smattering of glinting red sequins, and around her graceful, milky throat there rested a string of tiny red beads. Her cheekbones were high and sharp and the eyes above them were large and dark, staring straight out of the picture tube into Kyle's face, seeing him. Or so he liked to imagine.

"*That's* why you're watching this," he said, chuckling quietly to himself. He took another drink of soda and smacked his lips comically.

The woman on the television sat in a large chair, a throne almost, with a carved bat on the back of it looming over her head, its wings spread, its fanged mouth open. One long-fingered hand reached up and toyed with the red beads she wore as she said, " 'The Friday Night Frights' will continue in just a few moments. Hope you're enjoying the show." Her voice was soft and heavy, but not fake. Unlike other horror-movie hosts he'd seen, Kyle was sure that Xanthe spoke the same way off camera as she did on.

A newscaster appeared on the screen, identified himself, and said, "On 'Eyewitness News' at eleven, we'll bring you up-to-date on the rash of bizarre, bloody disappearances occurring across the nation. A San Francisco artist is the latest to join the rapidly growing list of victims. Also in the news tonight . . "

Kyle fought his way out of the hugging beanbag and carried the nearly empty bowl of popcorn to the kitchen. Rain shooshed frantically outside and there was thunder rumbling in the distance, too far away to be really threatening. Lightning peaked playfully though the windows.

Perfect, Kyle thought, as he stuck his hand in the cookie jar. All we need now is a werewolf. Or a beautiful woman in black. He smiled. Kyle's taste in entertainment was quite different from most of his peers'. Not better, he often thought, just different. He liked to read plays and poetry. He liked classical music and jazz and could tolerate little of the inebriating rock that was constantly blaring out of portable stereo speakers at school. He was the only student he knew of who liked—no, *loved*—foreign films. Not that he didn't enjoy a good old-fashioned car-chase flick now and then, or some slapstick comedy. He just didn't like them as much as *most* high school juniors did. There was, however, a genre of film and literature that Kyle thoroughly enjoyed—almost secretly. It was a genre usually disdained by those who preferred more thoughtful, intellectual forms of entertainment.

Kyle was a sucker for a good scare. He had cut his teeth on horror comic books and had never shed his taste for the macabre, the gruesome. He also had a weakness for Xanthe and her Friday and Saturday night horror-movie shows. Tacky, maybe, but *he* thought she was gorgeous. She was dark and mysterious, forbidding, and, boy, she knew her horror flicks. How many girls around knew that Alfred Hitchcock only *directed* the film *Psycho* and didn't *write* it? None of the girls *he* knew. How many were aware that Frankenstein was the name of the doctor who created the monster and not the name of the monster itself? None, that *he* knew. From the articles Kyle had read about Xanthe, he learned that she was something of an expert on movies in general, old and new, all kinds. Kyle liked that: having a knowledge of something, just one special subject, like a hobby, a forte. And besides all that, she was absolutely *gorgeous!*

On his way back through the darkened den, Kyle paused in front of his father's gun cabinet. In its smoky glass front, Kyle's reflection was superimposed over the row of guns that stood at attention against the racks inside. Lightning flashed, outlining his somewhat round frame. Tubby, he thought sadly; *tubby* is the word for it. He glanced at the three Oreos he'd taken from the cookie jar and decided he'd feel better if he ate them than if he didn't. Plopping back into the beanbag, he adjusted his glasses and bit into a cookie.

As he stared at the television screen, he thought that Xanthe's inaccessibility was probably a good part of her attraction. It was as if she weren't even real. In a sense, she wasn't.

Leslie Newell was very much the same way. Like Xanthe, she was inaccessible, out of reach—except the reach of a chosen few. Kyle, of course, was not among that chosen few. He was among the many who had to be content with watching Leslie walk about campus in her tight, colorful, fashionable clothes, watching her golden hair swing back and forth over her shoulders, watching her hands move in that excited way they did as she spoke to her friends—no, her *entourage:* all those girls who weren't quite as beautiful as she, but who hoped that, if they hung around her long enough, it would rub off on them.

Kyle, though, had some time ago come to the conclusion that he would never get a girl like Leslie Newell, let alone Leslie herself. *No* guy "got" Leslie, anyway; *she* did the getting. Somehow she always managed to make it look as if she were being pursued whenever she got together with someone, but in actuality she was engineering the whole thing, choreographing it like a Broadway show. There was something admirable about that, but Kyle was certainly glad it wasn't a trait common to *all* girls. He wanted to have some say in the matter.

As things were going lately, however, he had nothing to have any say about! He didn't know *any* girls. Not very well, at least; he just had a few acquaintances. There were a couple of girls who worked on the school paper with him (Kyle wrote a weekly movie review for the *Campus Voice*). They were kind of cute, but they didn't like him. At least, he didn't think they did. They never spoke to him. Of course, he never spoke to *them*, either, and he wasn't sure he wanted to. They were always giggling and fawning over Mitch Parker, asshole extraordinaire, who also happened to write the paper's sports column. Kyle didn't trust girls who went for guys like that, mostly because he didn't trust guys like that. But then, maybe he shouldn't be too picky. He wasn't looking to get married, for crying out loud. He didn't want a lasting relationship, or anything deeply meaningful. Of course, he didn't just want some shallow, one-night—

Oh hell, he thought, I just want to get laid!

In the seventh grade, a classmate had once told him that if you didn't get laid by the time you graduated from high school, your dick would fall off. Of course Kyle hadn't believed such a crock (well . . . not for very long, anyway), but there was a certain amount of inadequacy that accompanied his lingering virginity.

The Thing was back on, but Kyle's mind was now occupied by other things. Namely, sex. He began thinking of who, where, when, and various hows, all the while trying to keep from his mind the thought that there was probably no one out there who wanted to go to bed with a fat seventeen-year-old virgin who liked horror movies, old books, and classical music.

Leslie Newell, of course, was out of the question, although he would gladly have sold his soul for one night of lying between those deliciously smooth, firm thighs. Then there were those two girls who worked with him on the paper, Kim Wyman and Tina Something-or-other. But they probably weren't in his league either.

Do you *have* a league? he silently asked himself. *Is* there a league when all you want is some nookie?

Kyle suddenly felt a pang of distaste for this train of thought. How could he think this way, plan—actually *plan*—this sort of thing? He hadn't been raised that way! It all seemed so crass, so low.

He removed his glasses and rubbed his eyes with thumb and forefinger as he thought, Tell that to an unemployed hard-on.

Kyle often wished he had a therapist. Not because he was having any psychological problems, just because it would be nice to have someone to talk to about things like this. His father could afford one, he was sure, but he wouldn't dare ask him. Just as he wouldn't dare talk to his father or mother about something like this. He had no friends with whom he would be comfortable having such a discussion, either.

He pulled one of the Oreos apart and licked up the cream filling, then ate one chocolate half, ate the other. His forehead wrinkled with thought for a moment. He licked some dark crumbs from his lips. Perhaps he *did* have someone he could talk with.

He cleared his throat and, in a tone of rehearsal, Kyle said to the television screen: "Uh, Mr. Ellis? I have this problem . . ."

When Anne awoke in the cool darkness, the rain falling harder outside, she was moist between her legs. Her breasts tingled just a bit and she lifted a hand to one, gently massaging it, flicking a finger over the hardened nipple. She felt Donald's naked body beside her and had a sudden urge to embrace him, to be embraced by him. Had she been dreaming?

37

Donald stirred next to her, muttered something in his sleep. He felt damp; he was perspiring. He had his back to her now. She turned toward him, put one hand on his hip, pressed her breasts to his back. He shifted a bit more.

She chuckled deeply in her throat when she felt her thighs getting warm, felt the slippery juices flowing over the inside of one leg. Anne reached a hand over Donald's hip to his stomach, ran her fingers through the patch of hair, tickling, then touched his penis, flaccid now in sleep. She curled her fingers around it, pulled ever so lightly, squeezed ever so gently.

Donald moved again, turned a bit, groaned. But the groan was not one of pleasure. His head turned toward her. In the darkness, she looked at his face; his eyes were tightly shut, his brow furrowed, his lips pulled upward, as if he might be ill.

"Donald?" she whispered, her voice no more than a bit of down floating through the air. She chuckled again and pulled back the covers. "Donald, honey."

Another groan, his head turned right, left, right again.

Anne rubbed her hands softly over his chest, down his stomach. She got up on one knee, bent forward, lifted his penis with her hand, and kissed the head, touched her lips to it again. Ran her tongue over it.

Lightning flashed outside in the distance, turning Donald's body powder-white for an instant.

"Donald, my love," she whispered, her breath falling over his soft organ, warm and gentle. She took him in her mouth, sucking mildly. "Fuck me," she hissed. "Come on, Donald, honey, wake up. Fuck me, Donald."

The groan came again, rising in pitch; his movements were jerky and she felt him trembling, yet his penis remained limp. She lifted her head and saw that he was lying rigid, the muscle cords in his neck taut. His hands were wrapped into tight fists.

"Donald?" Her voice was a little louder, her tone uncertain. Then she smiled again. "Come on, Donald . . . fuck me."

"Jeee-zuuusss nooo!" he screamed, bolting upward, his eyes wide and his mouth stretched to its limit, his hands reaching outward, fingers open, imploring.

Anne threw herself aside, almost falling off the bed, too startled to scream or shout.

Donald was on his feet in an instant, crossing the room's darkness with his arms outstretched like a comic sleepwalker. He pressed his naked, sweating body to the opposite wall, hugging it, one hand over his face, his shoulders convulsing.

"No, god, not again, not anymore," he sobbed softly, one fist tightened, pushing against the wall in methodic thrusts.

Anne could do no more than stare at him for a few moments. Then she left the bed and walked over to his side, cautiously putting a hand on his shoulder.

"Donald, are you . . . are you okay?" She heard her voice tremble.

He backed away from the wall a couple of inches. A burst of lightning caught the tears on Donald's face and made them shine. "I'm sorry," he rasped, his voice hoarse. He gulped air and wiped at his eyes. "I'm very sorry. Go . . . go back to bed, Anne."

"I will not!" She slid her arm around both of his broad shoulders. "Is there anything I can do? Donald?"

He turned to her, moved his mouth as if to speak a couple of times, but said nothing for a bit. Then: "Talk to me. Just . . . just come talk to me."

She put on her robe and he slipped into his undershorts, then they went into the kitchen. Anne turned on the soft fluorescent light over the sink; it blinked and flickered before coming on fully. Donald sat down at her little round breakfast table.

"Would you like some cocoa? Coffee?" She stood behind him, lightly massaging his shoulders.

"Got any Scotch?"

She turned to a cupboard, opened it. "Yep." She pulled the bottle down and got a glass. "Want anything with it?"

"Straight."

Anne poured the liquor into the glass and set it before him on the table. Then she sat down.

"Was that a nightmare," she asked, "or do you have something against getting blow jobs in your sleep?"

He looked puzzled, stared across the table. "A nightmare."

"Well," She sighed, locking her hands together, putting her elbows on the tabletop and her chin on her knuckles. "Since we aren't going to be doing anything *else* tonight, why don't you tell me about it?"

He drank some of his Scotch and exhaled slowly, coarsely. "Sure you want to hear about it?"

"I'm all ears."

Donald closed his eyes, chewed on his lip, fiddled with the glass between his hands. He had to decide. Should he tell her? Everything? His tongue made a sharp little clacking sound in his mouth as he thought. Then he opened his eyes, looked across at Anne. He was trembling again and it was building; he was shaking the table some, causing the Scotch in front of him to lick gently against the sides of the glass that held it.

"Donald, what's wrong?" Anne's forehead was wrinkled.

"I'm . . . I'm scared."

Donald was almost through with his second glass of Scotch and Anne had poured herself a brandy by the time he finished talking about his nightmare, about the feelings that accompanied it, the feelings that would not allow him a moment's peace. He looked exhausted, drained.

Anne, however, was sitting stiffly in her chair, her lips pulled into a straight line across her face. She drummed her fingernails against the side of the glass, making little clinking sounds.

"Three weeks the nightmare has been coming?" she asked coolly.

"Every night."

"And you think it's something more than just a nightmare?"

He gulped loudly and exhaled with short, jerky rhythm. "I know, Anne, it sounds crazy, I know. But it's . . . it's a feeling I've had before, a feeling of something bad, like—"

"Like knowing a student has crib notes?"

He'd been looking down at his drink, but his gaze swung up to her again when she mentioned the crib notes. His teeth were nibbling again, chewing on his lip, chewing. "You think . . . you think . . ."

Anne leaned forward on her elbows. Her fingers stopped their drumming. "I think you should talk to someone, Donald."

He stared at her for a long while, his cheeks twitching, his hand toying with his glass, turning it around and around on the table. Then he picked it up and tossed the remainder of his drink down his throat and slammed the glass down. He stood, pushing his chair back noisily and walked into the dining room, stared out the window. Raindrops speckled the pane like little liquid diamonds. The rain had calmed outside, but its fresh, clean fragrance coming through the partly open window was as strong as ever.

"I knew it," Donald whispered coldly. "I *knew* you would think something like that." He put his hands on his hips, his elbows pointing outward.

Anne stood up and slowly walked into the dining room. "Donald, I don't think anything *bad*. I just think you need to

41

talk to someone who can help you better than *I* can. Someone—''

"*Nobody* can help me!" His head shot around and he threw her a sharp, knife-edged glare.

Air punched out of Anne, like a cough or an aborted laugh, and she said, "What do you *mean* nobody can help, Donald? You're okay. Just . . . tired, maybe, or overworked."

"Oh, Christ!"

"What about Harvey Blanchette, the school psy—"

"If I thought a psychiatrist *could* help me, he'd be the *last* one I'd go to. Son of a bitch thinks he's Sigmund Freud *and* Jesus Christ." Donald raked his fingers though his hair.

Anne wrung her hands together a couple of times, then stepped over to Donald and touched his arm gently. "Donald, for me, would you—''

"Goddammit, just drop it, okay? I'm sorry I said a bloody thing about it." He spun around on his heels and left the room.

"Donald . . ." Anne stood in the darkened dining room for a while, composing something to say, the *right* thing, something that would help. She heard rustling movements from the bedroom and went to see what he was doing. As she came out of the kitchen, he was walking to the front door, tucking his shirt in. He opened the closet and got his coat. "Donald, for crying out loud, will you—"

"No, I won't." He put on his coat and picked up his umbrella.

"Where are you going?"

"Out into the streets," he snapped as he went out the door, "with the rest of the midnight crazies." He slammed the door shut.

Anne groaned helplessly and slumped onto the sofa, burying her face in her hands. She felt tired, sad, and still very horny.

*　　*　　*

When Donald was a little boy, his mother had always told him that watching those "spooky plays" on TV—he'd liked shows like "Twilight Zone" and "Outer Limits"—would give him horrible nightmares, keep him up all night. But they never did. Oh, they scared him, there was no doubt about that. He fondly remembered sitting in front of the television with Julie (Bill was just a baby then), the two of them huddled close together, the volume low so their parents wouldn't hear the eerie music and come turn it off. They would sit Indian-style on the floor, slowly rocking back and forth, ready to hide their eyes during the scary parts.

No, those television shows never disturbed Donald's sleep. Neither did the horror comic books he liked to read, although his mother insisted that sooner or later they would. He supposed that, if she were still alive, she would tell him that the nightmares he was having now were just a delayed reaction, nothing more than the inevitable result of all those horrible, spooky plays.

He knew that wasn't the case, though. Maybe, back then when he was a small boy. But not now, a thirty-six-year-old man. This was something else.

When he got back from Anne's, the taste of blood faint in his mouth from chewing angrily on his lip, he turned on the television. After pouring a tall glass of scotch, he sat down and watched *Double Indemnity*, but without paying attention. His mind was elsewhere.

It was with a friend in a neighborhood theater on a Saturday afternoon in 1957, watching a Jerry Lewis movie. Donald remembered his friend—Toby, was it? or Jake—laughing happily, swatting his thigh now and then with his palm, which was spotted with chocolate from the candy bar he was eating, nudging Donald with his elbow whenever he found something funny. Donald was not laughing, however. He was a big fan of Jerry Lewis, thought he was very funny, but on that day his nine-year-old jackhammer laugh had been silent, the corners of his mouth turned downward a bit. Because something was wrong, something was out of balance. The movie made no sense to him, the theater—The Summit, where he spent almost every Saturday afternoon—kept fading in and out of familiarity. Even his seat felt different—smaller, or tilted, or something like that.

Those were not the things that really bothered him, though; they were merely additions to it, like subplots in a story. No, the thing that was most disturbing was the smell—the faint but definite smell of smoke, of something burning. He'd sat through the cartoon, the short, and the coming attractions, smelling it but saying nothing. He got halfway through *The Sad Sack* before turning to his friend to see if he smelled it, too. But he didn't. Finally, when he could not sit still any longer, Donald went into the lobby and found the assistant manager and asked if anything was burning. The man—tall, with a sort of pointy bald head—had become very nervous suddenly and told Donald not to say such a thing so loudly, told him that everything was just fine and he should go back to his seat and enjoy the picture. He didn't, though; he insisted that *something* was burning. His insistence got him kicked out of the theater.

That night, because of an uncomfortable feeling in his head—a light, sort of cloudy feeling—Donald had sat up in bed and stared out his window at the night sky, trying to ignore his discomfort. Until he saw the orange glow in the distance. Until he heard the sirens.

Due to faulty wiring, a fire had broken out that night in the Summit Theater right in the middle of a Bette Davis film, badly injuring several ushers and killing two customers. A number of others suffered from smoke inhalation, and the theater did not reopen for almost two years after that . . .

The clock on the wall said that it was now 4:37 in the morning. Donald's shoulders were beginning to ache with weariness, but his muscles were relaxed, thanks to the Scotch. He could not, however, rid himself of the knot of anger that remained in the pit of his stomach, a leftover from his encounter with Anne.

Anne, who he had *known* would not understand, would not *try* to understand. Why? he thought angrily. Why did I tell her, confide in her? How could she understand—how could anyone understand—what he was going through *now*, when she hadn't been there to see him go through it *before*, hadn't been there in that dark theater that smelled of doom, hadn't been with him that night he'd heard the sirens that made his veins fill with ice water.

Nor had she been with him on that misty November 1973 night in his little apartment in Healdsburg when he'd awakened to the faint sound of a child's voice calling for help. It was of no clear gender, it came from no one spot, and it seemed to be far away yet all around him, calling for help, crying in pain, begging for release. And then fading out. Gradually. He'd slept no more that night and was very tired when he went to work the next morning. He'd wanted nothing more than to forget the experience and teach his sixth-grade class well. But the memory of that frail voice would not leave him, and his eyes kept straying to the one empty seat in the classroom, wondering where that little girl was. Anne had not been there to see all the color leave Donald's face and to watch his knees buckle so that he had to sit down when the principal's secretary came in to tell him that one of his students had been found dead in a canal. She'd been raped and stabbed.

That night, Donald's sleep had been haunted once again by the voice of a child, almost a chanting plea for help. The words were muddled, but the intent was clear. It had happened again the next night, and the night after that, clouding Donald's thoughts during the day, robbing him of sleep at night. He dreaded going to work each day for fear of seeing another empty seat. And three weeks later, he did.

A little boy was found half buried in the woods by the Russian River after being missing for the weekend. He, too, had been raped and stabbed.

The killer was never found, but for more than two months, Donald had lived on coffee and No-Doz, sitting in front of the television at night hoping to drown out that phantom voice, not wanting to know that children were dying somewhere, not wanting to feel responsible because he was aware of it, yet helpless because he could do nothing. After four children had been killed, three of them from his class, the murders stopped, the voice went away, and he was able to sleep, to stop drinking so bloody much. And to live in peace. Of a sort.

No, Anne knew nothing, could understand nothing, because she hadn't been with him for the other times, either, all the countless *other* times:

—the times he'd told his mother she shouldn't leave the house just yet because she'd left the gas running on the kitchen stove, when there was no way he should have, or could have, known;

—the times he had known—just *known*—that a quiz or test was coming up when the teacher had meant for it to be a surprise, and the one time in particular when he'd inadvertently mentioned an upcoming test to a classmate—one that was meant to be secret—setting off a chain of events that ended in the principal's office where he'd had to lie about finding a copy of the test on his teacher's desk in order to avoid sounding crazy;

—the time Donald had told his father not to use the ladder to climb up on the roof of the house because two of the rungs were ready to give; he'd used it anyway, fallen, and broken his leg;

—and the time he'd had that dream, again and again, of his fiancée sleeping with another man—the custodian of the school Donald had been teaching at then—a dream with such detail that, when he awoke, Donald felt as though he'd actually watched them making love, heard their groans, their gasping breaths, had actually smelled their sex; he never married her.

Those and so very many other times, events that were big, and others that were trivial yet haunting, like knowing the dialogue in a movie before he heard it—in a movie he'd never seen before. Whenever he became ill, he didn't know if he was coming down with the flu or if something horrible was about to happen. He never knew if a nightmare was just a nightmare, or something else.

Like this one. This one had to be something else.

Anne could not know, would not understand. And if he sat her down right now and told her everything, every incident, every feeling he'd ever had, she *still* would not. And despite the anger he felt toward her now, the resentment and disappointment, he could not really blame her, he could not hold it against her. Because it was all so ridiculous. So insane.

Donald stood up with his drink and walked over to the front window in his living room, ignoring the voices on the television. The night sky was beginning to lighten. Soon the sun would be shining behind the fat, dark clouds that still floated about and threatened more rain. He drank, then leaned his forehead on the windowpane, enjoying the cold, hard glass against his flesh.

Suddenly he flinched. That vague reflection in the window's glass was not his, *could not* be his. He didn't look like that, surely. It was the face of a much older man. A man with many worries and a lot of fears. A man hanging from a rope

47

over a dark, black pit filled with whispering, slithering creatures that he could not see, knowing full well that at any moment the rope could snap and he could fall down into that darkness, fall right into the midst of those things that lay waiting for him at the bottom.

Donald's shoulders jerked twice with a cold, humorless chuckle. Yes. That face *was* his.

2

October was all around: the trees were coated with orange and yellow; the windows and doors of houses were decorated with cardboard skeletons and witches and black cats; the sky was a bully with dark puffy muscles that shifted and flexed, only occasionally letting the sun shine through, teasing it with freedom. The air was alive with that crisp chill that seems to come only in October, that playful chill that has more character that month than at any other time of the year, as if it's at first excited by the change of season and then calms down as the novelty wears off.

It was Donald's favorite time of the year. It was the time when the whole Napa Valley was scented by the crush, smelling like a freshly opened bottle of wine. Usually, Donald savored the aroma, like a wine snob smelling a bottle's cork. But today Donald was feeling as cloudy as the sky above him and hardly noticed the sweet fragrance. His ears were ringing slightly from the countless cups of coffee he'd had at the Season's Restaurant on Soscol, and his stomach still burned from all the Scotch he'd consumed before that.

The window of his Toyota wagon was rolled down and the icy air blasted his face as he drove through Napa, his elbow resting on the edge of the open window. It was almost eleven-thirty and Donald was not feeling in the least bit hungry; he was on his way to have lunch with his brother anyway.

Donald turned off of Jefferson, drove slowly into the dingy little trailer park where Bill lived, and parked in front of space 57. He got out of the car and climbed the creaky steps that led to the sliding glass door of the small mobile home. He saw Bill on the other side of the glass; the door slid open.

Donald froze for a moment and took in his brother's appearance. Bill, like Donald, had always been a big man— not fat, but strong, sturdy. He usually took big steps, moved quickly, stood straight. But the Bill who stood before Donald in the doorway of the trailer was different. He had a slight stoop, so slight that most would not notice it. He didn't fill his clothes as well as he usually did; they hung loosely on him. His shoulders, although still broad, were slumped a bit. His rusty hair, a little thicker than Donald's with fewer gray strands, was sloppy, unkempt, and his face was drawn and thin, his eyes hollow. A prickly chill scurried across the back of Donald's neck when it occurred to him that the disheveled appearance of his brother was very similar to his own.

"C'mon in and sit down, Donald." Bill gave him a quick, rather weak handshake.

Donald sat down on the end of a small, slightly ratty sofa and looked around the cramped but neat little room.

"Uh," Bill stood before him, shifting his weight from foot to foot, "I'm not much of a cook, you know, so I figured maybe we could go someplace a little later? Go for pizza or something, sound good?"

"Sure."

"Good. You thirsty?"

"No, not right now."

"Well. It's good to see you again. It's been a while."

"Yes, it has. Same here. It's good . . ." He tilted his head to the left a little, curiously. "Are you feeling okay these days, Bill?"

Bill shrugged in a quick, jerky way, and smiled crookedly.

"You look . . . well, no offense, but you look kind of washed out. Have you been working too hard?" Donald had heard those words directed at himself so many times lately, it felt good to be saying them to someone *else* for a change.

Bill rubbed his palms up and down over his blue denim thighs as he sat down in his easy chair, facing Donald. "Well, I just ain't been—I mean, haven't, *haven't* been . . ." He smiled broadly. Grammar was an old joke between them—one of the only old jokes between them. "I haven't been sleeping well lately. And yeah, I guess I been working too hard."

Donald's face tightened; his chest, his whole body tightened. *Haven't been sleeping well lately.* "Night . . ." He swallowed the dry lump in his throat. "Nightmares?" he asked, almost too softly.

"Ah, sometimes. Mostly just, I don't know, I've got a lot on my mind these days, it seems." He dropped his gaze to his lap and scratched the back of his head. "That, uh . . . that's what I want to talk to you about."

Donald was nodding absently. He was chewing on his lower lip again, wondering what was coming up, wondering what vile sore was festering in the near future, waiting to infect and spread.

"You know," Bill said, somewhat uncertainly, "you don't look so good yourself. You're a little green around the gills, and your eyes are bloodshot. How are *you* sleeping?"

"Well . . . I haven't been sleeping well myself, as a matter of fact."

51

Their eyes locked and there was a loud silence between them for a few moments, broken finally when Bill said, "Whatta ya feel like? Burgers? Pizza? Whatta ya say?"

The Pizza Pit was dark and murky inside, the air thick with spicy smells and loud with the beeps and bloops of video games in the back. Eric Clapton was singing about '57 Chevys and screaming guitars on the juke. Donald had not felt particularly hungry before, but the restaurant's aroma stirred his appetite; he hadn't had a pizza in some time.

They sat at one of the rustic wooden tables in the corner, each with a beer, waiting for their order. Bill held a cigar between his teeth and Donald was just opening a pack of cigarettes he'd gotten from a machine at the entrance.

"I don't know, Donald," Bill sighed. "Everything just seems sort of upside down. I guess I should've expected it. Had to come sooner or later. I mean, jeez, Beth and I have been divorced, what, four years now?"

Donald smiled around his cigarette as he touched the matchflame to it. "A woman?" he guessed, breathing smoke.

Bill nodded clumsily, one side of his mouth cocking up. "Yeah." His smile faded, though; his face darkened as he stared dully at his beer.

"Something wrong, Bill?"

With his thumb and forefinger, Bill twirled the smoking cigar back and forth between his lips, puffing now and then. "I don't really know, Donald. She's . . . she's different."

"Well, who is she, how did you meet her?"

"It's a weird story."

"Let's hear it." Donald leaned forward on the tabletop.

Bill fidgeted in his seat, a preparatory gesture, moving his hands down to his beer mug, a palm on each side of it. "Did you hear about that fire, the big fire a couple of weeks ago? East of town, in the woods by the river?"

Donald nodded silently.

"Well, I was there, working my ass off. Sure was a big fire. We never found out what caused it. Never found out what that smell was, either."

"Smell?"

Bill nodded. "Yeah, you didn't hear about that? There was a horrible smell there, awful. Really sweet and . . . well, it kind of stung your nostrils, you know? Anyway, we worked through most of the night, till we'd finally killed the worst of it. We weren't done, though, not by a long shot. Damned thing hung on.

"We were all ready to drop, you know? We'd started around nine-thirty and it was going on three in the morning by then. All of a sudden, we hear this scream. We all just froze, right where we were, staring at the dark around us, and we heard it again. It was goddamned awful, worst thing I ever heard. Even worse because, as soon as I heard it, I knew who it was and I almost threw up right there, cause Eddie . . . well, Eddie just wasn't the kind to scream like that. *No* man screams like that. Unless it's his last. And it was."

Bill wrapped his fingers around the mug handle, removed the cigar from his mouth, and drank half the beer, his Adam's apple bobbing up and down like a yo-yo. He put the beer back down, returned the cigar, puffed thick, bluish smoke as he shook his head from left to right.

"Eddie Monohan—he was a good guy, a drinking buddy of mine—he'd gone over to kill some spot fires, you know? He was alone, but hell, Eddie was no wimp, he could take care of himself, we all knew that." He shook his head some more. "When we heard the screams, we pretty much dropped what we were doing and made a run for Eddie. But we couldn't find him. It was still pretty dark, even with our headlamps. Then I happened to walk through a patch of bushes that hadn't burned, took off a glove to scratch my eyes—they were itching and stinging like crazy—and I felt something on my hand. Something wet and warm. Then I stopped. I felt the bush next to me and . . . I could see by the light of my headlamp . . . the leaves were dripping blood. I shifted my feet kind of, and . . . there was . . . it was on the ground . . . in a puddle." He shook his head and sighed. "Jesus."

Donald took a drink of his beer, then set the mug aside, as if it might interfere with his brother's story. His eyes were like wide windows and his eyebrows hung down over them tightly, like little awnings. "I heard something about that in the news, but I had no idea he was a friend of yours," Donald whispered.

"Yeah. They wanted to keep it quiet, at least until they found Eddie, or was sure he was . . . you know, dead. But when the same thing started happening to other people in San Francisco and . . . hell, all *over* the place . . . well, it was big news. A *mystery*. I stayed out of the spotlight, though. Didn't want to get involved."

Donald took a long drag on his cigarette, drank some more beer. "What does all of this have to do with your lady friend?"

Bill's mouth smiled, but his eyes remained dark. "That's where I met her. After we found all that blood, we spread out to look for Eddie. We figured he was hurt bad, or something. So I was walking around, poking into bushes, calling Eddie's name. There were a few patches of fire burning, and everything still reeked, and . . . I don't know, the lighting just made it kind of spooky, you know? And naturally, not knowing what had happened to Eddie, we were all of us kind of jumpy. So when I pulled back this bush and saw somebody crouched down behind it, I nearly shit in my pants." He chuckled and puffed on his cigar. "There she was, behind this bush, holding some clothes around her. I asked her who she was and she goes, 'Sshhh! Just leave me alone and I'll go!'

" 'Go *where?*' I asked her. 'What the hell are you doing out here? Are you hurt?' Her face looked kinda smudged, so I thought maybe she'd been burned, or something. And her clothes, they were really dark. There was something funny about the way they clung to her. She wasn't wearing them, whatever they were, she was holding them up in front of her. She was obviously naked, and that was kind of . . . well, distracting, because she was *beautiful*.

"She said she wasn't hurt or anything. 'And I haven't done anything illegal,' she says. 'Just pretend you never saw me and I'll go away.' But when I asked her what she *had* done to get stuck out there with her clothes off, she made this little sobbing-laughing noise and said, 'It's a long, *stupid* story.' Then she looked up at me with these big, beautiful eyes and said with the sweetest voice, 'Don't give me away and I'll tell you all about it over dinner tomorrow night.'

"I stood there a few seconds and just looked at her—god, she was an eyeful—and I realized, just then, how familiar she looked. Like I'd seen her someplace before, you know? 'Have we met before?' I asked her.

" 'What's your name?' she says. So I told her. 'No. We've never met before. But we'll meet again. Now, *beat it!*'

"So I smiled at her, turned, and started to walk away. Then I remembered what the hell I was doing, and I turned back to ask her if she'd maybe seen Eddie. And she was gone. She hadn't even told me her name! How the hell was I going to have dinner with her?'' He finished off his beer, then licked his lips thoroughly.

"We never found Eddie's body, of course,'' he continued after a few moments. "It was his blood, but damned if we could find his body. *Nowhere!* Turned those goddamned woods inside out. Nothing. He was just gone.''

"What about the woman?" Donald asked.

"She looked me up in the phone book and called me the next day. And we went to dinner. She explained to me what had happened. Seems she'd been to the river with some lover that night, some guy she'd been going with. They got into a booger of a fight and she refused to leave with him. So he left without her. And took her clothes with him."

"What was she holding in front of her when you met her?" Donald asked, feeling more and more uncomfortable with the story as it went on.

Bill shrugged. "Don't know."

"Wasn't it cold?"

"A little chilly, I guess. Yeah. Anyway, we got along really well. She ditched this guy, the one she'd gone to the river with. We started spending a lot of time together. But ever since I first saw her that night in the bushes, I knew I'd seen her somewhere before. Bugged the *hell* out of me. Up until late last week, I been beating my brains out, trying to figure out why she looked so familiar."

"All the while, though, you were seeing her pretty regularly?" Donald took a drag on his cigarette, without really knowing it, and let the smoke out easily, but very slowly.

"Oh, yeah. Nearly every night. Every *other* night, at least. She and I've been having a ball. She's a knockout, fun to be with . . . Last Thursday, though, I was kicking around the station; there was nothing going on, I had nothing to do, so I picked up a magazine. I came to an advertisement, an ad for women's cigarettes, and it hit me. Hit me like a wrecking ball." He fidgeted nervously, tugged at his lower lip, chewed on his cigar. "See," he continued, "Eddie Monohan and me, we played cards together a lot, went out, kicked back a few when we had time off. And we talked a lot. Being a couple of single guys, you know, we talked about women a lot. Women we knew, wanted to get to know. One night, Eddie and I were both at the station, shooting the breeze. He picks up a magazine, thumbs through it, and all of a sudden he smiles real big and says, 'Yeah, yeah, that's what I want. Right there.' He holds up the magazine and shows me the ad, the cigarette ad.''

Bill leaned to his right, reached his hand down to his hip and pulled out his wallet. As he opened it and removed a folded piece of glossy paper, he said, "I tore the ad out. I wanted to show it to you." He handed it over to Donald.

Donald carefully unfolded the magazine page. The creases were ready to tear, the corners were dog-eared, but the picture was very clear. It showed a thin young woman—long, tan legs topped by a skimpy pair of leopard-skin bikini bottoms, shimmering blond hair that cascaded down over her breasts—stretched out on a wet, glistening rock, luxuriously smoking a long, thin cigarette. In the slightly blurred background there stood a muscular, Tarzan-type man at the foot of a tall, sparkling waterfall, looking on. The ad read: "For the natural woman—Eden Cigarettes.''

"Eddie showed me that and he says, 'Billy, this is my idea of beauty. Eve: the perfect woman. Know what I mean, Bill? If I had my choice, that is exactly what my woman would look like. Except she'd have black hair. Black hair, not blond. I like my women dark and mysterious.' '' After a pause, as if to let what he'd said sink in, Bill opened another compartment in his wallet and removed a snapshot. "We had this taken in one of those photo booths, you know the kind? It's not very good, but . . . that's her." He handed it across the table.

Donald squinted at the picture in the dim light, holding it close to his face. He glanced at the cigarette ad. Then the snapshot again.

Bill stood behind the woman in the picture, a happy,

almost childlike smile on his face. The woman wore a comfortable-looking gray jacket over a white, blousy top. She was thin with a dark tan and long, cascading hair.

She was identical to the woman in the advertisement. Except for her black hair. Long, shiny black hair.

Donald's lips formed the word he wanted to say, but it didn't come out at first. He tried again. "Wh-what did you say her name is?"

"I didn't." Bill took his cigar from his mouth, held it between the knuckles of his first two fingers. He ran his thumbnail across his lower lip.

"Well . . . what is it?" Donald's voice was a bit weak.

Bill leaned forward just a little. "Her name is Eve."

Donald belched beer and pepperoni all the way home. He had the car's heater going full blast to fight off the chill that was making him tremble all over. He'd been able to eat very little pizza, much less than he'd expected. Bill's story had dampened his appetite.

His brother was in love with this woman, and had come to him for advice! "I don't know nothing about her, and . . . well, you gotta admit," Bill had said with a nervous chuckle, "it's kind of weird, the way we met. But, I think I love her."

What was Donald to say? How could he tell Bill to stay away from her, to cut all ties with her, when he had no reason, no explanation for his feeling—that razor-sharp feeling in his gut—that this woman was evil?

"She's different, Don," Bill had said, a drop of sweat glistening on his upper lip over the cigar, "but that's part of the attraction, know what I mean? She's beautiful and mysterious and . . . well, she likes me. She *likes* me, Donald."

Something about the way Bill said that made Donald feel very sad.

"We haven't, uh, done anything yet," Bill had continued.

"I mean, you know, slept together, or anything. She's . . . I don't know, she's different than other women. It'll wait, know what I mean?" He'd sniffed then, puffed on the cigar. "I don't eat much, I don't sleep well. Hell, I haven't felt this way since I was in high school. Guess I got it bad, huh, big brother?" He'd smiled and drummed three fingers on the tabletop anxiously as he said, "I got a date with her tonight. Dinner at Vivaldi's—like I can afford it, huh? She's really something, Donald. A real catch, you know?"

No, Donald didn't know. He didn't know anything, and yet he knew more than he wanted to. When he got home, he had another Scotch. For a moment, he thought that perhaps he was drinking a little too much, but then he flicked the thought away like lint off of his lapel. His drinks were becoming his friends now.

Somewhere in town, a creature calling itself Eve waited for its evening with Bill Ellis, looked forward to it eagerly . . .

3

The words QUEERS WILL DIE were scrawled across the reflection of Kyle's face, cut clumsily into the mirror in the men's room at school. He raced a comb through his hair, his straight, somewhat limp, dirty-blond hair responding with its usual indifference; he was in a hurry. He'd gotten into a rather heated discussion with Miss Cramer about his grade on the last algebra test—he was convinced he deserved better, but, of course, she thought otherwise—and he'd not heard the bell that signified the beginning of the next period, which was his English class with Mr. Ellis. Miss Cramer had been in a bad mood and especially difficult to reason with—more difficult than usual. She was a beautiful woman, whatever her age—a question that was the subject of a number of bets among several of her male students—but her beauty was outweighed by her almost intolerable personality. She was a barracuda in the classroom, ruthlessly grading her students with a total disregard for their grade-point averages. She was a cold one, all right. For a while, Kyle had thought something was developing between Mr. Ellis and the Barracuda. But if there *had* been something, it had apparently faded out, much to Kyle's relief. He knew Mr. Ellis could do a lot better.

Kyle stuffed his comb into his back pocket and was starting to wash his hands when he heard the bathroom door open. It wasn't until then that he realized he'd been alone. He heard the footsteps first, slapping on the hard floor, slow, easy. Then he saw the guy in the mirror, coming up behind him, his hands in the pockets of his dark brown leather jacket, the leather crinkling softly as he moved. The guy's face was tight, tense, as he looked around the bathroom, as he walked over to stand beside Kyle, staring into the long, rectangular mirror that was mounted on the wall above the row of sinks. He just stood there and looked at himself, jutting his chin, tilting his head, sniffing, flaring his nostrils. He was handsome, with black hair that swept back in a short, stylish cut, olive complexion, piercing brown eyes.

As Kyle scrubbed his hands under the water, he turned and smiled at the stranger, but was ignored. He'd never seen this guy before and thought he might be new.

The boy leaned forward, looking closely at his reflection, lightly touching his cheekbone.

"Something wrong?" Kyle asked, ripping a couple of paper towels from the dispenser on the wall.

The guy turned and looked at Kyle as if he hadn't noticed him until that moment. He stared; no expression, no reaction, just those eyes looking right into him, searing little holes into Kyle's head, like sunlight shining on paper through a magnifying glass.

Kyle turned, got his books from the shelf by the door, and left the rest room, feeling very uncomfortable.

The stranger's gaze turned back to the mirror.

*   *   *

Asshole, Kyle thought, as he hurried to class. What would guys like that do without mirrors? They couldn't look at themselves then—they'd probably go crazy.

He tried to be inconspicuous as he entered the classroom. It was dark inside, quiet, except for the dialogue coming from the television screen in front. Kyle found a seat and put his books underneath, trying to figure out what was being shown.

It was a video of *The Merchant of Venice*—looked like the PBS production. Kyle glanced around but could see Mr. Ellis nowhere in the darkened room. He leaned over and asked Randy Stone, "Where's Mr. Ellis?"

Randy was doodling on paper. "He's sick today. Didn't come in."

Kyle leaned back. Mr. Ellis *had* looked sick Friday, and he'd probably been sicker than he'd let on. Kyle decided to stop by and see him after class.

Donald hoped that he would receive no visitors as he dropped some ice cubes into his glass. They clinked and clattered, then popped and cracked as he poured Scotch over them.

The Roadrunner beeped and whizzed on the television in the living room. Rain fell steadily outside. Shades were pulled over the windows and the light was dim; the lamp by the sofa was on.

Donald shuffled to the sofa in his bathrobe, drink in hand, a cigarette held between his lips. He'd waited until noon to start drinking today; he thought that was only proper. It was about two-thirty and he was feeling the Scotch, the good old Scotch, his buddy and pal who helped him ignore the screaming ache in his joints, the feeling of some sort of fuzz—living, crawling fuzz—occasionally scurrying over his brain inside his skull.

He hadn't even bothered trying to sleep last night. He'd sat up drinking coffee, smoking, watching television. Twice he dozed a little. Around six-thirty he ate a little breakfast, even though he wasn't particularly hungry, but it made him ill and he threw it all up a while later. That was when he'd decided to call in sick. No way could he sit through classes today. He wondered how he would be able to do it tomorrow. And the next day. The next . . .

There was a knock at his front door and he winced as if he'd been pricked with a pin. Putting his drink down, he went to the door and looked out the peephole. Kyle Hubbley's face was contorted by the little lens, rounded outward nightmarishly. Donald unlocked the door and opened it.

"Hi, Mr. Ellis."

"Hello, Kyle."

"How . . . how are you?" He looked up at the taller man, eyes sharp with concern behind his glasses. He had obviously not expected to see Donald in such a disheveled state.

"Well, Kyle, to tell you the truth, I feel like shit warmed over."

"I'm sorry you're sick. I just thought I'd drop by and see how you were. I don't have to stay if you're feeling really bad."

"No, no, come on in, Kyle. I could use the company. If you don't mind a messy house." He stepped aside and let Kyle enter, taking the boy's coat and hanging it on the back of the chair by the phone. "Have a seat. Can I get you anything? Tab? A Coke?"

"No, sit down. You're sick, remember?"

"Oh, yeah. Almost forgot." Donald sat down slowly with a long, heavy sigh. "So, did you enjoy the video in class today?"

"Yes. Especially Shylock."

"Good performance. Very good." Donald's words came out a little slurred. He picked up his drink, the ice clinking gently. "The medicine you don't need a prescription for." He smiled, holding the glass up to Kyle in a half-toast.

"No, but you need an I.D."

Donald laughed at that, a genuine, spontaneous laugh, smoothed out by the Scotch-induced relaxation he was feeling. "How'd the weekend go, Kyle?"

"Boring. I watched television, slaved over algebra. I'm not doing too well in that class, and I think I deserve better."

"Anne's class? I mean, Miss Cramer's?"

"Mm-hm."

"Do you think she's in error in her grading?"

"Yes. But she doesn't. She and I had a talk about it today." Kyle chuckled coldly. "Quite a talk it was."

Donald did not pursue that; he just nodded. "Yes, she's very adamant about what she thinks, no doubt about it."

Kyle stared at the television for a few seconds. "You're watching cartoons?"

Donald nodded, smiled weakly. "I'm not a soap fan, and that's about the only other thing that's on right now. I'd go down to Videoland and pick up a couple of movies if I felt better." He hadn't even considered doing that, but he knew Kyle would like the idea and he decided that Kyle's company was better than sitting around alone.

Kyle's eyes brightened. "You want *me* to? I will, if you'd like."

Donald scowled in mock suspicion. "Shouldn't you be home studying, boy?"

"Nah, I have really nice teachers."

Donald got his wallet, gave Kyle some money, and told him to pick up a couple of whatever he wanted to see. Then he sat down in front of Daffy Duck and Porky Pig to finish his drink.

*   *   *

Barbra Streisand was singing on the radio and the wipers were sweeping back and forth over the windshield of Kyle's blue Volkswagen bug. The streets of Napa ran together in a blurry puddle through the watery glass; his wipers were not working properly and couldn't keep up with the rainfall.

Mr. Ellis looked as though he'd aged five years since Friday, Kyle thought as he came to a stop at a red light. Mr. Ellis's face had looked so wrinkled—as if it were about to slide off his head. And he'd been drinking. From the way he spoke and acted, he'd apparently been drinking for some time. Kyle had never known Mr. Ellis to do that, and he wondered what was wrong, what was eating him besides the flu, if he really *had* the flu at *all*.

If it were another teacher, like Miss Cramer or Mr. Reilly, Kyle would not have felt such concern. None of *them* had come to visit Kyle regularly in the hospital when he'd had his appendix taken out last year; only Mr. Ellis had. In fact, that was how they'd become such good friends. That was when Kyle had began to look at Mr. Ellis as more than just someone who stood at the head of the class talking and writing things on the blackboard. He became someone with whom Kyle had a great deal in common, and with whom he could talk easily, with more ease than he felt while talking to his parents, in fact. And yet, he didn't really know Mr. Ellis, didn't know a whole lot about him despite the feeling of closeness that existed between them.

Kyle pulled into the small parking lot in front of Videoland. He turned the ignition off and looked at himself in the rearview mirror. He wanted to look presentable at the very *least:* Leslie Newell worked at Videoland.

A James Bond movie was playing on the big-screen television. Leslie had wanted to watch *Body Heat*, but they weren't allowed to show R-rated movies in the store. Business was slow today, so she thought it probably would make no difference. But if Miss Pemberton, her boss, happened to drop in, she wouldn't be too pleased. And Gary Whittaker just couldn't appreciate good movies like *Body Heat*, anyway. Gary was the asshole she had to work with. He liked movies with exploding cars and high-speed chases, shit like that. No romance, no sex.

"Bond," Roger Moore was saying on the screen. "*James Bond.*"

Gary laughed joyfully, loudly, and pounded a fist on the counter by the cash register. "Yeah! I *love* the way he says that!"

God, what a prick, Leslie thought. Wouldn't surprise me a bit if Roger Moore turned the little queer on.

Gary leaned on the counter, his head craned forward on his skinny neck, his large, goiterlike Adam's apple bobbing now and then. He wore thick glasses, and when he smiled, his mouth was so big that it pushed the glasses up on his pocked cheeks.

Leslie stood at the far end of the counter, blankly watching the screen, wanting to be as far away from Gary as possible. She tried to bury the sounds of the movie and the thoughts of her co-worker (a title that sounded far too important and responsible to be tacked onto that little shit) with the anticipation she felt about the upcoming evening. She was going out with Dave Milken. He was supposed to have taken her out Saturday evening, but something had come up. Something had come up with Dave, not with Leslie, which was quite unusual. If any backing out was done, Leslie was usually the one who did it. Usually, guys with whom she agreed to go out were too grateful to back out of anything. She was going to give Dave another chance, however. She thought he might be able to make up for it, he might be worth it. God, he was good-looking. Not just attractive, but *hot*—like he was ready to fuck, anytime, anywhere. Most guys *were*, she knew, but she'd never known one to *look* that way with such appealing results. She hoped his looks weren't deceiving.

Like Jordy Gillis's. He looked fine, but what a wimp. She'd gone out with him last spring, thinking he would be a real sizzle, what with that big bulge in his crotch. He'd taken her to the drive-in to see a couple of kung-fu flicks, but of course they hadn't watched the movies. Afterward, Leslie wished they had.

He'd gotten her into the backseat of his Camaro, his hands going all the hell over her body, mostly over her tits. He wouldn't let them go, for god's sake! He'd kissed her for a while, then frantically opened the top she'd been wearing, almost popping all the buttons, and started slobbering all over her tits! She'd tried to divert his attention and eventually got his cock out. What a joke. It certainly hadn't been the cause of that bulge, although she'd never found out what was.

"Yeah, yeah, yeah," he'd hissed, straddling her with his knees.

"Wait! My pants . . ."

"No, no." His voice had quivered. "Your tits, I wanna fuck your tits, put it between your tits."

"But what about—"

"Your tits, baby, I wanna fuck your tits!"

That was when she'd pushed him off of her, buttoned her blouse, told him he was a goddamned perverted son of a bitch and stormed to the snack bar where she had called her girl friend Val to come get her. She'd seen to it that word got around about Jordy Gillis and his tit fixation, and he'd suddenly found it very difficult to get dates.

Then there had been Rodney Pearce. He was good-looking, of course, or she wouldn't have gone out with him, but he was shy, *so* shy. He'd taken her to dinner a few weeks ago and he'd sat across the table from her in total silence, saying nothing. So she'd just stared at him, giving him her best, using her eyes, her lips. When they got up, he'd been hesitant, then he'd walked sort of funny, bent over a little, and she'd known then that she'd gotten what she'd wanted: he was hard as a rock. When they got in the car, Leslie had turned to him, putting her hand over his hard cock, knowing that if she didn't do anything, he wouldn't either, and she'd said, "You know, this doesn't do anyone any good unless you share it." God, now *there* was a guy who knew how to fuck. He sure hadn't been shy once that beautiful pole was out in the open . . .

"Leslie!"

She started, taken from her thoughts, and turned to Gary.

"Jeez, what are you, asleep? A customer. *I* handled the last one, now it's your turn."

She'd been leaning her elbows on the counter, staring blindly at the screen. She looked over at the customer. It was that Hubbler, Hubbleman, Hubble guy, whatever the hell his name was, from school. The fat one who was always coming into the store. She wasn't sure what he came in for most of the time—to look through the video selection or to look at her. She walked over to him, joined her hands in front of her, pasted on a smile, and said, "May I help you?"

He turned to her and smiled back. The smile was a little too big, and Leslie supposed he thought he was making a good impression. He was probably undressing her there in the middle of that chubby little mind of his, as well.

"Yes, I'm looking for *Cat People*," he said, his voice a little too steady, his nod a little too pronounced.

Yep, she thought, he's trying to make a good impression. Fat chance, no pun intended.

"The original," he continued, "from 1942. Not the remake."

She reached for the tape and glanced at the number. "Right here."

"I'd also like *Tales from the Crypt*."

Creepy taste, this guy.

"Come over here," she said, leading him to the counter. She looked on the back shelf down the rows of cartridges until she found the ones he wanted, then rang them up on the register. Leslie looked him over a couple of times as he paid for the rentals. Without interest, of course. Chubby cheeks, sort of a pouty mouth. Nice eyes, very nice. Put those eyes on a good body and you might have something. She giggled inside, shaking her head back and forth slightly. They were all basically the same, guys. It's just that some of them came in better packages than others. She put the cartridges in a bag and handed them to him. "Have a nice day."

"I'll try. You do the same, Leslie." He smiled, actually blushed a little. "Um, I know your name because we go to school together. I'm Kyle Hubbley."

So fucking *what*, Porky? she thought. But she flashed a very brief smile and nodded silently.

"Well," he chirped—yes, it was a goddamned chirp, like some kind of bird—as he headed for the door, calling over his shoulder, "I'll see you later."

God, I hope not.

The bell over the door rang as Lyle or Kyle, whoever the hell, went out, and it rang again immediately as someone else came in. Out of the corner of her eye, Leslie saw Kyle stop just outside, turn, and look through the glass door at the newcomer, as if he knew him. Leslie's attention quickly focused on the next customer. He walked into the store—was that a walk? or a march, a strut?—his hands in the pockets of his brown leather jacket, which was flecked with raindrops. His black hair looked as if it hadn't been touched by the breeze outside. And was that a tan? Where the hell did he get

70

a tan in October, in *this* weather? His jeans were tight—deliciously tight: the seam that went through the crotch separated his balls and she could make out the protrusion of his cock pushed to the left. When he turned to look at a display of X-rated videos, she saw his ass—the most perfect ass she'd ever seen on anyone. God, it almost took her breath away. She felt her mouth quiver upward into an uncontrollable smile.

Gary opened his thin-lipped little mouth and started to come out with his "Howdy-there-what-can-I-do-for-you?" schtick, but Leslie beat him to it.

"May I help you?" she asked, walking around the counter again.

A car exploded on the television screen and machine guns ratta-tatta-tatta-ed loudly, quickly snatching Gary's attention away from the new customer. Leslie suddenly hoped the zipper down the front of her lavender jumpsuit was open enough to show some cleavage.

He looked up from the videos, his head moving slowly, almost dreamily, and she thought he was going to smile. It was as if the muscles in his face were preparing to pull the corners of his lips up in a friendly greeting. But they never did. He just looked at her. And yet something about his face changed, became warm, and she knew the change was for her.

"Just looking, thank you." His voice sounded as if it were coming from very expensive stereo speakers, like the ones her brother had. It was sharp, solid, very carefully modulated, perfectly balanced. He turned his head back to the display.

Leslie joined her hands together in front of her again, standing a little straighter, thrusting her breasts out just a bit, almost imperceptibly. "Looking for anything in particular?"

He raised his head again. "Something . . . hot. Really hot.

71

You know what I'm talking about?'' His eyes held hers this time, did not look away.

She gestured to the porn flicks in their cardboard packages. ''Well, I'm not too familiar . . .'' she began, but her voice trailed off. His eyes were still boring into hers. Then they were on her mouth, caressing her lips, licking them, then her throat; his eyes seemed to breathe warmly on her throat, her shoulders, her breasts, holding, squeezing, gently tweaking her nipples, which were growing, hardening like pebbles.

''Got any suggestions?'' he asked, one brow rising. He was looking into her eyes again.

''Nuh-no . . . I, uh . . .'' She wanted to speak, to sound intelligent, talk to him, but she couldn't. She just *couldn't!* Her knees were trembling. Was he going to stand there forever, looking at her like that, looking her straight in the eye as if he'd known her for years? He seemed to stand there for an eternity . . . another . . .

''I think I'll look around some more,'' he said finally, his voice so surprising, it was almost like a clap of thunder in Leslie's ears. ''But I'll be back.'' He turned and walked to the door, the sides of his ass moving up and down, up and down, the jeans clinging to his perfect legs.

She watched him saunter out the door, continued to watch him through the glass as he crossed the parking lot through the rain, as he rounded the corner on the sidewalk and disappeared. She stood there for a long time, even after she could no longer see him.

Nothing like that had ever happened to Leslie before. That was not the way she usually liked it; *she* wanted to be in control, to have the upper hand. She didn't like being rendered speechless. And yet, the experience had not been a bad one. There was something pleasurable about it, in a nervous sort of way. Something—

''Well, well,'' said Gary.

She turned to see him leaning against the edge of the counter, staring at her smugly. *Stupidly*.

"Have you been swept off your feet?" he asked mockingly.

Leslie's mouth, which had been open just a tiny bit, snapped shut and her eyes narrowed. "Whittaker," she said softly, coldly, "eat shit and die."

The creature rounded the corner, its boots clacking on the wet sidewalk. A chilling breeze fluttered its smooth, black hair, and tiny sprinkles of rain pattered on its jacket. It put its hands in the jacket's pockets, marveling once again at the strange feel of the heavy, thick material: so smooth and slick, with a flexible stiffness to it unlike any material the creature had ever felt before. It was an entirely new feeling. There was nothing like it where the creature had come from. It felt very good.

The creature looked to its right and saw its reflection in the windows of the shops it was passing. It watched itself carefully, but inconspicuously. It looked right, it moved right. The creature was pleased, as it always was when well-disguised. To be so different and yet fit in so easily made it very happy.

The air around it became warm and rich, and it suddenly sniffed, its nostrils flaring a bit. It turned its gaze from the windows as it walked. A couple passed by, a male and female, young, holding each other tightly, laughing, and the creature could smell their desire, their need for one another. It thought of the girl it had just left. She was right. It could sense a strength about her, and her passion was so strong that the creature could almost *see* it in a cloud, hovering about her, more definite than any it had ever encountered. It would pursue her, toy with her a little.

This is good, the creature thought as its boots continued to hit the wet cement. This is *very* good.

*   *   *

"Interesting little movie," Donald said as Kyle hit the REWIND button on the VCR. "Who did you say the cat woman was?" He'd asked before.

"Simone Simon."

"Ah. She was *very* pretty."

"I loved her accent," Kyle said, sitting down next to Donald again.

"I used to go to high school with a girl who had a French accent." Donald's sentences were beginning to sound like single words now, his speech was so slurred. He was a little too drunk to see the worried look on Kyle's face. "Dated her for a while. God, she was beautiful."

"Were you two very serious?"

"Nah, I never got serious with anybody in high school. I was having too much fun, dating too many different girls. I don't say that to boast, by the way. I think that's the way all kids should spend their high school years. Most of their college years, too. Plenty of time to get serious."

"Yeah." Kyle's voice dropped and he looked down at his hands in his lap.

"Do you have any romantic interests, Kyle?"

A chuckle. "I'm afraid not."

"How come? Why the laughter?"

"You don't seriously think I can just walk out and get a girl to go to a movie, or something, any day of the week, do you?"

"Why not?"

"Well, for starters, I'm fat."

"Oh, Kyle my friend, you're not fat. You're just—"

"If you say 'husky,' I'll forget that you're older than me and I'll hit you."

"No, no." Donald laughed, waving a hand at Kyle. "You're just a big guy. You could lose a few pounds, sure. But you're not grossly *obese,* you're not *fat.*"

"I'm not very tall, I've got ugly hair, and my teeth are kind of crooked."

"Jesus, Kyle, you're making yourself sound like Quasimodo. You are a good-looking young man, really. You look mature, intelligent."

"No disrespect, Mr. Ellis, but I'm afraid that's bullshit." The VCR finished rewinding with a loud click and Kyle went over to turn it off. Then he plopped onto the sofa again.

"If you keep talking that way, other people will start to believe it."

"I talk that way because other people *already* believe it. Have for years."

Donald took his glass from the end table. There was no more Scotch in it, but he shook the ice around and drank a bit of the water that had melted in the bottom of the glass.

"Mr. Ellis, I'm just not the kind of guy that attracts girls. I mean, I don't look good in tight designer jeans—in tight *anything*—I don't play football, and I refuse to appear in public unless I'm fully clothed, so that lets out beaches. I'm just not what they want."

"But not all girls *want* that, you know. Some actually *do* have brains." He smiled. "You don't want a typical girl, Kyle. You don't want a . . . oh, say, a Leslie Newell, or—"

"Yes, I do," Kyle broke in with a giggle.

"Well, sure, deep down inside, what guy doesn't? But honestly, Kyle, she's not your type. She's . . . oh, I don't know. You just want someone above that, *better* than that. That's between us, though. It's not good for teachers to talk about their students that way. Out of school." He smiled again at his pun.

"Look, Mr. Ellis, I don't really care what kind of personality she has. I don't have any experience with girls, you know? I don't know how to handle them, how to act around them, how to . . . how to *anything*. All I want now is a little experience. But I don't know how to get *that,* either. Know what I mean?''

Donald sucked on his lips and nodded his head slowly, crookedly. ''I see. You just want . . . you just want, um . . .''

''Experience.''

''Ex*peri*ence, of course.''

Kyle sighed. He was simply unaccustomed to seeing Mr. Ellis in such a giddy, disjointed state. ''It's like trying to get your first job; nobody hires you unless you have experience, and you can't get experience unless someone hires you. It's a real pain.''

Donald clapped his hands together suddenly and rubbed them together, laughing. ''Well, Kyle, lucky for you, I'm drunk. Maybe I can, you know, give you a few tips. So.'' He laughed again, the laugh sharp and uncharacteristic. ''What do you want to know?''

Dave Milken's van was carpeted and had a very expensive stereo installed in it, which was belting Joan Jett.

The lights were all off except for the soft green light on the stereo and they were naked in the dark, Dave and Leslie, moving together. He was sliding smoothly in and out of her, his face hovering over hers, one hand kneading a breast, the other hand buried in her hair.

''You like that, honey, you like what I'm doing?'' he gasped.

''Oh, yes, god, yes, keep it up, keep it moving,'' she replied thickly, her eyes closed, her hips moving with him. In her mind, however, the face above her was not that of Dave Milken. It was the dark, sharply featured face of the guy who had come into the store that day. It was *his* hand on her breast, *his* cock—the one she'd seen a hint of under those jeans—thrusting in and out of her, *his* hard, tense ass she was clutching so tightly with her hands.

If not tonight, she thought, then soon . . .

4

The next day, Tuesday, Donald stood in his classroom with a million marching bands in his head simultaneously playing everything John Philip Sousa ever composed. He'd taken some aspirin but it had only given him a stomachache. When the final bell for the period rang, it pierced his skull like a hot needle.

"If I could have your attention," he said to his students, trying to pronounce each word clearly, separately, "I'd like to get started as soon as possible. I don't feel very well today, so I'm not going to stand up here and verbalize a whole lot."

A couple of students applauded jokingly, and the rest of the class laughed. Donald held up a hand to silence them. He tried to smile, but it just didn't work.

"I'm giving you a couple of in-class essays to write—"

There were groans.

"—as much as I know you hate them. There are three, actually. I'll list them on the board. You only have to write one, though. Okay?" Several heads nodded in reply. Donald turned to the board and picked up a piece of chalk, lifted his lead-heavy hand and began to write. The chalk scuffed on the board, tossing tiny particles of white dust here and there. He heard the students talking to one another behind him. The classroom door opened; Donald heard the footsteps of someone coming into the room, heard the door close, but he did not turn around, assuming it was only a tardy student. He glanced now and then at the paper he held that had the questions written on it. He wanted to get them right, didn't want to copy them incorrectly. What he really wanted to do was sit down, get off his—

"I'll eat you if you like I'll eat you"

His hand slipped, scratching a downward line onto the board, crippling the *e* he was writing. He stopped, the edge of his hand leaning against the chalkboard, and listened to the chatter of the students behind him.

". . . to the party last weekend . . ."

". . . broke up months ago, didn't you know . . ."

". . . totaled the car, but he was okay . . ."

He lifted his hand from the dusty board, adjusted the position of his fingers around the piece of chalk and began writing again.

"we can lick and suck and fuck"

The chalk made a whiny screech against the board and a couple of students winced and exclaimed. Donald froze again, held his breath, felt his heart pounding frantically at his chest, as if to escape, and he listened once again.

". . . sound of chalk doing that *kills* me . . ."

". . . course you can't believe everything *she* says . . ."

". . . too drunk to say his own name on Saturday night . . ."

He was going to ignore it, it wasn't there, it just *wasn't*. He simply hadn't been getting enough sleep, that was all. He raised his hand again to continue writing.

"fuck me"

The chalk slipped from his powder-tipped fingers and clattered into the metal tray below. The soles of his shoes hissed as he spun around to face the class and his eyes met another pair of eyes, eyes that had been waiting for him to turn around, waiting for him to look, burning into the back of his head.

"May I help you?" Donald's voice almost cracked, but he fought it. He could not, however, fight the tremble that had crept into it.

The newcomer stood at the back of the classroom by the door, his back leaning against the wall, one knee pointing outward, the foot also against the wall. His arms were folded over his chest, his brown leather jacket making whispery crunching sounds in the sudden silence that had fallen over the classroom. His head went back, his chin jutted, one eyebrow went up.

"I'm here to see someone," he said coolly, his voice as smooth as the shiny scales on a snake. He pointed out Leslie with a jerk of his chin. "I'm here to see Leslie."

A few soft murmurs floated through the room.

"Well." Donald swallowed. The hair on the back of his neck was as stiff as the bristles on a hairbrush. His stomach was doing backflips. "Can it wait?" He struggled for control of his voice, fought down the unexplainable acidic fear that was burning in his throat. "She's busy."

The boy stood there and stared at Donald so piercingly that Donald felt as if his own eyes were being pushed back in their sockets. "Sure," he said finally. "It can wait." He turned and went out the door.

Donald looked at Leslie. The tip of her tongue was running over her glossy lips, her eyes were blinking with what looked like pleasant surprise, and there was a soft, satisfied smile resting on her face. He turned to the board again and picked up the piece of chalk, lifted his hand. It shook—no, *jerked*—uncontrollably like the tiny hand of a newborn baby, and he let it drop down to his side before anyone saw. He chewed on his lip so hard that his teeth clicked together. Sweat trickled over his forehead. With resignation, he tossed the chalk down on its tray and nearly fell into his chair.

"You can go," he said, unable to keep his voice from sounding coarse and dry.

None of them moved. They were staring at Donald and over his shoulder at the chalkboard, their faces icy with shock.

"You can go, you're dismissed." He wondered why they were staring at him so, why they looked so stunned. Did he look *that* bad?

One laughed. Another. A girl giggled. They began to stand and walk out.

"Um, Leslie?" He crooked a finger at her and she came over to his desk. "Who was that?" His voice shivered, as if he were cold.

Leslie shook her head back and forth, bouncing her hair loosely. "I don't know, Mr. Ellis. I met him for the first time yesterday at work. I'm sorry about that, about the interruption."

He nodded and waved her away.

She stayed. "Are you okay? Do you need anything?"

"I'm fine, fine." He sounded stern, more than he'd meant to. She turned and left as he sighed heavily, wetly, swiping a hand over his stony face. This wasn't going to work, he realized. He would have to go back home, maybe for the week.

He pressed his palms to the desktop and pushed himself to his feet. Turned. Blinked. His mouth fell open. He gawked at what he'd written on the board:

1.) Discuss the structure of the lick me suck me short story. What makes a fuck short story good, I'll eat you eat you if what makes one fuck me bad?

"Jesus," he hissed, sweeping his hand rapidly over the board, erasing his writing. He dropped the eraser; it bounced off the chalk tray and fell to the floor in a puff of white dust. Donald hurried clumsily across the classroom, knocking over one of the little student desks, shoving two others out of his way, almost tripping himself. He lurched into the corridor.

There were only a few students scattered around; the period was well under way and most were in class. A few of the students from his class were in the corridor and they stopped, turned, stared at him uncertainly.

The stranger, the one in the leather jacket, was nowhere in sight.

Donald gasped, realized he had not been breathing, had been holding his breath for several seconds. He closed the classroom door and walked down the corridor, trying to ignore the stares he was getting from his students, and went into his office.

He sat behind his desk for a while, his face in his hands, working his jaw, trying to moisten his sandy-dry mouth. He simply could not continue feeling this way. Maybe if he stopped drinking for a while, started eating right, even when he wasn't hungry.

"I'll eat you if you like I'll eat you"

Donald groaned deeply, pressing his face hard with his hands, trembling for a moment all over. "God, what's happening to me?" he breathed.

The creature was sitting on a bench across the street from the school. The bench was wet and a spot of dampness was spreading over the seat of the creature's pants, but it was too deep in thought to notice.

This was not right. There was something about that man—something wrong, something threatening. He *knew*. Or at least he had the power to know, the ability to find out. There was something different about him: he had something that the others didn't have.

The creature sat with its palms flat on its thighs, staring straight ahead. Its eyes were opened wide and when they blinked, it was a slow blink; they would close, open, close, open again.

Were there more like him? The creature wondered if it was the only one that knew about this teacher man and the strange power he seemed to possess, and if there were any more like him.

The creature felt the coldness that came with danger, with fear. It was a new feeling, one with which the creature was not familiar. It opened its eyes and looked around slowly, cautiously.

Things would be all right, it was sure. What could go wrong? What could one man do against all of them? Nothing.

It stood, put its hands in the pockets of its leather jacket, and began walking. It smiled automatically at an old man who passed by. And it thought about what it was going to do next.

"What can I do for you, Anne?" asked Dr. Harvey Blanchette, leaning back in his chair, folding his hands across his chest. His thick lips smiled and his bug-eyes crinkled. The overhead light in his office was reflected in a soft, white pool on his smooth, bald head; thin wisps of hair, horseshoe-shaped, edged the back of his head and fell over his ears. He wore a blue suit, his tie loose and his collar unbuttoned.

Anne sat before his desk with a cup of coffee, leaning forward with her elbows on her knees.

"Well, I'm not sure, really," she said. "This may sound like a big, fat cliché, but I'm here to talk to you about a friend. Donald Ellis."

"Donald?" Blanchette put a hand to his cheek, his index finger stretching up over his temple.

"Yes. He's . . . I don't think he's well. We had dinner last week and we talked. He doesn't know I'm speaking with you and would probably be upset if he did. But . . . well, after that talk we had, I think he needs to see someone. You, maybe." She sat up straight and, with one hand, smoothed out the wrinkles in her gray, businesslike skirt. "He's been having . . . feelings. And a nightmare, a recurring nightmare that has been keeping him from getting any sleep."

"What is this nightmare about, do you know?"

Anne described it to him: the street, the blood, the ocean of human bodies, whole and dismembered. Then she told him about Donald's opinion of the dream, his feelings of danger, of dread.

"He's becoming obsessed with it. He's started smoking again, he's lost weight. He looks terrible, really terrible." She lifted the Styrofoam cup to her lips, sipped some coffee, blew on it, making the steam puff up, then sipped again. "Donald seems to think he has some sort of, oh, I don't know, some sort of prophetic ability, a sixth sense. He accused a student of having crib notes recently, and he had no reason to, no proof. He claims to have had this . . . this *feel*ing before, about other things." She clicked her tongue and shook her head, making her black hair swing back and forth. "I don't know, I just think you should talk to him. Make it friendly, casual, but try to see if there's anything really wrong. I'm worried."

Blanchette's thick lips were pursed tightly, and his eyebrows, wiry bushes over his eyes, were huddled together. He nodded. "I will definitely see what I can do, Anne. Thank you very much for telling me. Donald Ellis?"

"Yes. English department."

"Of course. I'll talk to him as soon as possible."

*   *   *

Ruth Falsey had actually seemed concerned about Donald when he'd gone into her office that day and told her he was going to have to go back home.

"You don't look well, Donald," she'd said with motherly sternness.

"I don't feel well, Ruth. I think I should go to bed for a couple of days. Any problem with that?"

"Not if you're ill. It'll be no problem at all."

He'd nodded gratefully. "Thank you."

"If you need anything, Donald, don't hesitate." Her beady little eyes had sparkled then, and Donald knew she really meant it. He'd thanked her again, then left.

At home, he undressed, donned his bathrobe, poured a glass of scotch, and slipped a George Winston tape into the stereo. The soft, plinking piano music worked like a massage on Donald, relaxing his tense muscles as he lay on the sofa, his drink on his chest, his right forearm resting on his forehead, palm up. He dozed for a while, never fully dropping off, savoring the cloudy area between consciousness and sleep.

The rapping at his door startled him; he knocked the glass on his chest over, spilling Scotch down the front of his bathrobe.

"God*dam*mit," Donald grumbled, sitting up quickly. He put the glass on the coffee table and swiped at the wet spot on his robe with his hand. "Who is it?"

"Harvey Blanchette," came the muffled reply.

"Oh, terrific," Donald muttered as he walked to the door, still fussing with his robe. When he opened the door, he saw Blanchette smiling comfortably, smugly, his hands folded in front of him, one foot placed ahead of the other, looking like a homely department-store mannequin.

"Hello, Donald," he said, his mouth moving in an almost

exaggerated way. "I heard you came home ill and thought I would drop by."

"Well. Thank you." Donald's voice was not grateful.

"Do you have the flu? I didn't know it was going around." His prissy nostrils flared, twitched, and Donald assumed he was smelling the liquor.

"I don't know, really. I'm just feeling under the weather."

"Hm." He glanced over Donald's shoulder. "Do you feel like company?"

"Not really."

"Oh. Well, is there anything I can do for you? Get for you?"

Donald took in a deep breath and let it out slowly, wondering just how much Anne had told Blanchette, wondering just how crazy she had made Donald look. "Yes. There is. You can ignore anything Anne Cramer has told you about me. You can keep in mind that anything I've said to her has been meant for her alone, not for you or anyone else. Other than fatigue," Donald said with a shrug, "I'm fine. Okay?" He smiled coldly.

"You don't look fine, Donald. You don't sound fine. Would you like to talk?"

"No."

"You've been drinking."

"You've been prying."

"Look, Donald, please, I'm just doing my job. I'm concerned about your welfare and you—"

The phone rang.

"Excuse me." Donald turned, walked over, and answered it. "Hello?"

"Donald Ellis?"

"Yes, who's this?" He was impatient.

"I'm Dr. Wallace Craig at Queen of the Valley Hospital.

I'm calling about . . . Do you have a brother named William Ellis?''

Donald felt rather weak all of a sudden, and he sat down at the phone table. ''Yes. Yes, I do. Has something happened?''

''Your brother is here at the hospital. He was brought in last night after being hit by a car. He's been screa— He's been asking for you.'' The doctor paused. ''I think it would be a good idea if you came to the hospital as soon as you can, Mr. Ellis. I'd like to talk with you. Would that be possible?''

''Y–yes, yes, I'll get over there right away. I'll leave now. Thank you for calling, Doctor. Thank . . . uh . . . Queen of the Valley, you said?''

''Yes.''

''Thank you, thank you.'' When Donald replaced the telephone receiver, he realized that he was gripping it so tightly that his knuckles were bone-white. He released it and flexed his fingers a few times. He turned to see Blanchette still standing in his living room.

''Something wrong?'' Blanchette asked. ''Nothing serious, I hope.''

''Serious enough. I'll have to ask you to leave; I've got somewhere to go.''

''All right. But I'd really like to talk with you later, Donald. If you don't mind.''

''I do.''

''If you'd rather talk with someone else, if you're not comfortable with me . . .''

''Look, Harvey.'' Donald's voice was warmer, but will not terribly friendly. ''I don't necessarily have anything against you, okay? I just don't need to talk to anyone. *Any*one. I will take care of my problems *my* way. Now, please. Leave me alone.'' Then he turned away, went to his bedroom, and got dressed.

*   *   *

The hospital room was small, almost cramped. Bill's was the only bed. There was a window at the far end of the room, but the curtains were pulled, letting in only a sliver of light between them. A soft light over the bed was on, humming quietly.

Bill was on his back, restrained, with his right leg elevated and in a cast. His eyes were closed, so Donald was very quiet as he entered, silently walking around the bed to the only chair in the room. He sat down, chewing his lip again, studying Bill's face.

It was like a mask, stone-still, stiff. And, even though Donald knew it couldn't be so (could it? could it?), his brother's hair seemed grayer than when he'd seen him last (days ago that was just days ago).

Teeth. The doctor had told him that Bill had been screaming something about teeth when he'd run naked into the street the night before and been hit by a car.

"The driver said your brother practically threw himself in front of the car, screaming hysterically," Dr. Craig had said. "He's been asking for you, Mr. Ellis, that's how we got your name. We hoped you could tell us something about him, maybe explain why . . ."

No. Donald couldn't. Not yet. He felt a little sick. That fuzz was running over his brain again, scurrying around inside his skull.

Bill's eyes popped open and he looked straight up at Donald.

"It's got teeth, Donald," he hissed, "big fuckin' teeth like razors, sharp fuckers—"

"Bill!"

"Jesus, Donald, where you been, huh? Goddamned thing almost had me, with those teeth, those fuckin' teeth."

"What, Bill, *what* has teeth?" Donald found himself whispering, hissing, as Bill was, leaning forward to catch his brother's words.

Bill's face was screwed up, his eyes clenched shut, and he strained against the straps on his wrists.

"Jesus H. Christ, they shined in there, they glistened and dripped, those teeth—*fangs*, they were fuckin' *fangs!*" His eyes opened wide when he said "fangs," as if the word were a revelation. "And the smell, Donald, it had the *smell*. Fuckin' close, boy, almost got me."

"Bill, calm down, please, you're okay. You're fine. Just tell me what has teeth, Bill. What was it?"

He was quiet, breathing heavily, his forehead wrinkling, relaxing, wrinkling, relaxing. "Jesus, Donald, it was like nothing you'd . . . you'd ever believe, it was . . . Jesus!"

Donald thought he might throw up soon, thought that he would pass out if he didn't get out of that little room soon. He didn't want to see this anymore, to see his brother like this, but he couldn't leave. He had to ask first, had to know.

"Bill. Does this have anything to do with Eve?"

There was an instant of transformation, a brief change in his brother's face, as if he were suddenly all right, as if he were just fine and did not belong there in the hospital, in that bed. But then it left. Tears welled up in Bill's eyes and his face twisted again, sobs catching in his throat like short bursts of machine-gun fire.

"I thought she liked me, Donald," he groaned. "I thought she would be m–my . . . I thought she would . . . but she was, she was . . . Jesus, Donald." His shoulders convulsed with sobs, his face turned blood-red as tears flowed over his temples and into his ears.

"Don't cry, Bill, don't," Donald whispered, trying to sound comforting, but only sounding sad and frightened. Then he lifted his hand, put it on Bill's arm, and squeezed. "Bill, don't cr—"

The chair and the floor and the room and everything slipped away and Donald was touching nothing, he was feeling nothing, he *was* nothing—darkness, cold, emptiness, all around him, until he knew:

He *was* Bill and he was happy and felt good, like a kid, like a boy in high school with a new girl friend (girl friend girl friend) beside him, pretty, soft, she liked him, she liked to be with him, liked to touch him, but he could not see her, or feel her, he just *knew*, because he was so happy and he felt so excited, filled with that fluttery anticipation he had not felt since the day of his wedding, but just inside, there was nothing outside until (*"fuck me"*) he felt it, felt the softness, finally. (*"let's do it let's do it together"*)

It was a feeling that he knew, that he had felt before, but not in a while, no, it had been a long time, that was for sure, and he deserved this, wanted it, needed it (*"sweeeet sex together touching and licking"*) so badly, and now he was feeling it all, feeling everything, the softness, the wet rubbing, stroking (*"fuck me fuck me"*), the licking and the sucking and (*"I'll eat you if you like"*) suddenly it was wrong, something was wrong, and the darkness began to part, like curtains in a window, and things began to form and take shape and move and shine and glisten (*"licking and sucking"*) and drip and it was closing in, he couldn't see it yet, but it was going to have him if he let it, if he didn't do something, if he didn't didn't didn't—

A scream filled his head, cutting through it all like a laser, and Donald jerked his hand away, feeling cold, empty, terrified, his mouth like sandpaper inside. He was standing now, his knees quivering like Jell-O. He was standing a few feet away from Bill's bed, which now had a nurse beside it, and the doctor, Dr. Craig. Bill was jerking, fighting to escape the straps that held him down, screaming like a baby with a desperate, gasping wail. The nurse was giving him a shot— trying to, anyway, without hurting him.

"Mr. Ellis?" The doctor was beside him, touching his

elbow. "Why don't you step outside now." Donald followed him out into the corridor, almost colliding with a nun who was hurrying by. The doctor looked at him with concern, his soft face framed by silver hair, his thin mustache twitching slightly. "Are you going to be okay, Mr. Ellis?"

Donald turned and watched the door to Bill's room slowly swing shut, muffling his brother's cries. Then he looked at the doctor again, nodded jerkily. "Yes. Fine."

"Do you have any idea why your brother might—"

"No. No, I don't. I don't have any idea." He left the doctor and walked down the corridor to go home. He'd never been so frightened—filled with such pure terror—in all his life.

"Bye, Leslie," Gary said sweetly as he went out the door, his coat slung over his shoulder like he was cool, or something. The sweetness in his voice was pure sarcasm; he knew she despised him. How could he not know? She made no attempt to hide the fact.

With a sigh, she walked over to the Betamax and pulled out the *Smokey and the Bandit* cartridge Gary had put in. Thank god she only had to put up with him for two hours: he worked from ten to four; she, from two to eight. She returned the cartridge to the shelf, then began scanning the rows of video tapes for something *she* wanted to watch. The bell clanged as the door opened and Leslie turned to see Betty Pemberton, her boss, sweep gracefully into the store.

Betty Pemberton swept gracefully wherever she went. Despite her size—she weighed an easy three hundred—she always managed to glide smoothly, as if she were light as a feather. She was wearing a long, brown, furry coat and carried a brightly colored, flowery umbrella in her hand, using it like a walking stick.

"Hello, Miss Pemberton," Leslie said, turning from the shelves. "How are you?"

"I'm in a hurry, honey," she replied in her almost falsetto voice. She reached into her coat pocket as she walked to Leslie's side. "I'm going to ask a big favor of you, hon, I hope you don't mind. You see, my mother has finally had the decency to expire and I'm going to have to go back to Mississippi for the reading of her will, which I and my sisters have been awaiting for ages. The woman has been at death's door for nearly two years now, you know. Anyway, the lady who usually feeds my cat and fish while I'm gone is out of town, so I was wondering if you would be so good as to do that for me. Of course I would pay you. I really appreciate it. Here is the key and a little map I've drawn so you can find the place. Everything okay here? I hope so, because I haven't got time for *anything* right now. I've got to go to the parlor"— she carefully patted her full, plastic-looking, sandy hair— "so I'll look decent on the plane. I should be gone for about a week. Will you take extra care of the store for me? God knows that Whittaker child isn't responsible enough. I'll never know why I hired him. You really must talk me into firing him soon, Leslie, my girl." She started toward the door again, her broad back to Leslie. "Take care of everything, love, including yourself. You might say a prayer for *me*, too, having to get together with my sisters and all. *Gawd*, I don't look forward to it. Ah, well. Tootle-pip." And she was gone.

Leslie shook her head and smiled. The woman was like a strong gust of wind, in and out, never silent for a moment. Leslie took a tape from the shelf and walked over to the machine, slipping it into the deck. She punched the PLAY button, went over and sat down behind the counter. Images appeared on the screen, voices spoke, music played, but Leslie eventually tuned the movie out. Things were clicking together inside her head; a smile was materializing on her face.

A week. Miss Pemberton would be gone for about a week, her house in Leslie's care. She'd have it all to herself. She had never seen it before, didn't know what it looked like or how big it was. But what difference did that make? How big did it have to be to accommodate two people as long as it had a bed? But with whom would she share it?

What if *he* came back? The one who had come to class today? The thought of having him made her feel warm inside. Surely that was what he had in mind. After all, he'd looked her up at school, found out what room she was in, and disturbed an entire class to see her. The other girls in the class had sizzled with envy, she remembered with a smile.

But why hadn't he waited around for her outside? She'd searched for him after Mr. Ellis had let them go, but couldn't find him anywhere. He was probably afraid of getting in trouble with Ellis. Leslie had never seen him around school before. Maybe he wasn't a student. Maybe he was new. It didn't matter. He would find her again. Or she would find him.

"Yes." Blanchette cleared his throat. "I *do* think there's something wrong, but I don't know what." He turned slowly to Anne, who was looking at him questioningly. They were both seated in Ruth Falsey's office. Ruth was at her desk, listening intently. "Do you have any ideas, Anne?" Blanchette asked.

Anne's fingers toyed with each other in her lap and she glanced down at them a number of times. "Well, I think I might. Last year, Donald and I became very close. We . . . spent a lot of time together." She chuckled nervously. "Of course, you all know that. Anyway, at the beginning of our relationship, I tried to let him know that I didn't want to get serious, that I just wasn't ready for that. I was married once before and it didn't work out, and I tried to tell Donald that I didn't want to marry again, not for a while. If ever. But we just got closer and closer and . . . I guess I led him on. I guess I didn't make myself as clear as I should have. I started seeing other people when the opportunity arose and . . .'' She fingered the collar of her blue blouse. "Well, Donald was very upset. Very hurt. He'd thought I was going to be exclusive, of course. See only him." She shrugged. "Poor communication, I guess."

"How did he react?" Ruth asked, tilting her head, her expression dark. She was touching the eraser end of a pencil to her chin and looked more like a psychiatrist than Blanchette did.

"The first time I went out with someone else he became very angry. In fact, I'd never realized he had such a violent temper."

"Violent?" Blanchette bent toward her. "What did he do? Did he strike you? Threaten you?"

"He . . . well, he threw a few things in my apartment, broke a dish. He never threw anything at *me*, though. He was just angry. It was sort of a . . . a tantrum."

Blanchette sighed, and he and Ruth exchanged glances. "Does Donald drink heavily?"

"Oh, no. I've never even seen him drunk."

"He'd been drinking when I went to his house today. Quite a lot, from the look and sound of him. Not to mention the smell," he added softly with a sniff. He sucked at his teeth with a squeaky sound, then said, "So. You think Donald is still upset about the failure of your relationship."

Anne nodded. "I think . . . well, it was my fault. I let it go too far, even ending it when I did was too late." She smiled sadly. "He fell pretty hard for me. Oh, and I cared for him, too. I love him still. I just don't want . . . what he wants." She was staring at her lap again, speaking as much to herself as to the others. "Donald is a lonely man. He needs someone. I think that's what is wrong."

They were silent for a while. The digital clock on Ruth's desk hummed steadily.

Blanchette suddenly slapped his thighs and straightened his back. "I think we should wait awhile, see how he does. I'm going to pay him another visit tomorrow, I think. He got a phone call while I was there today and he had to rush off to the hospital for some reason."

Anne frowned, disturbed.

"But," Blanchette continued slowly, his thick lips moving precisely, "if he won't allow himself to be helped, we'll have to take it from there." He looked at Ruth, silently waiting for her approval.

"All right." She tossed the pencil down on her desk. "I'm worried about him, frankly. I kind of like Donald. Let me know if you get anywhere with him, Harvey."

"Yes," Blanchette replied, standing. "I'll let you know."

Anne returned to her office and got her things together to go home. She was dead on her feet and was getting a headache; she wanted nothing more than to lie down and stop thinking for a while. She turned from her desk and was starting out the door when Pamela Hoppe walked in, looking flustered.

The girl usually looked a little flustered, but today her condition was especially noticeable. Her short red hair was a bit of a mess and she was breathing rapidly, as if she'd been running. She had.

"Oh, I'm glad I caught you before you left," the girl gasped. "Here." Pamela held out a piece of notebook paper. "This is the assignment that was due yesterday. I'm sorry it's late."

"No problem," Anne said, taking the paper. "Of course, it'll be five points off." She tucked it into the folder she held under her arm.

"Yeah." Pamela sighed through tight lips.

"Rough day?"

Pamela nodded. "Yes. And a little weird. First my car wouldn't start this morning. I turned the wrong assignment in for Mr. Reilly's chemistry class. I threw up at lunch." She shook her head and chuckled. "Then in Mr. Ellis's English class—"

"Mr. Ellis? What about him?"

"Oh, he was just writing some weird stuff on the board. Really shocked everybody. Well, I gotta be going." She started to turn but Anne grabbed her shoulder, a little too hard.

"What stuff? What kind of weird stuff?"

Pamela looked a little frightened. "Well . . . some words, some, you know, dirty words, and stuff."

"Please, Pamela, *what* dirty words? Exactly what did he write, do you remember?"

The girl faced Anne fully now, her eyes puzzled. "Well, it was supposed to be an essay question, but it had lots of really crazy things mixed in, like . . . well, like 'lick me,' and 'suck me,' and 'f—,' well, 'fuck me.' Things like that. I don't remember what the rest of it said. Pretty weird, huh? Well, I really gotta go now, Miss Cramer. Um . . ." An expression of worry clouded her face and she took one step forward. "That's not gonna get Mr. Ellis into trouble, is it? I mean, I like him, you know?"

Anne shook her head twice, silently.

Pamela broke into a smile. "Good. Well, I'll see you tomorrow." Then she turned and left.

Anne digested the girl's words, remembering all the details of Donald's nightmare, the voices that said those things to him. But writing them on the board in the middle of class?

God, she thought, Donald really does need help.

* * *

When Leslie got home that evening, her mother was busy tidying up the house. She looked up from an ashtray she was emptying into a small paper bag to smile at Leslie. "Hi, kid," she said. "How goes it?"

"It goes wet," Leslie replied, tossing her books onto the recliner and brushing some raindrops off the sleeves of her coat. She noticed how nice her mother looked and said, "Aren't you ravishing this evening! Got company coming?"

"Mm-hm." Doreen Newell's eyebrows popped up twice and she smiled with her lips pressed tightly together, nodding her head quickly, almost like a child. "New dress. You like it?" She spun around, her arms spread wide, modeling the sheer wrap dress over a separate slip, both a soft, pleasing mauve.

"Looks great. What's the occasion?"

"Remember that guy I told you I met last week at the bank party? The guy with the little gallery in Sausalito?"

Leslie nodded.

"Well, he dropped by the bank this afternoon and said he would like to get together this evening and look over my pictures, then maybe have dinner!" She giggled conspiratorially, covering her glossy lips with the fingertips of her right hand.

Doreen Newell was an amateur photographer. Currently, she worked in the Napa Valley Bank, but her dream was to, some day, be able to make a living with her camera. She received a great deal of encouragement from Leslie, who honestly believed her mother's photographs—most of which were pictures of the surrounding valley—were quite good. A number of them decorated the walls of the house. Leslie did not, however, believe that the man her mother was seeing this evening was as interested in her pictures as he was in her.

"Wouldn't that be *marvelous*, Les?" Doreen gasped, clapping her hands together. "An exhibit of *my* pictures!"

Leslie managed to muster some enthusiastic agreement, but

it was not genuine. She believed her mother knew that her pictures were not the reason for the meeting just as well as she, Leslie, knew it, but the woman preferred to think and act otherwise. And perhaps something *would* come of it. Maybe some of her pictures *would* be exhibited. But it wouldn't be because this guy thought they deserved such treatment. It would be because he was grateful for a good lay, something for which Doreen Newell was notorious.

At forty, Leslie's mother was an exceptionally attractive woman. Leslie hoped *she* looked so good at forty. While Doreen's waist was perhaps not *quite* as slender as it once had been, her legs still turned heads, and her face was one to be remembered: firm and confident, beautiful round, blue eyes that could take on many expressions without causing a hint of change in any other part of her face. Since her divorce from Leslie's father thirteen years before, Doreen Newell had never been short of male company.

Leslie had inherited her mother's beauty and, like her mother, she was pursued by a good many guys. But that was where the resemblance ended. For although they'd never talked about it, Leslie knew—she just *knew*, somehow—that her mother feared being alone. She knew that Doreen would accept *any* proposal of marriage that came along, and had been ready to accept any for thirteen years. But none ever came because, in an effort to hold loneliness at bay, Doreen allowed herself to be used. She fooled herself into believing that each one was a potential Mr. Right when, in reality, none of them could be more worthless, more selfish. They were each just another of the many men who prayed to have those long, luscious legs wrapped around them for a night. Their prayers would be answered, and they would be on their way.

Leslie paid close attention to her mother's behavior and constantly swore to herself that *she* would never act that way. She would enjoy life to the fullest and learn to always depend upon herself and no one else. She would never be used, she would *use*.

"Well, I've got a little studying to do and then I'm going to step out, so I won't be in your way."

"Oh, Les, you're a sweetie. Cross your fingers!" Doreen giggled.

Leslie held up crossed fingers and smiled as she walked to her room.

Donald felt the friendly burn of Scotch as he swallowed some straight from the bottle before pouring himself a glass. He put the bottle down on the kitchen counter and turned to walk into his bedroom. He slapped a hand on the edge of the sink, though, to stop a fall. Some of the Scotch sloshed out of the glass and onto the floor. He stepped over the little puddle, almost caught his foot in the hem of his robe, but made it to his room. He sat down on the side of the bed and put the drink on the nightstand. He stared at the glass.

I should probably knock off the stuff for a while, he told himself. Too expensive. I can't afford to drink that much.

Donald thought of a former neighbor of his named Randy Keesler. He used to go through six hundred dollars a month in liquor. Six hundred, for Christ's sake! Nope, that would never do. Donald decided to make this his last bottle for a while. Maybe he wouldn't even finish this one. That would be good, noble. Sure.

The phone rang. Again. A third time. Donald made no move to answer it. If it was Anne, he didn't want to talk to her. If it was Kyle, he was in no mood to be friendly. And if it was the doctor calling about Bill . . . well, he was afraid of that. It stopped after seven rings.

Donald kept seeing his brother's face looking up at him pleadingly, his lips pulled back in that fearful grimace. His words echoed in Donald's head, again and again:

". . . they shined in there, they glistened and dripped, those teeth—*fangs*, they were fuckin' *fangs!* And the smell, Donald, it had the *smell!*"

His stomach hitched a little when he thought about what had happened in that hospital room when he'd touched his brother's arm, when he thought about what he'd heard, and what he'd almost seen. And he wondered what he would've seen had he not let go.

Would he have seen *it? Them?* Would he have seen whatever was tormenting him in his sleep every night? Would he have finally seen?

A chill passed over him and he hugged himself tightly. Did he *want* to see it? Yes, he did, if it would answer his questions, if it would make the nightmares stop, or at least make them clearer.

He ached for the glass, took a drink, put it back on the nightstand, swallowed slowly, pressing his lips together tightly.

If he went back. If he touched Bill again. If he didn't let go . . . what would happen? What would he see?

Donald's mouth opened in a long, slow yawn. He locked his hands together above his head and stretched, then lay back on the bed. He could easily go to sleep, but he didn't want that. Even if he didn't think he would have the nightmare, there was just too much to think about, too much to turn over and over in his mind.

What about that boy at school? Who was he? Where had he come from? Donald had never seen him before. What did he want with Leslie Newell? Probably what everbody *else* wanted with Leslie Newell. But he was different. When Donald had turned to face the stranger, he'd been able to feel the boy's stare, actually *feel* it. It was as if the boy *knew,* knew everything, and was mocking Donald, mocking all the things that had been happening to him. All the terrible things.

And then Donald had heard that voice. It had sounded so

close, as if it were coming from someone in the class behind him, from a student. Then he'd actually written those things on the board! His students probably thought he was some sort of . . . god knew *what* they thought. Some of them probably got a kick out of it, for Christ's sake. What if word got back to Ruth, or that asshole Blanchette? Or Anne? It would, Donald knew. It was only a matter of time.

He closed his eyes and rubbed them with the heels of his hands. He felt sticky again, dirty, and decided a shower would feel good. Or maybe a bath. His bedside clock said it was twenty till eight. He sat up on the bed again, stood, and walked to the bathroom, leaving the Scotch on the nightstand.

There were three short knocks at his door. Donald recognized them easily. They came again. He switched on the bathroom light.

"Donald?" It was Anne.

Donald stood by the tub, his hands in the pockets of his brown robe, trying to decide whether to take a shower or a bath. The bath won.

"Donald, I know you're in there. Please let me in. I'd like to talk to you."

He turned on the faucet. Water thundered into the tub, but he could still faintly hear the knock at the door again, immediately followed by Anne's voice.

"Goddammit, Donald, I can *hear* you! *Please* let me in!" Then, after a silent pause, her voice changed, became anxious. "Are you all right? Donald?"

He untied the belt of his robe.

She tried the door then, rattled the knob noisily. It was locked.

He let the robe slip to the floor in a heap.

"Donald. I talked to a student today. One of *your* students."

He bent down and sprinkled some bubblebath into the churning water.

102

"She told me what you wrote on the board today. In class. I . . . I haven't told anyone else, but it's going to get around. You know how things spread."

He put one foot into the hot, bubbly water.

"Things aren't good for you, Donald, and you're not making them any better. The way you treated Harvey? That's not helping you, Donald. And you *need* help. You're. Not. Well."

He turned the faucet off and sat back in the tub. Water dripped from the faucet for a while, each drop plopping into the bath.

There was silence for a long time before he realized that Anne had left. He closed his eyes and lay very still in the water, thinking about what he was going to do tomorrow.

5

The next day, Wednesday, was just as dreary as the local television weatherman had predicted it would be. A chilly drizzle sliced through the air for the first part of the morning, cutting through the fog that covered the Napa Valley.

Leslie yearned for summer: hot sun, blue skies, the smell of coconut suntan lotion. She clutched her books to her breast with one hand and held her umbrella with the other, hoping the cold dampness wouldn't damage the look of her hair. She yawned as she pushed open the glass doors and entered the school building. She closed her umbrella, looking around. The halls were practically empty. It was the middle of third period. She'd slept through her first class and was still tired.

She'd stayed up too late the night before, but it had been fun. She'd gone over to Miss Pemberton's to feed the fish and the cat—May Ling, a rather snobby Siamese—and to sort of look the place over. It was a small house, decorated rather gaudily, in keeping with Miss Pemberton's character: bright red lampshades covering bulbs suspended from the ceiling by brass chains, doorways with curtains of beads filling them instead of doors, a round bed covered with a blood-red spread, and a huge mirror on the wall above the headboard. Flaky woman. After feeding the pets, Leslie had begun looking around, not really snooping at first. But she eventually made her way into Miss Pemberton's bedroom, where she came across some diaries. Some of the diaries had snapshots glued to the pages. Leslie had read through some of the entries and found herself laughing aloud at the things Miss Pemberton had written.

This woman actually had boyfriends who flocked to her bedroom! If the diary was truthful, that is. Most of them, judging from the snapshots, were fat slobs, just like Miss Pemberton, but they did everything thin people did, Leslie had discovered with perverse delight. Not only that, but Miss Pemberton had *girl* friends, too! This woman was a bitch in heat!

Time had slipped by quickly and Leslie had gotten to bed later than she'd planned. Still, she'd had a bit of difficulty falling asleep despite the late hour; she was feeling anxious about having that little house all to herself. Herself and someone else, of course . . .

Leslie's umbrella, folded up to about a foot and a half, slipped from her hand and fell to her feet, tripping her. She tumbled forward and her books slid to the floor, her coat splaying around her like limp, flat wings. Before she even reacted to the fall, Leslie quickly looked about to make sure no one had seen it. Then she lifted herself to her hands and knees, then to a squat, and began retrieving her books.

Footsteps clapped on the floor of the corridor and Leslie hurried before she was spotted. As she picked up the last book and prepared to stand, two feet stepped in front of her face. Brown boots. Tight blue jeans. A full, well-defined crotch. Brown leather jacket. And that face, that sharp chin, that look of darkness and those eyes . . .

*   *   *

Kyle stepped out of the classroom quietly, not wanting to disturb Miss Cramer's lecture. He'd ruffled her feathers enough for one week. He headed for the bathroom and was just about to step inside when he spotted Mr. Ellis at the other end of the corridor walking toward him. He was wearing a pair of blue-denim jeans and, from the waist up, was sort of swallowed by his puffy down jacket.

"Mr. Ellis," Kyle said, approaching him. "I thought you were going to stay home for a while."

"I'm not here to work, Kyle," Mr. Ellis said, his voice clipped. He never looked at Kyle, just stared straight ahead as he walked. Kyle had to fall into step beside him, or the man would've walked right on by.

"Who you looking for?"

"I don't know. I mean, I don't know his name. New guy. Tall, dark complexion, black hair. Seen him?" He glanced at Kyle then, but just for an instant. His face was hard, craggy, his eyes sagging, his chin covered with stubble.

"Black hair, dark . . . yeah, I might have seen him. Saw a guy like that in the bathroom Monday. Kind of weird."

"Do you know his name?"

"No, I don't. Who is he?"

Mr. Ellis licked his lips dryly, sniffed. "Don't you have a class now, Kyle?" He glanced at him again.

"Well, yeah. Sure."

"I'll see you later."

Kyle stopped walking and watched Mr. Ellis continue down the hall. With a soft "Hmph," Kyle turned and went into the bathroom.

"Do you go to school here?" Leslie asked him as he walked her to class. He kept staring at her, paying little attention to where they were going, holding her books in the crook of his arm. He made her just a little uncomfortable, but it wasn't unpleasant.

He shook his head.

"Well, I don't know you. What's your name?" She tried to keep her voice warm and friendly, but it was hard not to sound nervous.

He smiled then, without speaking; his smile spoke for him. What difference does it make? the smile asked with a silent chuckle.

She tried to smile back, but felt she failed. "I'm Leslie."

"I know."

They were nearing her classroom and she slowed her pace. She wanted to see him again. "I'd like to see—" she began.

"Do you work today?"

She nodded.

"I'll be waiting for you when you get off. Eight." It wasn't a question.

She began to smile. "Yes, that's—"

"Excuse me."

Leslie turned to see Mr. Ellis standing right beside them. She hadn't noticed him. They stopped walking. The boy said nothing, but stared sharply at Mr. Ellis.

"Hello, Leslie."

"Hi, Mr. Ellis." He looked sick. And . . . well, something else as well. He looked frightened. His hands were in the pockets of his gray jacket, which was zipped all the way up, the collar pulled to his chin, making it look as if he had no neck. His hair was tossed and flecked with water; he must have just come in from outside. He turned to her companion, his jaw set tightly.

"I would like to know who you are," he said simply.

The boy smirked. "I don't go to school here."

"That doesn't answer my question. Who are you? What do you—where are you from?" His jaw worked frantically. He seemed to be chewing on his lip, something he did in the classroom frequently.

The boy's smirk remained, his stare never wavered. "Why should I tell you?"

Mr. Ellis took one step forward. "Because I already know more than anyone else."

A flinch? A blink? A slight shift of expression? Something about the boy's face changed. He turned to Leslie and handed her books to her, saying, "I'll see you at eight."

Something like a snarl came from Mr. Ellis as he fell forward on the boy. He grabbed the lapels of the leather jacket and pushed him across the corridor, slamming him up against the wall on the other side.

"Goddammit, *tell* me!" he roared. "Who are you? What do you want?"

Leslie dropped her books with a start and gasped loudly, slapping a palm to her chest. "Mr. Ellis!" she squeaked.

He shook the boy violently, slamming him against the wall again and again, but the boy's expression remained the same: icy-cold, with no surprise or pain.

"What are you doing?" Ellis demanded, his voice breaking, falling apart like dry clay. "What the fuck are you doing to me?" His words reverberated in the corridor. Classroom doors opened. There were hurried footsteps. Mr. Ellis raised a hand, curling it into a fist as he did so, and brought it down with a crack on the stranger's face.

Leslie screamed and hurried to the scuffle. The flesh over the boy's left cheekbone had split open a tiny bit.

"Donald!" exclaimed a voice from down the corridor. It was Miss Cramer. As she approached them, she winced at the gash on the boy's face.

Mr. Reilly dashed out of the chemistry laboratory, the tail of his white lab coat flapping, and grabbed Mr. Ellis's arms, holding him back from the boy. Ellis struggled, muttering something in a croaking voice.

"Calm down, Donald," Reilly was saying, his flabby jowls jiggling.

Leslie turned to the boy. He was calmly staring at Mr. Ellis.

"Are you all right?" Leslie asked. She reached up and touched his cheek. "He hit you hard."

The boy took his stare from Ellis and looked at Leslie, smiling. There was no longer a gash on his cheek.

Donald realized how weak he had become as he tried to break Reilly's grip. He knew he should be able to free himself from the old fart, but he just couldn't. He calmed down, never taking his eyes from the boy as he stood talking with Leslie. Leslie glanced back at Donald, frightened.

"Donald, for Chrissake, what happened?" Anne asked, appearing at his side, gripping his elbow.

"Nothing happened."

She put a hand on her forehead and groaned. "Oh, what have you done?" She looked over at the boy, then back at Donald. "You *hit* him!"

"Just a tap."

"What the devil is going on here?" Ruth Falsey was marching down the corridor, slicing her way through the crowd of students that had gathered. Blanchette wasn't far behind. "Desmond, what's happening?" she asked Reilly.

"I'm not really sure, Ruth. Donald was on that boy over there. He even hit him. I was holding him off."

Even though he wouldn't look down at her, Ruth studied Donald's face. "I think you can let go of him." She turned to the students who were standing around in the corridor. "And you can all go back to your classes. Whatever happened here is over."

"Donald," Blanchette said softly, shaking his head. His voice held no inflection, and yet he'd managed to pack a score of disappointed questions into that one name.

Donald kept his hands to himself, resisting the temptation to sock Blanchette. Instead, he turned and stared daggers at the man.

"Donald, I want to know what happened." Ruth folded her arms authoritatively.

He finally looked down at her. He opened his mouth, inhaled, paused, then finally said, "It was nothing."

"If it was nothing, then why did you hit him?"

"I didn't hurt him. Didn't hurt him at all."

Ruth turned around. Leslie and the boy were gone. "Where did he go?" she asked. No one answered. No one had been paying any attention to him.

"Really, Ruth, I didn't hurt him. It was just a . . . a little scuffle."

"You're a teacher, for god's sake, you don't take part in *scuffles!*" Her lips were tight as cables as she looked at Blanchette, holding a silent conversation in her head, deciding what to do. "I'd like to see you in my office, Donald." She turned and stalked back down the corridor.

Donald followed her, trying not to walk beside Blanchette, trying to ignore Anne's constant babbling about why he'd done it, what was wrong, on and on and on. "I really didn't hurt him," he mumbled with a very cold, humorless smirk. He *knew* he hadn't hurt the boy. The *thing.*

When Donald had hit him, the skin over his cheekbone had opened up just like anybody's would. But. It hadn't *bled* like anybody's would. And then. Seconds later. It had closed up. Just like a little Ziploc bag. Right before his very eyes.

When Donald walked out of Ruth Falsey's office, it was without a job. Oh, she wasn't firing him, she wanted to make

111

that clear. No, she was just giving him a leave of absence until he'd taken care of whatever was wrong.

"And there *is* something wrong," she'd insisted. "If you won't let Harvey help you, then get help from someone else."

"By all means," Blanchette had mumbled, standing slightly behind Donald.

"Look, Donald," Ruth continued. "Things go wrong for all of us at one time or another." She had glanced at Anne then, and Donald tried to imagine just how much Anne had told them. "I don't know exactly what problems you're having right now, Donald, but if there's anything I or Harvey, here, or Anne can do, *please* let us know. In the meantime, I'm going to try to take care of what happened out there quietly. I'll talk to Leslie and find out who her friend was, since *you* won't tell me. But I'm doing that in exchange for something, Donald. In exchange for the promise that you will *do* something. Do you understand? Get help, do *some*thing."

Donald had smiled then, looking down at the little lady sitting behind her desk. She didn't seem so big now. Not after that thing in the corridor, not after that feeling of confidence he knew that it had. The feeling of superiority, completely void of fear.

"Ruth, I *am* going to do something," he'd said with a nod. "I'm going to do something as soon as I leave here."

"Good, Donald. Good." She seemed unsettled. Perhaps by the cold, jovial tone of his voice? His smile?

Then they'd started to say their goodbyes, but Donald had turned and walked out, ignoring them. He braced himself for the cold as he went outside, crossed the parking lot, got into his car. Then he drove to the hospital to see his brother.

It was almost eleven-thirty when Donald approached the nurse's desk at the hospital.

"How is Bill Ellis doing today?" he asked.

A black nurse who was just hanging up the phone looked at him and smiled brightly. "Ellis?" She looked down at the desk, thumbed through something. "He's been very quiet today. Everything seems to be fine."

"Um, is it okay to go see him?"

"Oh, yes. Go ahead."

Squeezing the back of his neck hard with one hand, Donald slowly walked down the corridor, passing other hospital rooms, most with doors propped open, a few closed. He came to Bill's room. The door was closed. Donald pushed it open.

The little room was dim, as it had been the day before. It was deadly silent. The television, suspended from the ceiling and facing the bed, flickered, but the volume was off.

Donald turned to the bed, a smile ready for his brother, but Bill was not there. The bed was empty. At first, his eyes not fully adjusted to the lack of light, Donald thought that the crisp, white hospital sheets had been replaced with dark, unevenly colored ones. He took another step into the room. The door swung shut behind him. The plaster cast that had encased Bill's fractured leg lay on the floor, the top part of it leaning against the side of the bed, the plaster also drenched in darkness.

Red. Dark—almost *black*—red.

Donald's hand slapped over his mouth and his shoulders hunched. He swallowed hard again and again, taking deep, long breaths, trying to keep from vomiting. He squeezed his bloodshot eyes shut tightly, tried to calm the trembling that blanketed his body. He rubbed his eyes hard with his hands, then forced himself to look at it. His mouth turned downward in a tight, inverted U. His hands were fists at his sides.

"Jesus, Bill," he whispered raspily, "what did they do?"

There was nothing left of his brother but the blood that had, by now, soaked into the sheets, making them lumpy and limp. The smell clung to the air, the smell of his nightmare, that sharp, coppery smell that felt as if it would stay with him forever, stick to him like invisible tar.

Donald had decided the night before that he would have to see Bill one more time, touch him, hold him if necessary, to see what he had seen, to learn what had driven him into the street, naked, screaming about teeth and biting. Whatever it had been was now aware of Donald, aware that he was trying to find out more about it, trying to uncover it.

Donald looked around but there was no blood anywhere else: not on the floor, not on the walls. Just the bed, just the rails, just the empty, abandoned cast.

He slid his sweaty palms together a few times, stepped forward again, one step closer to the bed.

The door was pushed open and light fell in, followed by a young man dressed in white carrying a plastic tray of food.

Donald ignored him and reached out his hand, palm down, fingers splayed wide, moved it slowly, trembling, quivering like gelatin, down to the bloodied mattress.

"Lunch is ready, Mr.—"

The tray crashed to the floor, silverware clattered, a glass broke, apple juice splashed over the floor. The young man stood there a moment, the color leaving his face, his hands outstretched, as if still holding the tray. Then he was gone and his feet were thumping down the corridor as the door slowly swung shut again.

Donald pressed his palm to the sticky, damp sheet, pressed it until the mattress gave slightly beneath it. His eyes closed and his head tilted back, way back, his mouth opening, a low groan flowing from it, the fingers of his hand closing around the loosely fitting sheet, some of the blood wringing out of it, squishing between the fingers of his fist. His forehead creased like leather, and ribbons of sweat were left in the path of rolling, glistening beads that ran into his eyebrows, gathered in the corners of his tightly clenched eyes. His lips worked, his chin moved up, then down, as if he were silently speaking. His free hand raised from its limp position at his side and slapped down on the bed beside the other, rolled into a fist, clutched tightly. His head fell forward, tossing a few drops of perspiration into the air like little missiles. His knees buckled, clumped to the floor. He leaned his forehead against the edge of the bed.

"Nuh-no," he grunted, his eyes, hiding behind locked lids, seeing . . . seeing . . . "Christ, no. No, no. God . . . help . . . me." His face lifted again, looking upward, a patch of crimson on his forehead now, his mouth stretching, the lips tightening, posing for the scream that came from them, searing the mud-thick air at the same instant that the door slammed open and white-clothed people burst in to catch Donald as he fell backward, his scream crumbling into dark, empty unconsciousness.

Gary Whittaker was watching some goddamned Chuck Norris martial-arts flick today and he ignored Leslie through most of it. She was wading through a U.S. history chapter that she was supposed to have read the night before. She was getting very little out of it, though, because people kept coming into the store, Gary kept making joyous exclamations every time someone did something destructive on the screen, and, of course, she kept thinking about *him*. She kept thinking about being with him. In that big bed of Miss Pemberton's with the long mirror on the wall at its head.

He'd handled himself so well with Mr. Ellis. What a flake, that guy! What was his problem, anyway? Was he still pissed about his stupid class being interrupted the day before? No one would have gotten much out of it anyway, what with all that weird shit Ellis had written on the board. He hadn't been looking well, lately, and Leslie was beginning to think there was something very seriously wrong with him. Whatever it was, he'd certainly gotten himself into some hot water by the look on old lady Falsey's face that morning, storming down the hall like a little Matchbox bulldozer, while Mr. Ellis pounded on—

Leslie didn't even know his name yet! He wouldn't tell her! Well, like he'd said, what difference did it make? She blinked. *Had* he said that? she wondered, staring blankly at a diagram detailing the Louisiana Purchase.

She looked up when the bell rang and saw Miss Cramer walking smoothly toward her, a relaxed smile on her face. What is *that* bitch doing here? Leslie thought. She smiled.

"Hi, Miss Cramer. Can I help you?" She closed her book and stood up behind the counter.

"Well, I'm not here for a movie, today," the woman replied. She put her purse on the counter, directly between the two of them, then rested her hands, one on top of the other, right behind it. "I'm here to ask you a few questions, that's all."

"Oh. Well, if it's about what happened this morning, I already talked to—"

"Yes, I know you talked to Mrs. Falsey already. I just wanted to ask you a few questions of my own. Do you mind, Leslie?"

Not having much choice, Leslie shook her head.

"Do you have any idea why Mr. Ellis did what he did today?"

"No. I can't figure it out either."

"Surely he said something to you or . . . your friend?"

Leslie started to shake her head, then said, "Well, like I told Mrs. Falsey, he said he wanted to know who . . . who the guy was, the guy I was with."

"Who *is* he?"

Leslie smirked and dipped her head. "I don't know, Miss Cramer. He didn't tell me his name."

"Are you going to see him again?"

She shrugged. "I don't know. I have no idea where he lives, or anything *else* about him." It was the same lie she'd told Mrs. Falsey. She wanted no one to know she was seeing him again that evening.

Miss Cramer thought for a moment, looking around at the video displays along the walls. "He didn't say anything kind of . . . odd?" she asked finally.

"Well, yeah, there was something. But I told all of this to—"

"Please, Leslie."

Leslie sighed. "Mr. Ellis said something like, 'What are you doing? What are you doing to—' No, no, it was, 'What the *fuck* are you doing to me?' That's what he said. Then he hit him."

"Was your friend hurt?"

"Uh-uh." Leslie said nothing about the gash she'd thought she'd seen on the guy's face. She must have been mistaken, she decided, because it hadn't been there a few seconds later. "Is Mr. Ellis going to be canned?"

Miss Cramer's face hardened. "Mr. Ellis is having some problems, Leslie, and he's being given a short vacation. But he's not being *canned*. What happened today didn't make him look very good, though. That's why we're trying to find out exactly what *did* happen. And no one, including Mr. Ellis, is being very cooperative. So if you learn anything that might help, Leslie, please let me or Mrs. Falsey know." She tilted her head, her eyes narrowed. "Unless you *do* know something, but want to protect your friend?" Her jaw flexed as she clenched her teeth a couple of times. "I'll see you at school tomorrow, Leslie." She took her purse, turned, and left.

Leslie waited until the door was shut, then, softly, she spat, "Cunt."

A few minutes later, Anne sat in The Coffee Bean, a little coffee house across the street from Videoland, sipping a steaming cup of Irish mocha mint, thinking about Donald.

She would stay away from him for a while, leave him alone. If he wasn't even going to allow her to be concerned, she would force herself *not* to be. At least, she wouldn't show it.

Anne couldn't stop wondering who the hell that kid was, the one Donald had hit. He must have done *something* to provoke Donald. Anne had never seen the boy before. He'd looked . . . what was it? There had been something strange about him, something that disturbed her. He'd seemed so confident, so self-assured, even though Donald had attacked him. And there had been that gash. She was *sure* she'd seen a cut on his face. But the very next time she'd looked at him, just before he'd disappeared, it was gone. If it had ever been there.

Anne gently took another sip of her steaming coffee.

It was a few minutes before eight when Leslie put the CLOSED sign out and began turning off the lights. She got her books and purse together, then looked at her watch. Two minutes after. He hadn't come yet. She went out the door, made sure it was locked.

Her mother was seeing the gallery man again tonight. She was so busy trying to make another Mr. Right out of this guy that she gave no thought to what Leslie was doing. No problem there.

Looking at her reflection in the glass door, Leslie fussed a moment with her hair, relieved that the rain had let up for a while. The night was cold, though, and she shivered as she slipped the key into her purse. When she turned, he stepped directly in front of her and smiled. She was so startled that she almost dropped her purse.

"Hi," she blurted suddenly, feeling foolish.

"Hello." He stood with his hands in his coat pockets, as usual. Then he stared.

Leslie fidgeted, glancing around the parking lot over his shoulder. "Well, what would you like to do?" she asked him, smiling.

"I'd like to go someplace where we can be alone."

Leslie tried not to show her surprise—*pleasant* surprise. He wasted no time, this guy. "Do you have a car?"

He shook his head slowly. Light from somewhere caught his eye and sparkled. "Do you know of a place?" he asked, that strange, almost-smiling look on his shadowed face.

"Oh, yes. I do."

"Then let's go." He took her hand.

She almost recoiled, almost let go of his hand as if it were a writhing snake. Her eyes widened and she was suddenly very cold. It was so . . . so incredibly *smooth!* Almost as if his palm were lined with silk. He took a step, but she stood there for a few moments, just looking at him.

Who is he? she thought. Where's he from? Is he . . . okay?

She wondered if this one might be a mistake, if perhaps she should just turn and leave right then, go to her car and drive away, and never speak to him again.

He smiled. His eyes sparkled again. He squeezed her hand in his cool, eerily smooth palm.

Leslie smiled back and walked with him to her car.

The television was much too loud, but that was the way Donald wanted it: loud and distracting. He sat in front of it in his robe, the bottle of Scotch planted between his legs. He'd decided earlier that it would be his last bottle, and he chuckled coldly now at how very, very right he'd been.

Donald was relieved to finally be out of the hospital. He'd had a difficult time convincing the doctor that he was all right and could go home. The state they had found him in hadn't been a good one, but he'd come out of it rather quickly. All hell had broken loose at the hospital over the mess in Bill's room, over Bill himself and whatever had happened to him. They didn't know, of course, and Donald certainly wasn't going to tell them. He knew they would *never* believe him. So, he'd remained silent, although he'd left his address and phone number with a police detective—some guy named Walther—who said he'd want to talk with Donald later.

Out in the parking lot, Donald had sat in his car for a long time, thinking. When he finally drove away, he drove to Bill's trailer. He knew that, while he was married, Bill had always kept an extra key somewhere outside, in case someone got locked out. Donald hoped he'd not broken the habit. He found the key taped above the porchlight. He got inside and went to Bill's bedroom closet, searching the top shelf until he found what he wanted: Bill's .38, something of which Bill had been very proud.

He'd taken Donald out one Sunday afternoon a couple of years ago and taught him to shoot it. He'd promised Donald that someday he would buy him one. Donald hurt now as he thought about the "Yeah-sure-I'll-believe-it-when-I-see-it" way in which he'd responded to Bill's promise.

Once home, Donald had begun drinking, hoping to blot out what he'd seen and felt, knowing he would have to be drunk before he'd be able to do it. He'd decided it was the only thing left to do. He knew he couldn't face all of this, whatever it was, alone. And he had no one to face it with him, no one who would understand or believe him.

So Donald sat on the sofa, a bottle in one hand, a glass in

the other, staring at the gun. He'd cleaned it and loaded it, then put it on the coffee table in front of him, where it waited for him, waited for him to be ready. Soon, he knew, he would be drunk enough. Not yet, but soon.

The instant they were inside Miss Pemberton's, he moved close to Leslie, taking her face in his hands. His strangely smooth palms made her tingle as they had earlier. His eyes, staring without reserve into hers, told her that he wanted her. *Now*.

He leaned forward and lightly licked her lips, first the top one, then the lower one, his tongue flicking in and out of the corners of her mouth. Then he put his mouth on hers, his tongue probing deeply, sending shivers of electricity down her throat, through her breasts, between her legs, into her thighs . . .

When he stepped back, she was breathing heavily, licking her lips. She didn't even bother turning on the lights; she headed straight for the bedroom, and he followed her.

She led him through a curtain of beads and entered the short hallway to the bedroom. The beads clicked and rattled behind them, but the soft, gentle sound was blanketed by a sudden screech that made Leslie jump, turn.

Miss Pemberton's cat, May Ling, was squatting in the dark, her ears flat, her eyes burning, her teeth bared. She was looking straight up at him. A growl, low and rumbling in her throat, dissolved into a threatening hiss as one claw sliced outward toward his leg, and then she backed up, swiped at him again.

"Fucking *cat!*" Leslie snapped, kicking at it. With another piercing screech, May Ling shot through the beads.

"Cat?" he muttered behind Leslie, but she ignored him.

When they got to the bedroom, Leslie took off her coat and

tossed it over the back of a chair, turned to him smiling.
"You know, you *still* haven't told me your name."

He moved forward and took her in his arms, gently placing
one hand over a breast. "Is it that important?" He kissed her
again, longer this time. Then he began undressing her,
unbuttoning, untying, unzipping . . .

When she stood naked before him, the light from the street
outside shining through the small gap between the curtains
and glowing on her skin, he began kissing her throat, her
ears. She reached up and pushed his coat off him, began
unbuttoning his shirt, rubbed her hands over his firm body,
his hard shoulders, his tight back.

His hands moved over her breasts, his palms making slow
circles. He bent his head down, took one in his mouth, rolled
his tongue around and around, sucking gently.

She reached down and unbuttoned his jeans, pushed them
down. He wore no underwear, and she wrapped her fingers
around him, hard and thick.

He quickly sat down on the bed and removed his boots,
never seeming hurried, however. His movements were precise,
as if calculated. He stepped out of his pants and they pressed
themselves together, smooth and cool.

Leslie's legs were weak, quivering, her heart was firing
like a machine gun. She held him in her hand, caressing it,
pumping slowly.

They moved to the bed and he lay on his back. She looked
at him for a long moment, savoring him, like a gourmet
sitting down to a feast with approving, hungry eyes. The
tendons in his neck were taut as he lifted his head to look up
at her. His body rippled with tight, small muscles. His cock
stood tall, twitching impatiently. She leaned forward and
kissed him, kissed his neck, his shoulders, ran her tongue
over his firm pectorals, down the center of his abdomen,
delightedly rubbing her nose in the hair below, kissing the

base of his cock, climbing it with her lips, holding it with one hand like a lollipop so she could slide her tongue around the head several times.

She felt his hands on her head, the palms pressing against her temples, and then she began to feel it, to feel it *all*. It seemed to open up inside, that part deep inside her, in the very center of her, where it all began, opened up and quickly began to spread through her entire body, that stirring feeling that usually took its time and came out slowly. His hands tingled warmly on her temples and she began to suck him in a way she never had anyone before, enjoying it as she never had before, juices flowing freely from her, her hands, trembling childishly, reaching up and moving smoothly over his chest and stomach, feeling him move with her, feeling his muscles tighten, his *skin* tighten, almost as if it were about to change its texture, feel different. She lifted her head for a moment to take a deep breath, her tongue never leaving it, his hands never leaving the sides of her head, and then she went down again, her lips stretching over it, her tongue moving knowingly, a moan deep in her throat coming with the knowledge that— even though it made no sense, even though she *shouldn't* be—she was heading rapidly for a monster orgasm, a granddaddy, a real whopper to top them all, an earth-shaker.

He was moving, pushing, tensing all over, swelling inside her mouth, swelling more than anyone ever had before. He squeezed her head tightly between his hands, and she became numb with pleasure, pleasure that spread over her body in waves, and she knew he was going to come, and she was going to come, too, she *knew* it. It moved in her mouth, swelled, jerked, pulled, and suddenly there was thick, warm liquid dribbling down her chin and she had to pull her head back, lift it to swallow. But there was *more!* More and more and more, and she opened her mouth to let it spill over her lips, down her chin, down her neck.

With his hands still on her head, she opened her eyes and saw her reflection, dim and shadowy in the dark room, in the mirror over the head of the bed, hardly aware at all of the wet, sticky smacking sound beneath her, and she saw it shoot—actually *spurt*—from her mouth in a little stringlike stream and spatter on the mirror in front of her, and she saw that it was dark, very dark, and thick. She tried to speak when she realized that it was her own blood shooting from her mouth, but it was also flowing down her throat and she only gagged; she tried again, tried to form words in her mouth, but could not, no matter how hard she tried, because it was gone, her tongue was *gone*, most of her mouth was torn, and the chewing sound below her continued and her orgasm came, pounding and strong and continuous, and the hands held her head, and the blood continued to flow from her mouth, and his skin was tightening, it *was* changing, and she tried to move, wanted to get away, leave, scream, save herself, because she knew now that she was going to die, but she could not move because her legs were no longer there.

Donald was ready.

A live studio audience was laughing uproariously at something that he could not quite make out because his ears were ringing so loudly.

He leaned forward, thinking briefly about Anne (he loved her, he really *did* love her), about Bill (why couldn't they have been closer during all that time, all that wasted time?), about Kyle (good kid, he deserves to be happier than he is—hope he gets laid soon).

He reached a very unsteady hand forward, wrapped numb fingers around the cold, hard butt of the gun, and pulled it toward him, letting it rest a moment in his lap. His eyes stung with tears, his vision blurred as he lifted the gun, turned the barrel toward himself, slid it into his mouth, put his thumb over the trigger. With his index finger, he pulled the hammer back. It made a solid click . . .

"No!" a voice shrieked, making Donald start. "Don't! Please!"

Anne? No, too young. Who?

There was a pounding on his door, urgent, rapid. "Mr. Ellis? Donald? I'm here to help you! Don't do it, please, I need you!"

He lowered the gun and turned his glassy eyes to the front door.

The knob turned and the door opened. A thin young girl stood in the doorway, a pack on her back, almond-shaped eyes wide with fear.

"I need you to help me stop them, Donald! *We need each other!*"

But as she spoke, her mouth did not move.

two

REALIZATIONS

That fiend that goth a-night
    Women full oft to guile,
Incubus is named by right;
    And guileth men other while
Succubus is that wight.

—"Description of Wales"
in Caxton's *Chronicle*

6

Usually when the phone rang before Detective Lewis Walther awoke in the morning, he jerked from his sleep, sat bolt upright in bed, and grabbed the receiver from its cradle. On this morning, however, he came out of it a little slower, twisting under the covers a few times, grunting with dread. When he finally reached over and picked the receiver up, his wife already had it on the other end.

"He's still asleep, Mitch, he had a late night," she was saying.

" 'S okay, hon," Walther croaked, trying to sit up in bed. He heard her sigh, then hang up. "What is it, Mitch?"

"Sorry to wake you, Lew, but we got another one."

"Another what?"

"Over on El Centro. Somebody reported a strange car in their neighbor's driveway and said the front door of the house was wide open. The guys who investigated found the house—belonging to one Betty Pemberton—to be empty. The bed, however, was covered with blood. No sign of a body."

Walther cradled half of his head in one hand, rubbing a

129

little with his palm, pressing hard. "Jesus Jumpin' Christ with a Gucci bag, Mitch, haven't I got enough to do as it *is* today?"

"Somebody else can handle it. Thought you'd be interested, though."

"Yeah, I am, I am. Okay, give me the address and I'll get over there right away." He listened, ran the address through his head a few times until it stuck, then said goodbye and hung up. He wanted to stay in bed, just a few more minutes, but he knew that would only prolong the pain of having to get up. So he tossed the covers off and stood, stretching slowly. He shuffled into the bathroom while slipping his undershorts off, and got into the shower.

Only thirty-seven, mornings tended to make Walther feel about eighty years old. He was a staunch night person and often wished he had a job that would allow him to enjoy his nights without the constant need to remind himself that he had to get up at some godless hour the following morning. He'd majored in communications in college and had harbored dreams of hosting a midnight-to-six radio show on some soft-and-easy jazz station. That would indeed be the life: spinning records in a comfortable, darkened studio with the moonlight shining through the window. Ah, but God had wanted Walther to be a cop, a police detective, homicide division. Well, it *could* have been worse. At least God got *His* wish and Walther's mother didn't get *hers:* she'd wanted him to be a singing evangelist.

Walther stepped out of the shower, felt through the steam for his towel, and began scrubbing himself dry. Musical, high-pitched laughter came from the kitchen. It was Shawn, Walther's four-year-old son. He definitely does *not* take after *me*, Walther thought. The boy was always very alert in the morning. Slipping on his blue terrycloth robe, Walther went into the kitchen for breakfast before he dressed.

"Hi, babe," Nancy said cheerfully, kissing his stubbly cheek and reaching around to pat him on the ass. "Sorry about that phone call. I wanted to let you sleep a little longer."

" 'S all right."

"Daddy's awake!" Shawn exclaimed, holding his fork over his head and smiling broadly. His cheeks were chubby and rosy, his blond hair full of loose, floppy curls.

"Wrong, punkin," Walther replied, bending down to kiss the boy's head. "Daddy is *up*. Daddy is not necessarily *awake*." With a sigh, he sat down at the little breakfast table next to Shawn.

"Want your coffee black this morning?" Nancy asked, pouring some into a cup.

"Are you kidding? Why don't you leave out the water and I'll just eat it with a spoon."

"Strawberry waffles, Daddy," Shawn said, one cheek bulging with food.

"Don't talk with your mouth full," Walther told him through a yawn. He sipped his coffee and grimaced at his wife. "God, you took me seriously, didn't you?"

"I don't suppose you'll be able to make it to Sherry's play this afternoon, will you?" Nancy asked him, dishing up some waffles.

"Play? Oh, that's right. It's that Fall Frolic thing, isn't it? What time?"

"Two-thirty."

"I'll be there. Wanna go see your sis in a play today, Shawn?"

"Nah. I don't want to."

"How come?"

"Cuz, she never lets me win when we play Star Raiders on the 'tari. She *always* wins, cuz she's bigger."

"Oh, you just keep it up. Pretty soon you'll be blowing her

131

clear into the next galaxy, kiddo." He chewed his food, swallowed, then turned to Nancy, who was now sitting across from him with a cup of coffee. "Where *is* Sher, anyway?"

"She stayed over at Marci's last night."

Walther's brow wrinkled. He hadn't even known she was gone last night when he got home. He was a little disturbed by the thought that he'd been so busy, so preoccupied with work and all those goddamned disappearances, that he wasn't paying much attention to his own children. Sherry was already eight, but it seemed as if she'd been Shawn's age just last week. He found it very unsettling to know that by the time parents retire and have time to spend with their families, their families are busy struggling to make a life for families of their own. He wished he could be different, but he couldn't. He was the same as everyone else. What a shitty deal.

"Got a lot to do today?" Nancy asked.

Pulled from his thoughts, Walther looked over at his wife. Her blue eyes were compassionate, interested. Her face appeared rather expressionless, but there was a look there with which he had become familiar during their eleven years together. It was strong, supportive, and warm, and it usually got his day off to a good start.

"Yeah. A lot. I've got to go over to El Centro. Mitch says they found another patch of blood in an empty house. No body, nothing. Just blood."

Nancy clicked her tongue and shook her head a little helplessly.

"Then I've got to go talk to the brother of that guy who disappeared from the hospital yesterday and left *his* blood all over the place. Plus I've got about half a dozen others to talk to, also, and I'm sure there will be more. What about you?"

"Well, Shawny-boy here has an appointment with the doc—"

132

Shawn let out a groan and clattered his fork against the edge of his plate.

"It's just a checkup, honey," Nancy assured him.

"No needles?" he asked.

"No needles."

He still did not look pleased.

"Aw, c'mon, punkin, you can take it. We want to keep you well, you know. All the doc is going to do is make sure there's nothing wrong with you, make sure you haven't got the Sneaky Stuff or the Crawling Crud."

Shawn's laugh rang out just as the cuckoo clock went off eight times.

"Oh, Jesus, I better get going. I don't want to hold them up down there. Good breakfast, Nan." He stood and left to get ready for work. When he returned, he was putting on the overcoat that Nancy had given him two Christmases ago, partly as a joke because it looked, she said, like "such a detective kind of thing to wear." He picked Shawn up and gave him a hug and kiss. "You be good for Mom today, okay, kiddo?" Shawn's blond curls, which he'd gotten from his dad, Walther was proud to say, bounced as he nodded. Putting the boy down, Walther turned to Nancy and put his arms around her. "I don't know when I'll be home this evening. Why don't you skip dinner and take the kids out to the Sizzler, or something."

"Without you?"

"I'll let you know when I'm coming," he said, chuckling. "I love you." They kissed briefly, and Walther went to work.

Walther's thumb tapped lightly on the steering wheel, keeping rhythm with the reggae playing on the car stereo. It was Bob Marley, one of Walther's favorites.

The sky looked ready to rain again at any moment, and that

133

didn't appeal a whole lot to Walther. His mood was dreary enough without any help from the weather. He was under some pressure to get to the bottom of these disappearances. Officially, that's all they were so far: disappearances. There were no bodies, so they couldn't be classified as homicides, but everybody was anxious to prove that they *were* homicides, so it had been handed to that department, namely to Walther himself. The captain was breathing down Walther's neck—in a friendly sort of way, as usual—and everyone above the captain was breathing down the *captain's* neck as well.

Walther knew that in other towns and cities there were other cops like himself with other captains breathing down *their* necks, too, for the same reason. These things—these disappearances—were making the national news now. John Chancellor, Ted Koppel, all the biggies were talking about them. And Walther knew, as did everyone else down at the station, that it was only a matter of time—and probably not much time, at that—before the FBI took over. These things were far too widespread to be left in the hands of local authorities.

Yesterday, one William Ellis, fireman, and friend of the first Napa resident to vanish, Eddie Monohan—a point Walther thought possibly significant—had disappeared from his room at Queen of the Valley Hospital. He'd left blood spattered about his hospital bed, right under the noses of the nurses, doctors, nuns, and whoever else. Walther had wanted to talk to the guy's brother, Donald, who was present at the hospital—also significant, perhaps?—but the doctor had said to give the guy a break because he was pretty upset over the whole thing. Okay, fine. Walther would catch Donald Ellis today.

Now *this*, he thought as he pulled in front of the little house on El Centro. Other cars were already there. Reggie Gruenwald, from the lab, was just crossing the small, well-kept front yard when Walther turned his ignition off. Reggie

134

came over to the car and bent down. Walther rolled down the window.

"Still listening to that Negro music, Lew?" Reggie asked, jerking his head in the direction of the stereo.

Walther reached down and switched it off.

"Reg, you wouldn't know good music if it came up and kicked you in the balls, you know that?" Walther opened his car door, gently nudging Reggie out of the way, and stepped out, closing it after him. "What have we got here?"

"Oh, same old shit. Owner of the house, Betty Pemberton, has been contacted. She's on her way back from Mississippi now."

"Well," Walther said, slipping his keys into his pocket, "let's go play." He and Reggie walked across the lawn to the front door of the house and went in.

There was sunlight shining through Donald's window when he opened his eyes, and it hurt his already throbbing head. The window was open a crack and crisp, fresh morning air wafted into the otherwise stuffy bedroom. Donald clenched his eyes shut and smacked his lips, feeling the cottony coating on his tongue, and he stretched his arms out in front of him, flexing his fingers.

He smelled something cooking. Eggs were being fried, bacon was sizzling, coffee brewing. The sound of shattering glass came from the kitchen. She was still there.

Donald vaguely remembered the girl from the night before. In fact, he only vaguely remembered the whole evening. The whiskey, the gun, the girl.

He tried to prop himself up on one elbow, but the stiffness in his neck seemed to branch up into his head and wrap a few wiry fingers around his brain, giving it a painful squeeze. He lay back on the bed and pressed his temples with his palms, a sigh that was part groan coming from his chest, and he could see her once again, standing at the front door, shouting at him but *not* shouting at him, because her lips had not moved; it had not really been a voice he had heard, but something he had felt. She'd dashed in, taken the gun from his hand, thrown her arms around him, and held his head to her breast . . .

"It's okay, it's fine now." A *real voice,* a soft, musical voice; a faint whiff of perfume and breath mint; the warm softness of her small breasts against his cheek. "Oh, go ahead, Don, you go ahead and cry. You got somebody to cry *with* now, okay?"

She'd stood there forever, it seemed, holding him to her, stroking his hair, gently rocking him from side to side. He'd wrapped one arm around her tiny waist, listened for a while to her heartbeat. Then she'd led him, staggering drunkenly, into his bedroom, helped him undress, and put him to bed. She'd sat on the bed for a while, comforting him as he continued to sob. Then he'd looked up at her and asked who she was.

"I'm Freddie."

"Freddie? Where are you from? Why did you—"

"Shhh, we'll talk about all of that tomorrow. You go to sleep."

"No, no, I don't want to sleep, no sleep, please, not with those nightmares."

She'd stroked his face softly, soothingly, bent toward him, and smiled. "No, there'll be no nightmares tonight, Don. Promise. I'm gonna stay here with you, and I'll keep them away from you, okay? I promise. You just sleep, now. Just sleep . . ."

And he did. He slept better than he had in weeks. When he thought about it, it seemed that the nightmare had begun at one point during his sleep, but had simply faded away.

(". . . and I'll keep them away from you, okay?")

Donald's headache was rapidly giving way to his growing

curiosity. There were some clanking, clashing sounds, then silence. When he heard soft footsteps nearing the bedroom, Donald sat up, tried to fluff his pillow a little, and folded his arms across his chest.

The bedroom door was already open a couple of inches, and dark, thickly lashed eyes peeked around the doorway, the eyebrows high, partially hidden beneath girlish bangs.

"I'm awake," Donald croaked sleepily.

She pushed the door all the way open with her foot and stepped inside, holding a tray with breakfast on it. "Good, good." She went to his bedside and carefully put the tray in his lap. There was a small glass of orange juice, a cup of coffee, eggs, bacon, toast, and a banana. Having set the tray down, she stood and put one hand on her hip, chewing on the thumbnail of the other. "Um, I broke a dish out there. You probably heard. I'm really sorry, but it just—"

"Don't worry about it. This is very nice. Thank you."

"Well. I'm not much of a cook, and it's probably not that good." She tilted her head once, jerkily, and her smile sparkled.

Donald smiled back, but said nothing. He realized that she was younger than he'd thought, maybe eighteen or nineteen. Her hair was very dark and shiny, patches of it still wet from showering. Her eyes were two of the darkest he'd ever seen, almond-shaped and lively. Her lips formed a perfect bow, smooth and very kissable. Her small body was lost in a billowing sweatshirt, the sleeves pulled up around her elbows, but from the waist down, her figure was well-defined in the faded jeans she wore. Donald felt a twinge of guilt: this girl could be one of my students! he thought. He took a bite of his toast.

"Did you sleep well?" she asked, slipping her hands into her hip pockets.

"Yes, I did."

She sniffed hesitantly. "No nightmares?"

He stopped chewing. "No, I didn't have any nightmares. I think I *started* to have one, but . . ."

Those lips parted in another smile, and she exhaled with apparent relief. "Good, I'm glad."

What was it about the way she said that? She knew . . . ?

He slowly lowered his hand to his plate, put the toast down. *You know about them, too?* he thought, wordlessly. Just a hunch.

She nodded.

You have the nightmares?

She nodded again, got down on her knees beside him. *My name is Freddie. Fredericka Santos, really, but I go by Freddie because Fredericka sucks.*

They both laughed aloud, her laugh clear and fresh, his still hoarse from sleep, and she squeezed his hand.

"You know my name," he said quietly.

Freddie nodded.

"How?"

She adjusted her position beside the bed until she was comfortable, then propped one elbow up on the mattress and rested her chin on her forearm.

"A few months ago, I met a girl named Sandra Stillwell," she said.

"Sandra? She was—"

"A student of yours. I know. I met her through another friend of mine in San Francisco. Sandra moved there after she graduated. And that's where I'm from, too, by the way. One day, she was showing me one of her high school yearbooks. I saw a picture of you and . . ." She shrugged. "I just knew. It all came at once. I knew you were like me. And I felt . . . I don't know, I just felt *lonely* for you. Does that makes sense? I felt you were hurting. But I didn't feel you *needed*—I mean *really* needed me—until I started having the nightmares and hearing the voices. And I kept thinking of *you*, thinking I should find you, help you, that maybe you could help *me*. So here I am.''

Donald didn't know what to say. What *could* he say that wouldn't sound silly? During the last few months, this girl had been living an hour or so away from him, they had never met, he hadn't even been aware of her existence, and she was hurting for him, actually feeling his pain and fear.

He smacked his lips and sipped his coffee, turning the whole thing over in his mind. He wondered if she were reading his thoughts at that moment. Apparently she was much stronger than he; she had control over her sensitivity, unlike Donald. She could read his thoughts, but he couldn't read hers, it seemed, unless she wanted him to. That put him at a disadvantage. He had no way of knowing if she really wanted to help him, or if—

Donald blinked suddenly with the thought that she could be one of *them*.

Freddie gasped and tightened her fingers around his hand. ''No!'' she snapped. ''No, don't you think that! *Don't!*'' Her lips worked busily and her eyes began to glisten with unfallen tears. ''I've come to *help* you. You're . . .'' Her voice had lowered to a whisper. ''You're the only other one I know.'' She stood up, her eyes avoiding his. ''Your breakfast is getting cold,'' she said as she left the bedroom.

Donald finished his breakfast, then took a shower and shaved. He felt truly clean and fresh, a feeling that had been getting less and less familiar lately. He put on his robe, which was in need of a good wash, and walked out into the living room. The backpack that Freddie had been wearing the night before was leaning against the wall by the door. Water was running in the kitchen. Donald went in to see her standing at the sink, washing dishes.

"Thanks for breakfast," he said, leaning his shoulder against the doorjamb. "And for cleaning up. God, this kitchen was a mess."

"Sure. Glad to do it." She washed the last dish, set it on the drainboard, dried her hands, and said, "I don't know where you put your dishes, so I'll leave that up to you." Then she scooted by him through the doorway.

When Donald turned, he saw her gathering her pack up. "What are you doing?" he asked, taking a few steps toward her.

"I'm going. I've got enough money for a cheap motel. Or I can maybe stay with—" Her voice broke and she cleared her throat; she wouldn't look Donald in the eye. "I can stay with friends." She stood by the front door, shifting her weight from foot to foot.

"Now, wait a minute, Freddie," Donald said softly, stepping forward. "I . . . I'm really sorry about that. I've been through a lot, you know. It's only natural for me to harbor a few suspicions."

"I just want to help you," she whispered. When she looked up at him finally, her eyes were shedding tears.

Donald inhaled deeply, held the breath for a few seconds, then let it out slowly and quietly.

"After all these months," she continued, "you've been so . . . you've been so *important*. Then, when the nightmares started and I decided to come to you . . . well, I just never thought you might not trust me."

"Give me a little time. Please. You've got to stay, Freddie. There's too much I don't know. There are too many questions I want to ask you."

She wiped the back of her hand under her nose.

"Like . . . like, what do you know about this *thing*, whatever's been happening to us? What *is* it? And, and how did you do what you did last night? I mean, with the nightmare.

You *were* responsible for that, weren't you? For keeping it away?''

She looked down at the floor again, almost guiltily, and nodded. "I thought you needed the sleep."

"I *did!*" He stepped back and made a quick, excited gesture with his hands. He had suddenly become animated and was sweeping his arms in front of him as he spoke, accentuating his words. He felt *refreshed*, suddenly. The solid night's sleep and the hot breakfast had fortified him, and he felt the rationality and the logic—the confusion and disbelief of all that had happened to him—begin to come out of the box it had all been locked up in lately. He wanted his questions answered. "I *did* need the sleep, and I want to know why I *got* it! All of this is so . . ." He touched his fingertips to his temples and shook his head. "It just doesn't make sense."

Freddie slipped the backpack off once again, lowered it to the floor, bent down to open it. She pulled from it a number of newspaper clippings that had been folded carefully, neatly packed together, and she began taking them apart, unfolding each one separately and handing them to Donald. "Here. Read these."

Donald took the clippings and began scanning them. He moved over to the sofa and sat down.

The first one was from the Los Angeles *Times* and told of a man in Ventura who came home from work to find his bed drenched with blood, the covers torn back, the blood leading nowhere, coming from nowhere, just covering the bed, soaking the mattress. The blood was found to be AB negative, his wife's type. Other than the blood on the bed, no trace of her could be found.

The next, taken from the Chicago *Sun-Times*, was about a car found parked near a popular lookout point, its backseat saturated with blood. The car's owner, a male college student,

had been seen earlier with an unidentified young girl. Neither
of them could be found, but the blood type in the backseat
matched the young man's.

The other clippings described similar incidents involving
people of various ages in cities like New York and Seattle,
and three in San Francisco.

"It may not make sense," Freddie said, "but it's happening all over the place."

Donald looked up slowly, feeling weak, thinking once
again of Bill, and of Bill's drinking buddy, Eddie Monohan.
He leaned back on the sofa and let the papers drop into his
lap. He rested his hands on top of them. "You don't understand this any better than I do, do you, Freddie?"

The girl slipped her fingers into the pockets of her jeans
and shrugged her shoulders. Her face was still red from
crying, but she had stopped. Her eyes, now puffy and tear-
stained, avoided Donald's. "I know I'm scared shitless of
them, whatever they are. Because they're very strong. And
they're very secret. They're good at disguising themselves, I
think. Sometimes when I'm in a crowd of people, I can *feel*
them. I know they're nearby, but I can never see any sign of
them. Of course, I don't know what they look like anyway,
but they seem to blend . . ."

"Just a theory," Donald said after a few moments of
silence. "One theory, something to start with . . . *that's* what
we need."

As if suddenly remembering something she'd intended to
do earlier, Freddie quickly reached into the backpack again.
"Here, read this."

Donald took from her another clipping, a smaller one,
something the papers use to take up space, a filler.

"It was in the *Chronicle* just a couple of days ago," she
said before he started reading. Then she sat down next to
him.

DISAPPEARANCES HAVE HISTORICAL COUNTERPARTS

Cornell Hamilton, San Francisco author and historian, gave police historically based information today concerning the recent bloody disappearances taking place across the U.S.

Hamilton, 78, stated that similiar incidents were recorded in English history during the 16th, 17th, and 18th centuries. According to Hamilton, it's difficult to tell how widespread the occurrences were, and there is apparently no explanation given.

The historian accused the police of "apathy toward the situation" after he was dismissed from the station.

Donald looked up silently from the article.

"His name is in the phone book," Freddie said pointedly. "I looked it up before I left."

"I'd like to speak with him," Donald said. "Maybe we should pay him a visit tomorrow. He could be just a crazy old man." He stood and walked over to the window, leaving the clippings on the sofa, folding his arms before him. "Then again, he *could* know something everyone else *doesn't*."

There was a long silence between them in which Freddie rose and walked over to stand beside Donald. Instinctively, almost without realizing it, he put his arm around her shoulders and she leaned against his sturdy frame, lay her head on his shoulder. Donald caught the vague, flowery fragrance of her hair.

I think they know about me, he thought to her. *They know what I can do and that I'm . . . suspicious of them.* Both stared silently ahead through the window. *Do they know about you?*

I think so.

Donald squeezed her to him just a little. *We need to stay together, then. It's safer.*

A reggae beat pounded through Walther's modest car speakers as he drove toward Eberhardt High School that afternoon. His thumb was tapping on the wheel again and his head began to throb. He didn't need a headache now, only halfway through what was turning out to be a rather long day. He leaned over and rummaged in the glove compartment until he found the little tin container of Anacin. It was the coated kind that went down easily. He worked up some spit and swallowed a couple.

Things weren't getting any better. The car in front of the house on El Centro belonged to one Leslie Marie Newell, who had been seen entering the house with a dark young man by a neighbor. He had not reported it, though.

"Are you kidding?" the meaty man had said to Walther when asked why he hadn't called the police. "If I reported every punk I saw doing something suspicious, I'd be on the phone twenny-four hours a day."

The man who *had* reported the car early that morning *was* on the phone twenty-four hours a day. Well, almost. He seemed to do nothing but sit at his window and report to the police everything that moved. How he had missed the arrival of Leslie and her friend the night before was a mystery.

No one had been seen leaving the house, and no other car had been seen parked there.

Walther had remained there awhile to speak with some of the neighbors, but someone else, thank god, was assigned to tell Leslie's mother. Walther was on his way to see Ruth Falsey and ask her a few questions about the girl. He would talk to anyone else he thought might be able to help him, too.

144

He wanted to learn as much as he could about this dark young man she'd been with the night before.

This was getting out of hand. If these things were happening just in the Napa Valley, that would be one thing. But they were happening in other cities, too. Same goddamned thing, no rhyme or reason. Quite frankly, Lewis Walther thought it was getting just a little bit spooky.

Ruth Falsey greeted Walther at the door of her inner office and offered him coffee. He declined, they sat down, and he began, first answering her questions about what exactly had been found in the house on El Centro, then asking her some questions.

"I don't suppose you would have any idea what Leslie's plans were for last night, what she'd intended to do?" he said.

Ruth shook her head apologetically. "I have no idea. Now, I'm sure that if you asked some of the students, some of her friends . . ."

"Yes, I'm planning to do that a bit later." Walther reached into his coat pocket and took out a pad with a few notes he'd made earlier; he scanned them quickly. "A neighbor said that Leslie was seen last night going into the Pemberton house with a young man: tall, dark. Not much description, I know, but was there someone she hung around with a lot?"

"Yes." Ruth leaned an elbow on her desk and rested her cheek in one hand wearily, as if she'd expected Walther to say something like that. "There was a boy. He came to the school yesterday, apparently to see Leslie, because he wasn't a student here."

"His name?" Walther produced a pen quickly and prepared to write.

She shook her head. "No one knows who he is or where he came from. After the fight in the—" Realizing he knew

145

nothing of that, Ruth stopped and took a deep breath. "There was a scuffle between the boy and one of the teachers. No one involved—neither the teacher nor Leslie—would give his name. Leslie repeatedly denied knowing it. She claimed she'd just met him at work the day before."

"What was this scuffle about?"

"No one knows that, either."

The creases in Walther's brow were deepening.

"Well, who *was* this teacher?"

Ruth tugged at her lower lip hesitantly. "It was Donald Ellis. He's been having some—"

"Donald *Ellis?*" Walther practically snapped, leaning forward.

"Yes. English teacher."

"Could I . . . I'd like very much to speak to him."

"Well, as I was saying, he's been having some problems lately. Personal problems. Until he works them out, he's taken some time off from work. He's at home now, as far as I know."

Walther sat there for several seconds, trying, as he too often did, to put things together before he had nearly enough information; he was running ahead of himself. He twitched his head a couple of times, as if to toss away all the muddled, crowded thoughts going through it.

"Mrs. Falsey, I appreciate your time. Thank you very much." He stood, returning the pad and pen to his pocket.

"Well, would you like to speak to some of the students, or other faculty members, perhaps?"

"Later. I have other things to do now. I'd planned to speak with Mr. Ellis this afternoon anyway, about something else. Now I've got *two* reasons to talk with him."

Ruth's face clouded immediately and she stood with Walther. "Is he in some kind of trouble?"

"Oh, no. I just need to get some information from him

146

about another case I'm working on. I'll ask him about this, too. Um, I'll be back later, though.''

''Anytime.'' Ruth walked with him to the outer office and smiled as he left. But her smile quickly disappeared and her face became tight and firm. Without taking her eyes off the door, she said to her secretary, ''Marjorie, would you please tell Anne Cramer to come to my office as soon as possible. I need to talk to her.''

Donald's house took on a whole new personality with two people in it—no, no, with *Freddie Santos* in it. The walls seemed to relax in the knowledge that she was going about the house, cleaning it up here and there like a little housewife. And she *did* look like a housewife. When he asked her how come she seemed so comfortable with such tasks, she told him she used to do housecleaning now and then for a little extra money. She'd become quite good at it.

Freddie insisted Donald rest while she cleaned up, and she insisted he let her know if he wanted anything. So he sat in front of the television for a while, then read a bit, sipping a Tab. But whatever he was doing, he never entirely took his attention from the girl.

He mentally chided himself all day long for the pathetic way he had been handling himself—sitting around drunk, tearful, and afraid—while this girl had been remaining alert, reading the papers, cutting out all those clippings, keeping track of her enemy, even though she didn't know who or what it was. He hadn't even had the presence of mind to stay abreast of the news. Had he done at least that much, he would have known that, whatever was happening, it was not limited only to his area, only to those close to him. And with that thought, he'd turned on the radio to catch one of the afternoon newscasts.

That was when he first heard about Leslie.

''Oh, Jesus Christ,'' he'd whispered after hearing the story.

147

Freddie had come over and sat next to him, a dust rag in her hand. "A student," she'd said.

He'd nodded.

Later in the afternoon, there was a knock at Donald's door.

"I'll get it," Freddie chimed.

"No, no. Please, let me." Donald opened the door and Detective Lewis Walther smiled brightly at him, holding out a friendly hand.

"Mr. Ellis," he said, shaking Donald's hand, "we met last night at the hospital."

Donald looked confused for a moment; not because he didn't remember Walther, but because he didn't know how he might explain Freddie's presence or his involvement with Leslie Newell and her . . . friend, which, in light of what had happened to her, Walther would no doubt be bringing up.

"Sure," Donald said, smiling.

"I was wondering if I could talk with you awhile, ask you a few questions."

"Oh, of course." Donald led the detective into the house and offered him a seat. He noticed Walther's surprised blink when Freddie walked into the living room. Donald introduced the two of them. "Freddie is a former student of mine," he explained, glancing at her.

She smiled at Walther. "I clean his house for him. Mr. Ellis isn't very domestic. Can I get you something to drink? A soda, or something?"

"Sure, a soda would be nice."

Freddie disappeared into the kitchen.

"I'm really sorry about your brother, Mr. Ellis," Walther said, leaning forward and locking his hands together. "Everybody is still rather confused as to what happened."

Donald nodded silently. He took a pack of cigarettes from the end table by the sofa and lit one.

"I need to know everything you can tell me about what

you saw in that room. You probably know that there have been other similar, uh, incidents in the news. We're all baffled, and we want to get to the bottom of it. What did you see?"

Donald shrugged politely. "I can't tell you much. Just that I went into the room, saw the blood all over . . . and that's it."

Ice clinked into a glass in the kitchen.

"The orderly said he found you on your knees by the bed."

Donald nodded again. "I was, uh, rather upset."

Walther stared a few moments, his eyes never wavering, seeming to hold his breath. Then, quietly, "Yes. That's understandable."

Freddie breezed in and handed Walther a soda.

"Thank you." He sipped it, then held it between his palms. "I understand you had some sort of row with Leslie Newell's friend yesterday."

Donald's eyebrows popped up, but he did not register any nervousness, although he *felt* some. "Where did you hear that?"

"Ruth Falsey. I talked to her earlier. About Leslie Newell . . ."

"Yes, I heard on the radio."

Freddie had retreated to the kitchen where she sounded busy, but Donald knew she was listening intently to every word.

"Who was this guy she was with?" Walther asked, sipping his soda again.

Donald chuckled and slowly exhaled some smoke. "Sorry, but I don't know that, either."

"Well, what was the problem, what was the scuffle about?"

"Ah"—Donald waved a dismissing hand through the air—"it was nothing, really. I was having one of those lousy

149

days and this kid mouths off to me. Just caught me at the wrong time, I guess. I'd never even seen him before.''

"I don't mean to pry, but, uh, how come you're taking some time off from work?" Walther's eyes were locked with Donald's and they didn't stray.

Donald was quiet for a few moments. "Personal problems."

"Mm." Walther looked down at the floor a bit, then swallowed the rest of his drink and stood up. "Thank you for your time, Mr. Ellis. I'm sure you'll be seeing me again, soon, as questions arise. I've got a lot of things left to do today, though, and not much day to do them in, so I'll be off now."

"Sorry I was no help," Donald said, also standing, taking Walther's glass.

"You may have your chance yet, Mr. Ellis."

Walther was confused and excited. Confused because he felt he was onto something, but didn't know what, and excited because something was better than nothing.

Ellis was lying, plain and simple, no doubt in Walther's mind about that. He doubted the girl was just cleaning house, because there was a backpack leaning against the wall by the door and in it he saw a hairbrush, toothpaste, and some makeup. She had stayed, or was going to stay, the night.

Walther knew he would get no more out of Ellis right then. Later, when he had more information, when he could add more meat to his questions, he would return to Ellis. And he would bring up the other fireman, too, the one who had disappeared a few weeks ago . . . Monohan, or whatever his name was. Walther had a feeling Ellis probably knew something about that, too. He probably knew a *lot*.

A thin coating of sweat shone on Donald's face. Small beads of it speckled his upper lip. Freddie sat next to him.

"He's suspicious of me, isn't he?" he asked her. "He doesn't know why, yet, but he's suspicious, isn't he?"

She nodded.

"He'll be back. He'll want to know more. And I don't know what the hell I can tell him without sounding like a lunatic." He stared straight ahead from his position on the sofa.

"Maybe after we go see the old man in the city tomorrow, we'll know more," Freddie suggested. "Maybe we'll feel better."

Donald said nothing.

"Don, why don't we do something tonight? Why don't we go out to dinner, or something? Maybe a movie."

He turned to her and his lips twitched as if he wanted to smile. "Sounds good."

She smiled brightly. "Okay. Whatever you want to do is fine with me, but I think we need to do *something*. You know?"

"Yeah. We'll do something."

By evening, the rain had returned. The clouds regrouped to continue their intermittent downpour. There was an occasional flash of lightning in the distance and a light wind whispered secretly through the orange leaves of the trees.

Anne Cramer sat in her dining room looking out her window. One candle illuminated the dinner she had before her: take-out Chinese food. She ate slowly, not digesting well.

Thoughts of Donald haunted her like ghosts. She'd called him twice, but there was no answer. She would keep trying until she got him, and then she would plead with him to let her come see him. She'd abandoned her vow to forget about him and his problems in favor of a determination to do whatever she could for him. She'd changed her mind when Ruth told her, earlier that day, that the police were interested, for some reason, in Donald. What in the world had he done?

Of course, he could not help wondering if he might have had something to do with the disappearance of Leslie Newell, or if he knew anything about it.

(". . . a feeling . . .")

She took a bite of prawns.

("It's a feeling I've had before, a feeling of something . . . something bad . . .")

The little dining room was lit for an instant by a far-off blink of lightning.

(Something *bad*. BAD! BAAAAAAAD!)

Without a second thought, a little surprised at the suddenness of the thought, Anne decided to have a talk with Barry Sereno.

Donald and Freddie went to Alfredo's for dinner that evening. Donald ordered spaghetti and Freddie had lasagna. They were relaxed and quiet, having dismissed all thoughts of their problems for the evening. While they were eating, however, while music played softly over the speakers above them and the soft sound of conversation at other tables mixed with their words, their mild, almost domestic banter somehow swerved onto the topic of their unique abilities. And, for the first time, Donald was comfortable with the subject.

"If I could *use* it," he said, "*control* it, maybe, it wouldn't be so bad. But *it* uses *me!* It's like an ulcer: it flares up without warning, and there's no way of supressing it. And in *this* situation, it . . ." Donald's sentence remained suspended as he realized it was the first time all evening that either of them had approached the subject of their problem. "Well, it's nothing but a handicap." He took a bite of spaghetti, then dabbed at some tomato sauce on his lips with his napkin.

"But if you didn't have it, you wouldn't know—" Freddie began.

"I don't *want* to know!" Donald broke in. "I wish I *didn't* know! I'd rather be blind to the whole thing." He swallowed his food and took a sip of wine.

After a brief silence, Freddie took in a breath and said, "Well, I've decided that, since I've got it, I might as well use it the best I can. So, I've tried."

Donald looked at her across the table, ignoring his food for a while. There, she'd done it again. Earlier, he'd realized that by trying to stay abreast of her unknown enemy, she'd approached the situation in a far more mature manner than he. Now, without meaning to, he was sure, she had shown him up again, accepting the hand she'd been dealt and trying to play the best game she could with it, while he remained forever unsatisfied. It would be easy, Donald thought, for one to become confused as to which of us is nineteen and which is thirty-six.

"You're a remarkable young lady, Freddie," he said. Unintentionally, the words came out in a whisper.

Freddie stopped chewing a mouthful of garlic bread and her head moved back on her slender neck, her eyes widening in mild surprise. And, although the lighting was very dim, Donald thought she blushed. She looked at him for a long time, then smiled and continued chewing.

Donald went on eating his spaghetti, his mind wandering here and there, thinking about how nice it was to be away from work for a while, wondering what Kyle was up to, noticing how good the food—

This is nice, Don.

His head jerked up; he was not yet used to such a strange and intimate form of communication, and it still startled him each time he experienced it.

Her elbows were on the table and her hands were folded

gracefully under her chin. A smile rested luxuriously on her lips.

I'm glad we came.

Me, too, he replied, his eyes on hers.

They remained that way for some time, and the longer they looked at one another, the quieter became the music from the speakers, the more distant the nearby voices, the more the surroundings disappeared entirely for Donald. His attention focused more and more on Freddie, until she was all that he saw, all that he knew. He felt rather warm, and he assumed it was from the wine he'd had. But then Freddie's smile grew a bit wider, her teeth sparkled a little, and he could have sworn she was touching him . . . *inside*. Embracing him, not physically, but mentally, and he wanted to return the gesture, but he didn't know how. He wanted to touch her, hold her, *really* hold her. He'd been attracted to her from the moment he'd first laid a sober eye on her, but he'd been holding it in, suppressing it. Now it was gushing like a geyser, his feeling for her.

I loved you before I met you, Don. Before I even met you!

And he knew she was telling the truth. He could feel it. He didn't just pick up the words; he could feel the emotion as well, and it was strong. It wrapped around him like a warm, comforting blanket, soft and familiar, an old friend.

Donald pulled back slowly, moved away from the invisible cloud he'd been in, and waved the waitress over for the bill.

Kyle wondered why Woody Allen was taking himself so seriously these days. He'd just seen Allen's latest movie and was walking out of the Uptown Theatre, finishing off his popcorn as he thought the movie over, ignoring the cold drizzle that was falling. He passed a green metal newspaper-vending machine, THE NAPA REGISTER lettered boldly on the side, and slowed to look over what he could see of the front page through the plastic and wire-mesh front. There was nothing about Leslie.

God, that was weird, he thought, slowly chewing the popcorn. No one knew for sure if she was dead or not, but apparently there had been a lot of blood.

He walked across the corner parking lot, wishing he'd known her better. Even though she had a reputation for being a bitch, people had been speaking highly of her all day, what with the news. If no one ever says a good thing about you all your life, Kyle thought, they'll shower you with nice words when you die. He took his keys from his pocket and unlocked the door of his blue VW, got in, and shut the door with a solid *thunk*. Not a moment too soon, either, because large raindrops immediately began exploding on his windshield, slowly at first, then with frantic rapidity.

He started the car up, turned on the wipers, the lights. And then he saw her. Walking quickly through the beams of his headlights across the parking lot. Her body, warped by the rain on the glass, was tall and looked slender despite the long, heavy coat she was wearing. Her hair was wet, but obviously full. Her walk . . .

Kyle craned his neck forward, squinted, tried to see her more clearly. He quickly rolled down his window and stuck his head out, watched her for a couple of seconds.

"Leslie?" he shouted, not very loudly at first, but louder the second time. "Leslie, is that you?"

The young woman's pace never slowed; she continued across the parking lot and around the corner, down the sidewalk, until she was gone.

Kyle sat there for several seconds before he realized his head was getting soaked. Was that Leslie? She hadn't answered. Maybe she hadn't heard him. He first considered getting out of the car and going after her. Next he toyed with the thought of going to the police to report the potential sighting, but

155

then, with a brief shake of his head, he decided not to. Pulling out of the lot, he told himself that the person was most likely not Leslie Newell, and if it was, those concerned would know soon enough. They didn't need his help.

Kyle drove home.

Once it was around the corner and out of his sight, the figure that Kyle Hubbley had thought was Leslie Newell stopped and turned to peer around the corner of the building at the blue Volkswagen that had just pulled out of the parking lot and was moving slowly through the angrily pouring rain. The soft face was expressionless, the eyes squinting piercingly in the dark.

He had called out the girl's name. Perhaps the resemblance was a bit too strong. Surely if there was a hint of recognition even at *that* distance . . . No. This form would remain. The boy was baited.

Lewis Walther whispered good night to his son, switched off the light, and backed out of the little bedroom, leaving the door open a crack. He walked down the hall in his robe, stuck his head into his daughter's room for a moment, and said: "Good job in the play today, sweetheart. You'll be winning Oscars in no time. 'Night.'' Then he continued his slow walk to his bedroom, scratching his back lazily.

He'd been relieved from the case earlier that day, the disappearances. *Everyone* had been relieved, in fact, because, as they'd all known would happen sooner or later, the FBI was taking over. This business of puddles of blood and people missing all over the place was just too widespread *not* to attract the feds. Walther was surprised it had taken them this long to get in on the case.

But it was just getting *interesting*, dammit! Really interesting! Walther's talk with the Ellis guy had set off the old internal detective warning system. The man knew something. And it was just too obvious for Walther to ignore, to turn off his curiosity and step back so someone else could take over.

He went into his bedroom, let his robe drop to the floor, and crawled in beside his wife, immediately clicking off the light. He sighed. Nancy scooted over next to him and began rubbing a hand down his chest and stomach, which seemed to be growing softer every day. She kissed and nibbled his shoulder.

"I know this is probably going to come as a great shock to you, honey," he said gently, "but . . . not tonight. I've got a jobache."

"Oh, babe. Still upset because of the feds."

He nodded in the dark and she just seemed to know his answer was yes.

The phone rang.

"Hello, Walther speaking." He sounded official; it was a difficult habit to kick.

"Hi, Lew. Reg at the lab. Got some results for you."

"Yeah, well, I'm off the case. Efrem Zimbalist, Jr., and his buddies are taking over. But I appreci—"

"I know you're off it, Lew. I just thought you'd be interested. I know how you get into your work." The man chuckled. He was obviously chewing gum. "And this is pretty weird. The blood from the house on El Centro? Same type as the girl's. But something else."

Walther waited while Reggie performed his usual dramatic pause.

"Found some vaginal juices in the blood. How do you like that? Quite a bit, too. But that's not the *really* weird part. Found something else that's got me stumped. Closest I can come, though, is, believe it or not, saliva. It's not actual saliva, it just resembles saliva a whole hell of a lot. And there's a bunch of it, too." He chuckled again. "Pretty

157

fuckin' weird, huh? Even *weirder*, Lew. There was some of the same stuff in the blood from that hospital room. Saliva. Can't figure it. I'm sure the fee-bees are gonna love it. Not to mention the press, if they let it get to them, which I don't see how they can avoid. You know the press. They're like a bunch of goddamned—"

"Thanks a lot, Reg. I really appreciate your thinking of me. I owe you one."

"Anytime, buddy."

Walther hung up slowly, his hand moving automatically to the phone beside the bed.

"Something wrong, babe?" Nancy asked.

After a second or two, Walther said, "Something strange, Nance. Something really *strange*."

Everything inside Donald turned to hot melted butter when he cuddled up next to Freddie's naked body in his bed. They were both breathing slowly, but loudly, hotly. They'd both been insane to touch since leaving Alfredo's. They hadn't said a word on the way home, but there had been communication: warm, liquid communication that had passed silently between them, touching that had surpassed anything known to the flesh.

They pressed against each other between the crisp, cool sheets that Freddie had put on the bed earlier that day. Their hands passed over each other's backs, she feeling the hardness of his muscles, he feeling the smoothness of her silky skin and the roundness of her shoulders. He kissed her neck and her tongue flicked at his earlobe, her trembling breath rumbling in his ear.

You've been so lonely, Don . . . you've needed me . . . so much, for so long. And I've needed you, too. Wanted you. And now . . .

Donald was unable to compose a reply, even in his mind,

but he knew that the feeling was transmitted, that she caught it, felt it *with* him. And he felt hers, too, knew the pure happiness she felt at being with him.

Freddie turned to lay on her back. She looked up at him, and a faint, almost unnoticeable spark of distant lightning illuminated her loving smile in a soft electric blue.

Donald's hands traveled over her smooth, compact body, felt her heartbeat, her every breath. He kissed her breasts, sucked on them with care, his lips teasing her nipples. She spread her legs and he knelt between them, pressing the tip of his erection to her vagina for only a second, not entering her just yet. He put his hands between her legs, running his fingers reverently through the night-black triangle of hair as if it were a newly discovered orchid, circling one finger around her clitoris a few times, simultaneously slipping another finger inside her, feeling her heat, her softness, gently separating the slick, fleshy lips which, without any hint of warning, suddenly opened up of their own accord, pulling back over glistening white fangs that dripped wetly as they opened up wide, moved out of Freddie's vagina, and, with a heavy, sickening *crunch*, bit off Donald's right arm just below the elbow. In the room's murky light, Donald could see blood shoot from the ragged stub like water from a child's squirt gun, splattering on Freddie but receiving no reaction. The teeth, now smeared with blood, snapped again and again, like the jaws of an angry dog.

For an instant, his breath was taken completely away from him and he could only open his eyes and mouth to their fullest and gasp for air, lifting the half-arm until the warm, thick blood was landing on him and he was feeling it trickle down his skin to the ivory-white sheets. And then he screamed, long and horrible, guttural at first, but then shrill and piercing, like a child waking from a nightmare, his face turning almost as white as the linen below him, his whole body trembling so hard that the action was almost invisible, his tongue stiff and sticking straight out of his mouth, like a misplaced erect penis. Freddie and all of the other surroundings disappeared from Donald's attention; only his arm, the bone sticking out beyond the defiled flesh, which was torn and black-red, like a steak that had been cooked for only a very few moments, held him. The arm jerked from left to right convulsively, out of control, tossing the strings of dark blood about like confetti.

"DONALD!"

Silence. Total silence. No one moved or even breathed for a moment.

Freddie's horrified scream had been lika magic finger-snap and suddenly Donald's arm was back, there was no blood, the teeth were gone, and Freddie's vagina glistened wantingly in the dark. There was just total silence and bewilderment. Donald still kneeled between her legs with his right arm, now whole, held out before him, his eyes wide, his mouth gaping, Freddie pressing herself back against the fat pillows in fear.

"Donald . . ." she whispered.

Then he broke, the tears and trembling began, and he fell forward on Freddie. She held him as he cried, rocking him, stroking his hair, cooing over him, *It's all right, Don . . . not real, it's not real . . .* , like a mother comforting the frightened child that he now seemed to be.

He eventually slept, lying there in her arms, his mouth open, a bit of spittle dripping over her breast unnoticed. Freddie lay awake, though, still stroking his hair, even as he slept.

She lay that way all night long, keeping the nightmares away.

7

Donald was very quiet during the drive to San Francisco. Freddie turned the radio from station to station, stopping whenever she came to a song she liked. She sat close to him in the front seat.

They had spoken little that morning over the breakfast of pancakes and eggs she'd made. Donald had turned on the clock radio that sat on the counter under the cupboard, and a morning call-in show had served as conversation.

Freddie knew he was frightened.

"So," she said amiably, gesturing to the radio that was playing something by the Police, "what do you think of this stuff us kids listen to today?"

"*We* kids," he replied flatly.

She turned to him and stared for a moment, her head cocked to the right.

"I'm an English teacher, remember?" He half smiled at her.

"I'm *not* a student, though. Remember?" She tilted her nose upward in mock haughtiness. When Donald turned his

161

eyes back to the road and the pleasantness that had begun to grow on his face disappeared, Freddie moved closer to him and said, "Don, I wish you'd let go of whatever happened last night." She'd managed to get a brief description that morning before they got out of bed, but it hadn't been much. "That sort of thing comes with the territory. You know . . . with being sensitive." She hoped to comfort him with these words, but, as soon as she spoke them, she realized that *that* was the source of his discomfort.

"But what if it happens?" he asked quietly, his face turning a little pale. "What I saw . . . what if it happens?"

Freddie put a hand on his thigh and made a couple of short but warm, friendly strokes. "Might. Might not."

"You're a virtual tower of assurance."

Freddie giggled and the joy in it was contagious. Donald chuckled and tossed her a sidelong glance which prompted her to lean over and kiss his cheek.

"That's better," she said.

Nice, Anne thought. Be nice, or he won't tell you a damned thing.

"Would you like some coffee, Barry?" she asked him as he sat down in front of her desk. She was pouring herself some from a thermos.

He shook his head, a little nervous.

"You're not in trouble or anything, Barry. Don't worry. I just want to ask you a few questions." She smiled at him, managing to get a small one from him in return.

"Sure," he said with a shrug.

"Do you remember a day last week in Mr. Ellis's English class—it was a test day—when Mr. Ellis asked you if you had crib notes?"

His eyebrows scrunched together a little and he nodded uncertainly.

"Well," she said, lowering her voice a bit and folding her hands on her desk, "I need to know . . . Look, Barry, you won't get in trouble, I promise. This is just between the two of us, it's something *I* need to know for personal reasons and it has nothing to do with the school. *Did* you have crib notes that day?" She tucked her lower lip under her front teeth and waited for his reply, hoping he would tell the truth, hoping she would know if he were lying or not.

Barry squirmed in the chair, leaned to one side, then to another. "Well . . ."

"Really, Barry, it's very important. You'd be doing me a great favor." She tilted her head, a mildly pleading gesture.

"Well, yeah," he said, a worried look on his face. "Yeah, I had them."

"How did Mr. Ellis know? I mean, did you have them out where he could see them?"

He shook his head. "I hid them well. I can't figure out *how* he knew. He just did."

"Did anyone *else* know? Could someone have told him about them?"

"No. I didn't tell anyone. I never do when I'm gonna cheat." His eyes widened then, and he leaned forward quickly. "Not that I do it often, Miss Cramer. I don't, really, I just—"

Anne held up a palm. "Don't worry about it, Barry. Thank you for telling me. Thank you very much, you've helped a lot."

He stood nervously. "Is that all?"

"Yes."

Without speaking, he nodded clumsily at her, then left.

Anne leaned back in her chair and sipped her coffee. She was suddenly thinking about the first time she and Donald had made love. It was at her apartment on a Friday night. It had been in the works for a couple of weeks, but the right time had simply not come up for a while. When it finally did, they were more than ready. And it was wonderful. It had been the first time in a while for her, which made it even nicer. When they'd first started making love that evening, Anne had naturally thought of Rick a bit at first, but those thoughts had faded quickly. Later that evening, however, when she and Donald were sitting around smoking and drinking wine, he had asked, "Who's Rick?"

She'd blinked and said, "My ex-husband. Why?"

"Just wondered."

"Did I . . . say his name?"

He shrugged. "I just wondered."

She knew she hadn't said his name while she was in bed with Donald, and she knew she hadn't talked about him earlier. But she was so happy and so tipsy that evening that she hadn't pursued it. Hadn't even thought about it again. Until now.

How had Donald known? Someone *else* could've told him, of course. He might have asked around about her before they got together, but . . .

With a sigh, Anne picked up the phone book, found the number she wanted, dialed, and waited for an answer.

"Detective . . . uh"—she closed her eyes a moment and tried to remember the name Ruth had told her—"Walther, Lewis Walther, please." She waited some more.

"Walther here."

"Detective Walther, this is Anne Cramer."

"I'm sorry, who?"

"Anne Cramer. You don't know me. I'm a teacher at Eberhardt. I understand you were here yesterday asking some questions about—"

"Yes, but I'm off that case now. The FBI is taking over."

"I heard. But I thought you might . . . well, I need to talk to you. You were asking about Donald Ellis?"

There was a momentary silence on the other end. "Yes, I was."

"Well, I'm a good friend of his." She stopped, knowing that sounded stupid—what did he care?—and not knowing how to go on.

"Yes?"

"I need to talk to you. Could you meet me for lunch?"

"Name the place."

The door opened a crack and, somewhere in the midst of several chain locks, a pair of tiny, wrinkled eyes peered dully out at Donald and Freddie.

"What?" a voice croaked.

"Mr. Hamilton?"

"Well, it's *Doctor* Hamilton, but if the papers don't get it right, I can't expect anyone else to."

"I'm Donald Ellis, Dr. Hamilton. I called you earlier today?"

He made a little grunt of acknowledgment behind closed lips, then snapped the door shut and slid the chains off. "Come in," he said flatly. He opened the door and stepped aside.

"Thank you," Donald said, allowing Freddie to go in ahead of him.

Hamilton nodded at Freddie as she came in, his thin, crooked lips twitching into a brief smile.

"This is Freddie Santos, Dr. Hamilton," Donald said as he entered the apartment.

"Pleasure," Hamilton replied, closing the door. He was a thin man; his clothes seemed to balloon around his spare frame. He had a high, creased forehead that was topped off by stringy white hair; his cheekbones were high and sharp, and his nose was a vulturelike beak perched over a bushy white mustache with yellow nicotine stains. Dirty-looking stubble covered his sharp jaw, and a long-ashed cigarette dangled from his lips. His shoulders sagged and he stood stooped forward a bit. A thin, musty odor hovered about him as he shuffled down a short hall, leading them into a stuffy, dusty room that was piled high with well-used books.

Somehow, Donald had expected that.

"Now," Hamilton said, his voice gravelly, as he slumped into a ratty armchair. Beside it was a small table with a squat lamp that dimly lighted the little room; beneath the lamp lay an open book, face down, with a pair of reading glasses resting on it. "What is it you want?" Ashes fell from the cigarette, which was nearly a butt.

Donald fidgeted a bit; he and Freddie were very uncomfortable, standing before the old man like a couple of schoolchildren reporting to the principal. "Well, uh, we happened to read—"

"Sit down," Hamilton broke in, sounding irritated, gesturing to a nearby loveseat.

After they'd seated themselves, Donald, trying not to sound too eager, explained that they had read the filler in the paper about Hamilton's information, and that they wanted to hear about it in more detail.

Hamilton slapped the air in front of him with a knobby hand and scowled at them. "They thought I was trying to *explain* the whole thing," he grumbled. "Treated me like a goddamned crank. I was just trying to be helpful."

"But you *were* telling the truth?" Donald asked, leaning forward. "I mean, about the disappearances happening before?"

"Of *course* I was telling the truth!" he boomed, pushing himself out of his chair, lifting the reading glasses to his face and positioning them on his sharp nose. "Didn't get where I am by making things up." He shuffled over to a messy stack of books and began rummaging through them, muttering to himself. "What are you, writing a book or something?" he asked Donald over his shoulder.

"No, um . . ." Donald stood, Freddie followed suit, and they walked over to the old man until they were standing just behind him. "I, uh, have a personal interest."

"Oh." He sounded as though he didn't really care. "Here we go," he said, his cigarette bobbing up and down. He removed a book from the stack and walked back to his chair. He sat down, paging through it with fingers clawed by arthritis, then stopped and patted the book softly. "Here," he said, "some of the stuff's in here."

Donald stepped around to the back of the chair and looked over Hamilton's shoulder, struggling to read in the poor light. The pages of the book were grainy and old-looking, but Donald made do. As he read, his eyebrows drew together.

Freddie was bent over one of the book stacks, her hands on her knees, scanning the titles, tilting her head back and forth so she could read them properly.

"Is there any more of this?" Donald asked.

"Lots."

"Would you mind if I borrowed it, Dr.—"

"I don't loan books to close friends," he snapped, "let alone total strangers. Most of these books are impossible to replace." A bit of ash fell from the tip of his cigarette and Donald noticed, surprised, that he'd replaced the butt with a fresh cigarette. Hamilton stood and handed the book over the chair to Donald. "There's a Xerox machine at the drugstore down the street, though," he said grudgingly, crossing the room again. "You're welcome to copy the stuff off. *If* you pay for it, of course." He started fumbling through more of the books.

"I'd appreciate that very much, Dr. Hamilton," Donald said, tucking the book under his arm.

"Yeah," Hamilton grunted. "Let me find the others."

Donald looked over at Freddie. She was standing by some books, leaning toward the light, a volume open in her hands, a disturbed look on her face. He stepped over to her and said, "What's this?"

She glanced up at him, her lips pursed, and held the book toward him so he could see. One whole page was taken up by an old drawing of a nude man lying on a bed, his back arched, his eyes clenched, and his mouth wide. Crouching over him was a finely shaped female figure, weblike hair draped over her shoulders, with large, slanted eyes, black lips open fully, a long, thin tongue flitting from the mouth, forked at the tip. Her long, black fingernails were clawing at his chest, and his rigid penis was stabbed into her strangely large and furry vagina.

"What the hell is *that?*" Donald asked.

"A . . ." She squinted at the text. "A succubus."

A throaty chuckle came from Hamilton as he stood for a moment and glanced at them over his shoulder. "Incubi and succubi. Surely a pretty young lady like yourself has no interest in such things. Old trash." He chuckled again, setting books aside one at a time. "Religious bullshit. Scare tactics to keep folks from playing between the sheets." The chuckle again, crumbling into a cough.

Donald took the book gently from Freddie and paged through it, scanning the text and looking at the dark, brooding pictures. "You don't think there was every anything behind it, then?" he asked Hamilton.

The old man laughed. "Are you kidding? Of *course* there was nothing behind it. Just a bunch of old, self-righteous sons of bitches trying to force their opinions on others. Still being done today, but they're using different strategies now. All bullshit." He stood slowly, pressing a hand to his lower back and gesturing to a small stack of books at his feet.

"There they are. All the books with the information you want."

Donald said nothing. He was still reading about the demons. "Uh, pardon me?" he said, looking up.

Hamilton pointed to the books again. "The books you want. Have to walk down to the drugstore and copy them off."

"Fine." He nodded slowly, closed the book he was reading. "I'd like some copies of this, too."

Perry's Deli was busy at lunchtime, as usual, but Anne and Walther managed to get one of the little round tables by the large window facing Third Street.

Walther did not strike Anne as a detective; he looked more like an accountant to her. But, of course, such categorizing was silly. She had to keep telling herself that, because she did it so often. He pulled her chair out for her in a very gentlemanly way, surprising her. He had a high forehead, pleasant eyes, and a slightly crooked mouth that made him look as if he were perpetually swallowing with his lips pressed together.

"So," he said as he sat down, putting his roast beef and cheddar sandwich on the table and adjusting his chair, "you have something to tell me about Donald Ellis." His left eyebrow arched high over his eye and Anne had to hold back a smile: she thought the gesture made him strongly resemble Mr. Spock. Walther's face was not as long and thin, though, and he was better-looking.

"Yes, I do," she said, glancing out the window at a very fat, hairy man who was walking a pit bull down the sidewalk. She suddenly felt rather foolish. What *did* she have to tell this man about Donald? That he guessed right about some kid in his class who had crib notes? That he was going off his perch? That maybe he knew something that the rest of them didn't?

(Something BAAAAD!)

"If you don't mind my asking, Miss Cramer," Walther said around a mouthful of roast beef, "why me? I mean, I'm off the case, I no longer—"

"You told Ruth Falsey yesterday that you wanted to talk to Donald about something other than Leslie Newell's disappearance. I'd like to know what."

He dabbed at his lips with a paper napkin, wiping off a spot of mayonnaise, then took a drink of his 7-Up. "Well." He sniffed, hesitated. Then he told her about Bill Ellis, about his accident, and about the incident in the hospital, and that he'd needed to find out what Donald knew about it. "Then, of course, there was that business with the Newell girl and her boyfriend, the one Ellis slugged in the corridor."

"And did you learn anything?"

He shook his head.

"Donald told you nothing about the boy?"

"No."

"What do you think? I mean, do you think he knows more than he's telling?"

"I think so. Yeah." He started to take another bite of his sandwich, then chuckled and shook his head slowly. "You know, I've never even *met* you before, and here I am talking over police business with you. *I'm* the detective, Miss Cramer. *I'm* supposed to ask any questions that get asked. You're ruining my image!"

"Sorry." She smiled and took a drink from the glass of milk in front of her.

"Now what, if anything, can I do for you?"

She'd called him impulsively after talking with Barry, and now she didn't know what it was she wanted to tell him. She thought quickly, trying to come up with something that wouldn't make her sound like an idiot, and finally told him all about the change that had taken place in Donald's personality, about the nightmare he'd shared with her, about his "feelings," and about her own suspicions, like Walther's, that Donald was holding something back. When she finished talking, she was unable to look Walther in the eye because she felt so stupid. She began eating her sandwich.

Walther sat there silently for a few moments, running his tongue over his teeth to get pieces of food from under his lips. He smacked his lips once as he took in a breath. "I know I've asked you already, but why tell *me* all of this?"

She shrugged and raised her eyebrows a bit. "I don't know *who* to tell. I told the school shrink, and he only seemed to make things worse. Then I heard you'd been asking about Donald, and I thought . . ." Her voice trailed off and she closed her eyes, shaking her head helplessly.

"What do you think he knows that he's not telling, Miss Cramer? Surely you must suspect something, have some theory?"

"You won't believe me. You'll think I'm crazier than Donald."

Walther chuckled. "Miss Cramer, I used to have a friend named Ted. He was a detective on the force in San Francisco. He retired, came to Napa to live. I met him through a mutual friend and got to know him well. He died last year in a rest home, but he once told me something that I've found to be a big help. He said, 'In our business, Lew, we've got to *believe* everything we hear, and we've got to *doubt* everything we hear. Sooner or later, we'll hit it on the nose.' So. Try me." He smiled.

And then Anne told him that she was beginning to believe everything Donald had been telling her. And that she was beginning to get a little frightened.

*   *   *

It waited for the young one outside The Doghouse. It sat on a stone bench watching others pass by, smelling them, smelling their desire, watching their movements, some clumsy, some sinuous. As always, it took joy in its inconspicuousness. It held the same form as the night before, wore the same clothes, waiting for the boy, knowing he would see it and notice as he had the night before. It was patient.

Kyle sat at one of the small square tables in The Doghouse, finishing off a deluxe cheesedog and a Coke. He'd taken no lunch to school with him and hadn't felt like going to the cafeteria that day, so, after his last class—English, which in Mr. Ellis's absence, was now being taught by a woman who looked as old as God—he'd driven over here for a bite.

He wondered as he ate and glanced through his chemistry book how Mr. Ellis was getting along. He was certainly missed in the classroom. Aside from that, though, Kyle was concerned. Maybe he'd go see him today.

Kyle rose from the little table and put on his coat. He picked up his book, carried his trash to the wastebasket, and went outside. He rounded the corner and—

His mouth fell open and he froze in front of the little stone bench beside the building. There she was! The girl from last night, he was *sure* of it! She wore the same coat and—yes, it was she. He was standing in front of her, staring at her like a fool. It wasn't Leslie, but the resemblance was chilling.

"Yes?" she said, looking up at him curiously. "Something wrong?"

"Uh, well, no." He shifted his weight from the right foot to the left and cleared his throat. "No, it's just that you look so much like someone I know."

Her eyebrows rose.

Kyle chuckled and held up a reassuring palm as he said, "I

know that sounds like some kind of line. But it's true. You could . . . you could be her twin sister almost. I saw you last night, I think. Over on Third, by the Uptown?"

She nodded silently.

Kyle stared at her a bit more, then chuckled again, shaking his head with amazement. "Sorry, but, god, you look so much like her."

"Well, who *is* this girl?" she asked, cool yet friendly.

"Um, her name is Leslie Newell. Well . . . maybe *was*, now. She's disappeared."

"Ah, yes. I read about it in the paper."

It began to sprinkle and Kyle stepped forward, ducking under the slanted shelter that stretched out from the building over part of the sidewalk, covering the bench.

The young woman patted the place beside her. "Sit," she said with a soft smile.

He did, a little cautiously, afraid of making the wrong move. "Are you waiting for someone?"

"No. I was shopping and just decided to rest awhile."

She had no shopping bags, but Kyle didn't mention it; it would sound stupid. "Do you live around here?" he asked instead, realizing that *that* sounded stupid, too.

She tilted her head and looked at him from an odd angle, smiling as if she sensed his nervousness and was amused by it. "Yes. But I'm . . . new to the area."

"Oh, um, I'm Kyle Hubbley."

"Nice to meet you, Kyle." She held out a graceful hand and Kyle took it.

Instant dizziness came with a tingle in his arm. Her skin was so cool, her palm so smooth. Incredibly smooth, like nothing he'd ever touched before. He took in a breath and held it as he shook her hand gently. He pulled his hand back then, slowly, waiting for her to introduce herself. She didn't.

173

"What's your name?" he asked.

She watched him silently for a few seconds, then said, "Betty."

A nervous smile twitched across his face, and then he looked away from her. She continued to watch him, though.

"Did you go to the movie last night, Betty? At the Uptown?" His voice was strained; his mouth was getting very dry.

"No. I was late, so I didn't go in."

He watched cars whoosh by on the wet street. He wanted to ask, he wanted *desperately* to ask! He knew it was a perfect time, the opportunity was there, but he was afraid. He was afraid he would stammer and stutter, afraid his voice would shake or crack, afraid she would say no. The question was inside of him, just waiting to be released. He knew that if he allowed too much time to pass, the question would sound forced. He had to ask now, *right now*, this very—

"Would you like to go *tonight?*" He glanced at her, but quickly returned his gaze to the street in front of them.

"Mmm, no. Thank you for asking, but I think I'd like to spend a nice, quiet evening in front of the television. A little wine, maybe."

Kyle's head spun like a top. At home . . . in front of the television . . . *his* television, maybe? He was so naïve, so bad at reading things girls said. How *angering*, how *frustrating!* Was she trying to tell him something? His parents were going to be gone again. For the whole weekend, in fact! He could at least *ask* her . . . His heart was ready to burst inside of him. His palms were slick with sweat. Tingling . . . his right hand was still tingling . . . she was so soft, so smooth . . .

His mouth was full of cotton and the aftertaste left by the cheesedog had suddenly become rank. Before he even thought about it, he was standing, his hand tightly clutching the spine of his chemistry book, his knuckles white.

"It was very nice meeting you," he said quickly, the

words tumbling out of his mouth like water over rocky falls, his eyes nervously avoiding hers. "I need to be going now. Take care." He turned on his heel and hurried down the walk, bending his head against the sprinkling rain.

She was so pretty, so nice, what the *hell* would she want with *him*, for god's sake! He'd come very close to making an absolute ass of himself. He felt so stupid, so damned *stupid!*

So close, and yet so far . . .

The creature smiled—a gesture that held no meaning for it, had no significance as anything other than an addition to the disguise—as it watched him rush down the sidewalk, leaving in his wake the scent of his need, so strong that it was almost tangible. He was so frightened, so afraid of what he wanted, that he was comical. The creature knew, as it stood and followed a short distance behind the boy, that this Kyle Hubbley was going to enjoy his death far more than he *ever* enjoyed his life.

Neither of them felt like going into a restaurant for lunch, so Donald and Freddie found a Carl's Jr. with a drive-up window, then sat in the parking lot to eat, the car radio playing softly, Freddie looking over some of the material they'd gotten from Dr. Hamilton.

"These people really believed this stuff," Freddie said quietly, shaking her head over one of the Xerox copies. "This says that incubi and succubi were thought to be angels that had fallen from heaven because of lust, and they came to earth to drag the mortals down to hell with them by seducing them, making them sin. Incubi seduced women, and succubi seduced men. There's a story here about a big-shot nobleman in the seventeenth century who left his wife to go on some long trip. Four years after he'd left, he died in some faraway place. A bit later, his wife had a baby. She claimed that her husband came to her in a dream and the child was conceived. For a long time after that, the local clergy argued over whether it was really the husband who'd come to her in the dream—which would then make the baby his legal heir—or if it was an incubus *disguised* as her husband. It never occurred to anybody that this chick had been screwing around!'' She laughed softly with her head back on the headrest, then looked over at Donald, who sat at the wheel eating a burger, staring at her blankly. ''Can you believe that? They really took this stuff seriously.'' Her smile faded, though, as she watched him. He did nothing, did not react, did not speak for a while, just sat there and chewed.

Then he said: *''We're* taking it seriously.'' There was no anger or malice in his voice. In fact, there was almost a tone of dark humor in it. But he was not trying to be funny.

''Yeah,'' she said quietly, shrugging. ''I guess we are.''

''I can't believe we are.'' It was a sigh, tired and soft. ''But we are. *Demons,* for Christ's sake.'' He reached over and picked up a small stack of the blurry copies and looked at the illustration on top. It was a drawing of a reptilian creature that stood upright like a man, horns sprouting from its head just above its sinister, catlike eyes, an enormous erect penis jutting from between its legs; from the penis flitted a thin, forked tongue. Beneath the picture was the caption: ''The legions of hell come to claim their own.'' Donald chewed his lip as he stared at the picture, one elbow propped on the steering wheel. He shook his head slowly, mumbling: ''It sounds right, but I don't think so. I just don't . . .''

Freddie licked a bit of ketchup from her lips as she chewed up some fries. Her slightly upslanted eyes squinted as she leaned toward Donald to hear what he was saying. He'd been very quiet and withdrawn since their visit with Hamilton. He'd spoken little about the incubus idea, although she'd gently tried to get his opinion of the whole thing. If he were going to start talking about it now, she wanted to hear what he had to say.

"What, Don?" she asked.

"I'm just . . . thinking."

What? About what?

He blinked, looked up. *My brother. Bill.*

Donald had told her about Bill after Walther had paid them his inquisitive visit. He'd told her about Bill's accident, about his ravings, and about his death—Donald knew Bill was dead even if everyone else looked upon it as a disappearance—but he had not told her what he'd seen while kneeling by the bloodied hospital bed. He thought she might have picked it up already, since it was on his mind so much. But he wanted to tell her about it now.

The day I went into his room and found his blood on the bed, I touched it. I put my hands in his blood and opened up to whatever might come. And I saw it. I saw what Bill saw before . . . breaking. I almost had it the day before when I touched him on the arm, but I got scared and pulled back. I didn't the second time, though. I held on and I felt the touching that he felt, the warm touching. She'd seduced him. He'd planned to seduce her, but it didn't work out that way. She knew just how to touch him, just how to hold him.

Words became insufficient. Coherent thought was pushed aside as Donald closed his eyes and saw once again, with his mind's eye, the dark patch of hair that had grown between the legs of the creature that called itself Eve up like a mouth turned on its side, and he saw the glistening fangs he'd seen while he was with Freddie the night before. And Freddie saw it, too.

"It was trying to seduce him because it *wanted* him," he said, turning his gaze blankly to a large tire display in front of a service station across the street. "It wanted to *devour* him, *eat* him, for Christ's sake." His skin tingled. "So," he continued, his voice taking on a little more life, as if he'd set aside the nightmarish images, "this incubus idea fits. Sort of. They used to seduce their victims, men and women alike."

"But they didn't *kill* them."

"Not according to the legends, anyway."

"*Something* was going on, though." She looked at the papers again. "People were vanishing, leaving blood everywhere, just like they are now. There are only a few instances here," she shuffled the stack, "but I'm sure there were many more. They probably didn't get all of them recorded. I guess communication wasn't at its best then." She smiled.

Donald nodded, chewing his lip again, staring out the window at things that weren't there, only at thoughts that were racing through his head. He took another bite of his hamburger and chewed it slowly. "Whatever's happening now," he said with deliberation, "*did* happen then. I believe that. But, although I can't explain *why*, I don't think demons are, or were, behind it."

Freddie crushed her empty cup in her hand after finishing the shake. She let her head slump to the right and fall against the window with a thud, and her shoulders slumped wearily.

"Then *what?*" she asked in a weak voice, sounding worn, tired of the whole thing. "Communists? Things from outer space? You know any experts on aliens we can talk to?" Her shoulders bobbed as she laughed humorlessly.

Donald was only partially paying attention to her. His mind was going over and over the things he'd read from Hamilton's books, the folklore, the superstition. It all sounded so empty, so superficial. There was something askew. Something wrong. They were looking in the wrong places, perhaps. But just in case, Donald decided to stop by a shopping mall in Concord where there was a large bookstore that carried a very wide assortment of occult material. He reached down and turned the key, starting the car.

*   *   *

"I wouldn't be a bit surprised if you were to laugh and walk away right now," Anne said, staring at the daiquiri in front of her. She and Walther had retreated to a bar around the corner from Perry's Deli for a quieter place to talk, and talk Anne did. She did *all* of the talking, in fact. Walther listened, very patiently. Now Anne turned to him, silently awaiting his response to all she had told him about Donald, and about her own feelings.

"Well." He lifted his gin and tonic a couple of times and tapped it down on the hard, shiny bar. "I have no reason to doubt anything you've told me. *Nobody* has any reason to doubt the existence of . . . of extrasensory powers, precognition, whatever you want to call it. Hell, even television networks use psychics to plan their programming, so I've heard. But neither do I have reason to *believe* anything you've told me." He turned to her. "Do I?"

She smiled. "Nope."

"Then I'm going to follow the advice of my good friend Ted and stay right in the middle. That way, I've got a fifty-fifty chance of being right." He swallowed the last of his drink. "The question, of course, is what do I *do?* I'm off this case. Officially, I'm pretty useless. But I'm interested."

Anne turned her body toward him a bit and lifted her head, sort of looking down at Walther over the bridge of her nose. "You're more than just interested, aren't you, Mr. Walther?"

He sniffed, tugged at his earlobe, looked away from Anne for a moment, down the bar to his right. "Professionally, I have to approach something like this with a good deal of neutrality. Can't just run around chasing nightmares and 'feelings.' But . . . well, there's a little bit of Gypsy blood flowing through my veins, so I'm naturally kind of, you know, superstitious. And, uh . . . I'm afraid I *am* more than just interested, Miss Cramer." He sighed and folded his arms on the bar. ''Maybe we could go see Mr. Ellis together today. I think your presence would help. *I'd* like to get to him before the *feds* do.''

When Kyle got home, his parents were just leaving.

''You're late, Kyle,'' his mother said at the door, her small blue traveling case in one hand, her purse in the other. Kyle picked up the heavy fragrance of the perfume she always wore. ''You almost missed us.'' Her smile was pleasant, but the tone of her voice suggested there were other things on her mind.

Kyle knew immediately, as he took his mother's case, that his parents had been fighting.

''Oh, thank you, Kyle. You're such a gentleman.''

Just then, Kyle's father came out onto the porch, a large suitcase in one hand and a garment bag slung over his shoulder. He held his favorite pipe between his teeth and sweet-smelling smoke wafted from the bowl as he spoke. ''Kyle,'' he said with a nod.

Kyle knew that, coming from his father, this was the equivalent of, ''Hey, Son, how's it going?'', and he accepted it as such.

''Hi, Dad,'' he replied, walking to the car with the bag. He put it in the backseat of the Volvo.

''Thank you,'' his mother said again, following close behind him. She turned to her husband. ''Well. Do we have everything?''

''Yes.'' He put the suitcase and garment bag into the trunk and slammed it shut. Then he stood straight, wrapped the fingers of his left hand around the lapel of his overcoat, held the bowl of his pipe with his right hand, tilted his head back a little, and puffed smoke.

He always seems to think he's posing for a portrait, Kyle thought.

"Well, Kyle, we're going to be off," his father said, a few strands of his carefully styled, graying hair getting caught in the icy, sprinkled breeze. "We've left a number where you can reach us by phone."

"Same hotel as usual?"

"No, no. We're staying with the Schalos this time."

"In Palm Springs?"

"Yes."

"I thought you were going to San Bernardino."

"*Business* is in San Bernardino. We're staying with the Schalos. I can take care of business in one day." He sniffed and puffed.

"Oh." Always pleasure before business.

He removed the pipe from his mouth and held it up in a sort of salute that he always performed for Kyle before they left. "Hold the fort, Kyle. Get in the car, dear." There was no affection in his words.

Kyle's mother turned toward her son, rested her chin on her shoulder, and scrunched up her face comically, as if to say, "Oh, listen to him—thinks he's boss." Then she got into the car, shut the door, and rolled down the window. "Having anyone over this weekend, Kyle?"

Kyle put his hands on the edge of the window and leaned his weight on it as he thought of the beautiful, blond Betty he'd met a little earlier. He hesitated longer than he'd meant to before answering.

"Nope."

"Oh," she said, a little regretfully. "Well, you really must do something fun, dear. All work and no play, et cetera, et cetera. We'll be back Sunday night. If you need anything, just call." She lowered her voice a bit. "Even if you just want to talk." Then she nodded, as if there had been some secret agreement between them.

The car backed around and went down the drive, the wipers moving smoothly over the windshield.

Kyle stood in front of the house for a while, allowing the sprinkles of rain to cover the lenses of his glasses, as he thought some more about Betty. She looked *so damned much* like Leslie Newell. But there was something there that had been absent in Leslie. Beneath the aloof, almost arrogant manner, there was a certain amount of . . . oh, what was it, *concern?* Friendliness was more accurate. She'd not been put off when he'd asked her to the movie (God, had he really *done* that?), and yet she'd not gushed all over him with excuses and apologies for turning him down. She just . . . *did*, and that was it. Kyle liked that.

He turned rather quickly and hurried into the warmth of the house, realizing that he was just wasting his time with any further thoughts of Betty.

Once inside, he called Mr. Ellis and rang eight times. He got no answer.

It moved confidently among them, watching them carefully, unnoticed, inconspicuous. It enjoyed the feel of the materials it wore: a smooth, dark velvet coat over the cool, silky clothes it had taken from the place of its last feeding.

The last one had been a female, lively and firm. She had fought violently, unlike most of them. Before that, there'd been a male, a bit too thin, but with a mind full of vivid, colorful pictures and a strong will that had been invigorating. Still, it had not been as frantic as the female; it had not been as passionate as the female during the kill, during those last few glorious moments when their minds and bodies had flowed together in the most violent feed the creature had ever experienced.

It was a bit weary now. The last two had been closer together than it preferred, and it had decided to rest for a while, securely hidden by its disguise. It was amused, as always, by the walkers, gathered here in this large marketplace, this "shopping mall." It watched the old ones, tired and slow, smelling of decay and waste. And it paid careful attention to the young ones, vibrant, quick, with a musky, delicious aroma about them as they moved. It looked into the shop windows with curiosity, smelled the wide variety of foods and sweets. It moved with relaxed ease, in no hurry, feeling no tension. Simply resting up for the next kill.

The dim lower-level parking lot of the shopping mall was filled with the cars of Friday shoppers, but Donald managed to find an empty slot. Their feet clacked on the red brick pathway that led from the edge of the parking area to the entrance to the mall. Once inside, Freddie took Donald's hand and smiled up at him briefly.

"I love malls," she said. "I love to shop, *anywhere!*"

"Yeah. It runs in your gender."

She reached over with her other hand and playfully smacked him on the shoulder. "Chauvinist."

They passed an old couple sitting and eating cookies on one of the many benches; a very fat woman pulled hard on her little boy's arm as she hurried past the shops, hissing at him angrily about his behavior; groups of young girls, sexy and shapely before their time, were standing around talking and giggling; a couple of men in nondescript business suits came out of a small Chinese restaurant, talking animatedly; women and men, together and alone, were window shopping, relaxed and in no hurry; security officers were here and there, keeping an eye on things; and sugary-sweet music bled quietly through it all.

"Where's this bookstore?" Freddie asked.

"Well, I'm not really sure," Donald replied, looking right and left. They slowed to a stop and he chewed on his lower lip as he decided which direction to take. "I don't come here often, and one end of this place looks just like another. I think it's by a bakery." He squeezed Freddie's hand and they went to the right, around a corner. The bookstore was at the far end of that wing of the mall. Donald walked through the aisles of books to the section labeled OCCULT/ASTROLOGY.

"We're looking for incubus stuff, right?" Freddie asked.

Donald nodded as his eyes scanned the display, finding nothing at first.

After a few minutes of searching, Freddie sighed. "I don't see anything."

Donald picked up a book on demonology and looked through the index. He found a very small chapter on incubi and succubi, but it told him nothing he didn't already know. "Come on. I think we're barking up the wrong tree, anyway."

As they turned to leave the store, Freddie said with a smirk, "Maybe they have a section on fanged vaginas."

Donald looked at her from the corner of his eye, not really turning his head, not a trace of humor on his face.

"Oh, c'mon." She nudged him in the ribs with her elbow. "Have a sense of humor. Maybe there's a book called *Deathtwat!*"

Donald smiled and shook his head. She amazed him. She was somehow able to laugh about it all. Such an attitude *could* come off looking immature or irresponsible. But Freddie made it the exact opposite: she was handling things in the most mature, responsible way anyone could. A way Donald had not yet been able to adopt. He put his arm around her shoulders as they walked out of the bookstore and was squeezing her to his side affectionately just as she bumped into a tall, thin black woman wearing a burgundy velvet coat, its collar turned up around her long, elegant neck.

A shocked, guttural gasp came from Freddie as she froze in place, her whole body stiffening under Donald's arm, her shoulders raising in a protective shrug. He turned toward her to see that the blood had gone from her face, leaving her dreadfully pale. Her eyes were wide, staring directly ahead of her at nothing, and her hand had slapped over her mouth, as if she might be sick.

"What, Freddie?" Donald stepped in front of her and put his hands on her shoulders. "What is it?" He gently backed her up so she could lean against the hard, cold wall.

Her hand fell away from her mouth and she began to whine softly, her lips working around the whispery sounds, trying to form words.

"Thuh-th-that, Don, Don, th-that woman!"

"Freddie, calm down, calm down!"

She lifted her hand and pointed, her eyes still wide and staring. Donald looked over his shoulder, following the direction of her trembling index finger, and saw the tall black woman walking at a hurried pace, looking over her shoulder once, twice, again, walking faster.

"C'mere," Donald breathed, quickly leading Freddie to one of the benches and sitting her down. "Wait here, Fred, you wait here for me, okay?"

She shook her head and clutched his arms in her hands. "N-no, Don—"

"Please! I'll be right back, Freddie, just *stay here!*" Without waiting for any further reply, he pulled himself away from the girl, turned, and hurried after the black woman.

The creature had felt the exchange up and down the entire length of its body. One of them knew. The young girl it had bumped into: she was able to know, able to see; she had a power that was not shared by all the others.

Some of the creature's confidence chipped away and it felt itself tensing up, felt threatened. It had been seen. No, it had been *felt*. It tossed a graceful glance over its shoulder. The male had moved the young female to a seat and was turned toward the creature. It faced front again, its mind racing. It was surrounded by them, therefore it could not afford to do anything that would draw attention to it. It glided around a corner and headed for the center of the mall.

The woman was several yards ahead, and it was easy to lose sight of her; Donald did a couple of times at first. He had to stop, stand on his toes for a second, then, after spotting her again, continue.

He had one of them cornered, he was *sure* of it! Why else would Freddie have fallen into such a state? This time, he was determined not to lose her, as he had lost that boy who'd been with Leslie Newell.

Up ahead, he saw the woman go around a corner. He picked up his pace, only to find himself caught behind a large group of elderly people. One had a walker, some had canes, one was in a wheelchair.

"Excuse me," he said, his voice too soft. They were talking to one another and paid no attention to him. "Please, excuse me!" This time he shouted and was heard; two of the old people in the group limpingly stepped aside and Donald rushed through the slow little crowd.

He rounded the corner, then stopped. He couldn't see her at first. Then he saw the lithe, dark form ascending the escalator. Dodging a little boy with a sticky blob of taffy, he hurried toward her.

The center of the mall was a large circle. In the middle of it was a rather impressive fountain with color-changing lights under the water. Streams of water spewed from its center; they changed formation periodically and seemed to be performing a sort of ballet. To the left of the fountain was an escalator that went up to the second level of the mall, and to the fountain's right was another that came down; beside each escalator was a regular stationary staircase.

By the time Donald reached the softly splashing fountain, the woman was no longer on the escalator. He dashed to the staircase and took the steps three at a time, almost stumbling once, but managing to keep his balance. At the top, he brought himself to a clumsy halt and quickly looked around him.

She was gone.

The creature was on its way down the opposite escalator, its head held high, one hand resting on the hard rubber railing. It hoped to leave the shopping area before the man could find it again. But, just in case that was impossible, it was considering all its options.

First, it needed a new disguise. Feedings were quite conspicuous, but perhaps it could pick one of the bystanders and lead him to a more private location where it could go about the kill without drawing attention to itself. It would, however, be in a very sluggish state afterward, considering the fact that it had just eaten not long ago. But that would have to be overcome. It was unavoidable.

The creature knew that the ideal solution would be to capture and feed upon its pursuer. But that was probably very unlikely. It would simply have to outwit the human, it thought with delighted anticipation.

Donald ran in a half-circle along the guard rail, frantically looking for the black woman. He stopped, closed his eyes a moment, took a deep breath, then put both hands on the railing and leaned forward, looking down at the fountain below and the people around it. There was a woman helping her toddler toss a coin into the water; some of the old people he'd passed were now sitting on benches beside the fountain;

some teenagers, one with a portable stereo, were standing around some indoor plants.

And then he spotted her. She was getting off the down escalator, apparently in no hurry whatsoever, moving with the ease of an ordinary shopper.

"Shit!" he hissed, breaking into a run, gliding down the stairs opposite the black woman. Through the bluish-white tentacles of water shooting up from the fountain, he saw her walking away from him toward the mall's exit, her back to him, her gaze straight ahead, as if totally unaware that she was being followed. Still running, Donald reached the fountain without hearing the shrill female voice shout "Tommy!" as the toddler he'd noticed earlier waddled right in front of him. Suddenly Donald was airborne, his limbs splaying outward wildly, as he dove over the child, knowing full well how ridiculous he must look to the people gathered around, but not for a moment caring. When he hit the floor again, his feet went in different directions and he fell, rolling. But without pausing, he was on his feet again, ignoring the flustered mother's voice as she called after him, "Mister, are you okay? I'm awfully sorry!" Her words faded behind him as he continued the chase.

Donald had lost some ground; the woman was considerably farther ahead of him than she'd been just seconds ago. With a very smooth glance behind her, she picked up her speed a bit, widening the gap even more. Then, for no immediately apparent reason, she veered to the right and slowed down. Donald, chewing his lip madly, slowed also, tilting his head curiously.

She was approaching someone! Some fat guy who was leaning against the wall outside a women's clothing store called Nikki's and eating a corndog. He was wearing a red and white Coors cap, a denim jacket, a baggy pair of green pants, and black boots. He seemed to be waiting for someone. The woman?

Donald came to a halt, wondering if Freddie had been wrong. Maybe this woman was just . . . a woman! But she'd acted so fearful, so guilty. What the hell was she up to?

It needed an ally, a cover, and this fat one looked as if he would serve perfectly. The creature was becoming rather familiar with these animals, and it seemed the ones that looked like *this* really thrived upon attention and affection. Yes, he was perfect.

The creature approached him without hesitation. It put one hand first on his chest, then slid it lightly up to his shoulder and squeezed ever so gently. It smiled, showing its straight, pearly teeth.

The man jumped with surprise, his eyes growing wide, his fleshy face trembling nervously. He started to speak, but was interrupted.

"I need help," it whispered to him softly, holding its full, glossy lips close to his ear, which was partially covered by strands of dirty-blond hair.

"Wh-what?" he sputtered, almost dropping his corndog. A few crumbs of yellowish batter clung to the corners of his puffy mouth.

"I need a friend, *now*. I'm being followed. Act like you know me. Act like you *really* know me."

"B-but, my wife . . ." He pointed a pudgy finger at the doorway to Nikki's.

The creature leaned closer, its whisper huskier: "I'll make it worth your time." It looked quickly over its shoulder and saw the man standing there, several yards away, just watching. It decided that simply *talking* to this fat one was not going to work fast enough, so it lifted its hand from the soft, round shoulder and touched its fingers to the fat one's temple, sliding them gently underneath the band of the cap. Its shadowed eyelids lowered and its face relaxed as it felt the slight loss of energy.

The fat one relaxed then, too, leaning toward the creature, his head resting back against the wall, his lips turning up in a smile from which came a low, breathy moan. He wrapped one arm around the creature and held it closer to him, bending his head forward to kiss its forehead, then its cheek.

The woman's cautious glance at him, combined with the fat man's obvious apprehensiveness, swept all doubt from Donald's mind and he began to move forward. The man's discomfort left quickly, though, melted like butter, and he began to *kiss* the woman, *hold* her! Their lips had joined and the woman was holding the man's face between her delicate hands, massaging his temples, by the time Donald was close enough to put his hand on her shoulder and spin her around to face him.

Her face registered what seemed to be genuine shock at first, but a flame of anger quickly lit up her dark eyes as she spat, "What the hell do you think you're doing?" to Donald in a quiet but firm voice.

He opened his mouth to speak, but realized he didn't know what to say! "I . . . I want to know who you are."

"Oh, yeah?" The fat guy stepped forward, letting his corndog fall to the smooth, tile floor with a soft *splat*. Close up, Donald saw that his face was whiskery and his eyes . . . his eyes seemed to be sort of *flat,* as if he wasn't really looking *at* Donald, but *through* him. "Well, *I* wanna know who *you* are!" He stabbed an angry finger at Donald, accenting the "I" and the "you."

"Look," Donald said, holding up his hands in a placating gesture, but trying to keep a determined, stony look on his face, "I'm not too sure what's going on, but there's *something—*"

"Problem here?"

Donald cut his sentence short and jerked his head to the right. Beside him stood a tall, broad-shouldered security guard, one hand on his uniformed hip, the other at his side holding a large walkie-talkie with a short, wobbly antenna sprouting from one corner. The man was bald on top with a wrinkled brow and thick eyebrows, which were now elevated questioningly.

"Uh . . ." Donald began.

"Yeah!" the fat guy interrupted. "There's a problem here. *This* guy's giving my lady here a hard time!"

Donald looked at the black woman and was chilled by the victorious glare she gave him, her head back, her chin out, as the security guard said, "Is there something *I* can do for you, sir?"

Looking at the guard, Donald could tell he was not asking the question with any polite intent.

"I, uh," Donald took a step backward, "I thought she was someone else." She was still giving him that icy look, with an added hint of a smile. "I thought I knew her." A brief, forced smile flashed across Donald's face as he continued to back up. "Sorry. My mistake. I'm sorry." Before he turned away from them, Donald saw the guard step forward and say something to the black woman. But she never took her eyes from Donald as she stood there in the hollow of the fat guy's arm, one of her dark, long-fingered hands resting on the side of his head.

Donald walked away, having no destination in mind, just wanting to get away from them. He looked back a couple of times to see the guard keeping a watchful eye on him. The woman and her "friend" had gone over to a bench and sat down. She was still clinging to him, casually running her fingers through the stringy hair above his temple, having removed his cap. She did not lose sight of Donald, however, and frequently glanced in his direction.

Spotting a cookie stand to his left, Donald walked over and bought a couple of chocolate chip cookies, then leaned on the wall nearby and nibbled one slowly, watching people pass, trying to look unconcerned, but also trying to keep track of his quarry, of whom he was still very suspicious.

"Let's go someplace."

"Hmm?" the fat guy replied heavily.

"Let's *go* someplace. Is there a bathroom around here? I want to repay you. For helping me." It kept its fingers over at least one of his temples at all times as it spoke to him, softly, its breath hot in his ear.

"Yeah. Let's go someplace."

She was speaking to him. Whispering, leaning close. As she spoke, she glanced at Donald once, for a split second, and then Donald looked away, his gaze passing quickly over the security guard who had, by now, mixed into a group of shoppers, but was still surreptitiously watching Donald, walkie-talkie in hand.

The black woman stood up, closely followed by her companion. They moved a few steps away from the bench, stopped, and she leaned forward and said something into his ear, caressing the side of his face (her hand has never left his head, it just stays there, rubbing, rubbing . . .), and then they continued.

Donald stopped chewing the dry cookie and watched them, no longer too concerned with remaining inconspicuous; he didn't want to lose her. The couple blended quickly with the shoppers and Donald had to stand on tiptoe for a moment to keep them in sight. He looked for the guard quickly, couldn't find him, then began to follow her, tossing the cookie into a garbage can. They were moving quickly now. She must know I'm still following her, Donald thought, dodging a middle-aged woman who was trying to walk and light a cigarette at the same time.

There was a momentary break in the group of people strolling ahead of Donald and he saw her, one arm snaking across her companion's back and shoulder, her other hand still on the side of his head. She was thin and moved so smoothly that Donald thought for a second that she might be a dancer. But she wasn't. He didn't know *what* she was.

They were heading for the exit! It was a side exit that led to the lower-level parking area, where Donald had left his car. They pushed their way through the glass double doors, which slowly swung shut behind them.

When Donald stepped out, he was greeted by the loud, reverberating sound of a car starting, and for a moment he thought he'd lost them, thought they were driving away. But he was relieved to see them hurrying through the murky, cool parking lot toward the rest rooms. He stopped and watched them, his eyes narrowing curiously, the tip of his tongue running back and forth over the rough, bitten area of his underlip.

They paused a moment before the two rest-room doors; she leaned closer and said something to him, and then they went into the men's room.

Donald took a few steps forward, his shoes sounding off on the red brick path, then the concrete of the parking area. He stopped, looked around, slipped his hands into his pockets, then out again, chewing his lip all the while. Then he slowly walked over to the rest room, standing in front of the door. It had looked innocent before, ordinary. But now it was ominous because it held beyond it something that Donald was not sure he wanted to see. Or experience. Setting his jaw and taking a deep breath, he wrapped his fingers around the cold, dirty knob, turned it, and went in.

It smelled, as public rest rooms do, of urine and air freshener. The music that played in the mall was also piped in here, coming through a speaker in the ceiling, tinny and weak. The door clunked heavily as it closed behind Donald and he started nervously, his muscles tense.

There was a row of three sinks to his left, with mirrors above them, and, to his right, a tiled wall that ran into the room for a few feet, then ended, revealing three stalls and three urinals. At first the only thing Donald heard was the soft, syrupy music: a poor rendition of ''Somewhere My Love.'' Then he heard breathing, heavy and slow. He put one palm flat against the tile and looked at the center stall. It was the only one that wasn't open. He bent down slightly to see two booted feet with green pants bunched in a heap around the ankles. The woman was there, too, her feet facing the opposite direction. And she was moving slowly.

''Mmm,'' she moaned, barely audible. ''Sweeeet sex, fucking, wet and hot . . .'' It was a neutral whisper, without gender.

Donald stood erect suddenly, his forehead pearling with sweat, the back of his neck tingling. There was something very familiar about that whisper. Horribly familiar. He bounded forward suddenly and reached his hands up, wrapping his fingers over the top of the stall door, shaking it violently. The lock on the inside rattled, but held. He stepped back, his chest rising and falling rapidly, and plowed his hand through his hair, then threw himself at the door. He bounced off, but felt the lock give somewhat. He stumbled backward, his hands coming to rest on the edge of one of the sinks.

There was another moan, this one from the man; it was soft at first, but it rose in pitch, then faded into a heavy, rhythmic pant. At least the man wasn't in pain. But Donald couldn't understand why they didn't *stop*, why they seemed to be totally unaware of him. He swept the back of his hand across his forehead and rammed the door a second time. It opened inward, but was immediately slammed shut again. Donald pushed against it, only to find that it was being held closed even more firmly than before.

He stood staring at the door for a few moments, his hands clenching and unclenching, again and again, as he listened to the sounds they made in the stall. At one point, the woman's pleasure-filled gasps turned into a deep gurgling, immediately followed by a wet tearing sound and a thick crunch. And then. Chewing. Sloppy, frantic chewing.

"Fuh-me, fuh-fuck me, babe," the man gasped tremulously.

Something in the stall snapped once, twice, a third time, and Donald, suddenly weak-kneed, leaned back against the sink again, hopping he would not become ill. He'd heard that sound once before when he was twelve, standing at the bottom of a tall tree in his backyard, waiting for his friend Larry Bonertz to come down. And come down Larry did, screaming all the way. At the end of the fall, Larry's right leg broke with a loud, resounding snap, and when Donald saw the jagged bone sticking out of his friend's flesh, he promptly bent over and threw up.

He wouldn't, now, though. He *couldn't!* He had to do something! Trying to ignore the horrible crunching and tearing sounds, he straightened up and swallowed the lump in his throat. He braced himself to rush the stall door again, but his mouth fell open when he looked down at the floor and saw the pool of blood that was spreading beneath the stall, spilling over the tile toward him as if it were alive. It also ran to the right and left, going under the other two stalls, all the while accompanied by the man's ecstatic gasps and groans.

She was tearing him apart and he was apparently not feeling it! And if he *was* feeling it, he was *enjoying* it!

"Jesus Christ," Donald croaked, diving toward the stall. He grabbed the top of the door again and pulled himself upward, his legs pedaling, his feet kicking against the metal door as he tried to climb over it. He craned his head forward, looking over the edge and downward, getting only a flashing glimpse of violent movement and gushing blood before a long, wiry arm, gray and leathery, swung up at Donald, supported by a horrid squeal, and hit him hard in the jaw with its sharp claw.

Donald was knocked away from the stall to the floor, face up. He opened his eyes to see the bottom of the sinks, rusted and dirty. When he tried to get up again, his hands slipped in the blood on the floor and he fell flat a second time. As he rolled over on his hands and knees, he felt some of his own blood trickling down his chin where one of those claws had caught him.

Claws? Jesus God, what *is* it? he thought fearfully. What the hell is *in* there?

Donald clutched the edge of the sink, his only ally in the room, and pulled himself up. The room spun around when he tried to stand, so he remained on his knees for a few seconds, his forehead resting on the cool porcelain.

"Goddamn you," he muttered breathily, finally standing. He turned around slowly, trying to keep his balance, but did not approach the stall again. Because it was silent. Dead silent. The moans had stopped, the breathing, the gurgling. Only a faint dripping sound remained. Blood. Donald cocked his head to listen some more. There was a whisper of movement, a breath was taken in, let out. Bending down just a little, Donald saw the two boots, both tipped onto their sides, both empty. The pants were there, too, soaked with blood, and abandoned. What looked like the velvet coat the woman had worn lay in the mess as well, along with some other unidentifiable articles of clothing. But that was all he could see.

Until two bloody bare feet lowered themselves slowly to the floor as if someone had been sitting on the toilet with feet up, out of sight. For a moment, there was absolute silence in the rest room. Donald lifted his head and took a step forward, another . . .

The stall door burst outward with an explosive *boom*, breaking off of its hinges and falling loudly to the bloody floor. A huge figure bounded out of the stall, a blond man, naked, with broad shoulders and firm bulging muscles, his large imposing body covered with splotches of blood.

Donald let out a short exclamation of shock, frozen in place, lifting one arm protectively.

The man pulled back his right arm, clenched his great hand into a fist, and swung it forward into Donald's face.

Donald was unconscious before he hit the floor.

The creature was sure that if it ate this human lying unconscious on the floor, it would be far too weary to get out of there, and it *had* to get out. Surely *somebody* had heard the noise. And even if they hadn't, there was a very good chance that someone would be coming in any time. It hurried to the door, not used to this hard, bulky body it had acquired from the fat one, and opened it a crack, looking out.

A man and woman were leaving the mall, arguing, having a difficult time keeping their voices down. The creature waited until they were in their car, driving out, before it opened the door and stepped out of the rest room. It had started walking quickly toward a row of parked cars when it heard the wet smacking noise its feet were making. It looked down. There was a trail of dark prints behind it, left by the blood on the soles of its feet. It quickly scraped its feet back and forth on the cold cement until it was confident there would be no more prints, then ducked between a row of cars and one wall of the lot. Making sure no one was in sight, it tried the doors of each car it passed. First, a small pickup truck: locked. Then a sports car: locked.

It heard laughter and footsteps nearby and immediately dropped down on its stomach, rolling under a station wagon. It watched four pairs of feet walk by: young people, laughing and talking. It didn't move a muscle until it heard the car doors slam, the engine start, and the car drive away. Then it rolled back out and tried the door of the next car. It opened! Getting into the backseat of the green Comet, it closed the door quietly, making only a small click, then lay down on the floor. To wait.

Possibilities traveled through the creature's mind: what if it were seen before the owners got into the car? What if it were outnumbered? What if it were somehow captured, hurt, even killed? If that were to happen, then there would be danger for the others.

For a moment the creature was afraid. But it resisted the feeling, knowing that it was dangerous, it brought weakness. And it needed to be strong now.

When Donald opened his eyes, they felt as if they'd been glued shut. He had only been out for less than a minute, but it seemed like hours. As he turned his head to look around the rest room, pain shot through his jaw and down his neck, making him wince. But he had to ignore it. He had to stop feeling it for a while and get the hell out of there. If someone came in and found him in that bloody mess, he knew he'd be in big trouble.

Slopping through the thin coating of blood on the tile floor, now getting sticky and thick, he tried to pull himself up, but couldn't. He was still too dizzy to stand.

Once on his feet, however, he turned weakly toward the

horrible center stall. The clothes were still there, the boots still on their sides. Behind the toilet, hanging on the silver handle, was the red and white Coors cap. The blood on the floor was streaked with clear places, the tile showing through where feet had slid over it. There were lines of blood on the sides of the stall which had run in little rivulets down to the bottom, where they still dripped to the floor. Near the back, though, on the left side, was a much larger splash of blood. And in it was a handprint, a big one, fingers splayed wide. Donald staggered a little closer and squinted at the handprint, realizing it was too big to belong to the fat guy, so it had to be the blond giant who had burst out of the stall and hit Donald. Odd. There was something odd about it, but Donald couldn't figure out what it was.

The creature tensed as it heard footsteps stop just outside the car. It tensed when the door on the driver's side opened, then the other door.

"I *still* don't understand why you paid such a ridiculous price for it when you could've bought the *exact* same thing at Mervyn's for much less!" A woman's voice.

"But they're *not* exactly the same, I told you! This one is much prettier. The collar looks *so* much better." Another woman.

"Well, if you say so."

As it listened, it silently sniffed the air. They were not young, these females. Nor were they old. Middle-aged, perhaps. Moderately healthy. They would do. They would *have* to.

It heard the key slip into the ignition and knew that it would have to move immediately. Smoothly, quickly, and without a sound, the creature sat up, grabbed the hair of the woman behind the wheel with its left hand, pulled her head back over the edge of the seat, and, with blurring speed, brought the outer side of its right hand down on her throat like a blade. This it did so rapidly that the passenger had no time to react before the creature had clamped its palm tightly over her mouth. The shopping bag that rested in her lap slid to the floorboard as she struggled. The creature put its other hand on the back of her head, wrapping its thumb and four fingers around it until they pressed the sides of her skull, but not hard. In an instant, the woman was limp, sighing pleasurably into the creature's hand. The creature, too, became less tense, closing its eyes, letting its head sag forward a bit, but only for a moment. Opening its eyes, it looked over at the other woman: lean, nicely dressed, her head still lying backward, her mouth and eyes gaping, garbled choking sounds coming from her crushed throat, her hands clawing at the collars of her coat and blouse for air.

While it knew the feeding would only further sap its strength and dull its sharp senses, it also knew it had no choice.

The strangled gasps for breath came to a halt. The driver of the car sat behind the wheel wearing her simple blue coat with its collar pulled wide, her hands still clutching it desperately, even in death.

After a sweeping look around the parking area outside to make sure no one was nearby, the creature lifted the other woman, whose breathing was becoming heavy, into the backseat, but with some difficulty; it was quite weak from its last kill. Laying her down on her back, its hand still holding her head, it watched for a few brief seconds with amusement as the woman, her head rolling slowly back and forth, pushed her pelvis out slightly, methodically, her movements gradually becoming more pronounced.

The creature positioned itself, and began . . .

What if someone were outside the door and saw him like this, covered with blood, a bruised, swollen face . . .? He would have to be very careful. As for that . . . *thing*, he had no intention of going after it now. He was in too much pain and knew it would be useless, even if he could find it, which he doubted.

After making sure no one was in sight, he stepped out of the rest room. He wondered what to do about Freddie. Certainly he couldn't go into the mall looking the way he did.

"Donald!" cried a gloriously familiar voice, as if on cue.

Donald turned to see Freddie hurrying toward him. Her face was red; she looked as if she'd been crying.

"Jesus, Donald, what *happened?*" She cautiously took one hand, as if she were afraid she might hurt him.

"Let's get out of here."

"But—"

"Let's just get the hell *out* of here!" He sounded angry without meaning to. "Really, Fred. I need to get home."

They began walking quickly toward the car, Donald hoping they wouldn't be seen, and Freddie protesting all the way.

"*Home?* You need to go to the hospital, Don, you're hurt!"

"I'm not hurt *that* bad. And if I told them what happened, they'd lock me away in the psycho ward!" He was glancing around nervously. He heard voices from the other side of the enclosed lot, and he saw a plain-looking woman wearing a blue coat walking away from her car. But no one noticed him, thank god. "Let's just go home, and then I'll tell you all about it."

The creature did not even look at them when it passed. It wanted to avoid another incident. It walked across the lot toward the mall. It needed to get inside and sit down for a while. It was very weak and needed to rest.

That had been a very messy situation, one it would rather avoid repeating. But it had gotten out of it. Unharmed, unidentified, and with a new disguise. The challenge had been enjoyable. But now all the creature wanted was rest.

Later, it would warn the others in this area about the two humans, especially the young female, who could sense them, detect them. They would *have* to be stopped.

8

Walther's chair squeaked in protest as he leaned back in it, the telephone receiver to his ear, one hand on his stomach, which was beginning to rumble hungrily. Nancy's voice came on the line after the third ring.

"Hi, babe," Walther said.

"Lew, how are things?" Walther could hear one of the children's voices in the background and he could hear the edge in Nancy's. She was having a hectic day.

"Well, they're quieter than they seem to be over there."

"Trade you places. You coming home for dinner?"

"Doesn't look like it. I've got to go meet someone this evening."

"Is she pretty?"

Walther laughed quietly. "As a matter of fact, she is. But it's purely business, as always."

"You keep it that way, hombre."

It was the sort of banter they indulged in when neither of them really had the strength for serious conversation. Walther rather enjoyed it.

"Actually, I'm going to be seeing Donald Ellis, if he's home this evening. He wasn't earlier today. I'm going over there with a friend of his."

"But I thought you were off that case." The sound of kitchen utensils clattering together came over the line. Walther guessed that Nancy had pulled one of the kitchen drawers out too far and it had fallen to the floor.

"I am. This is sort of unofficial. I'll see you when I see you, hon. Maybe I'll get that drawer fixed this weekend."

"Where've I heard that before?" she replied, only half good-naturedly.

"Bye-bye." He hung up the phone, stood, and walked out of his office, taking his coat from its hook by the door and slipping it on. He gave the others in the station the impression that he was going home. It was time, anyway. He stopped at the candy machine by the front desk and got a Milky Way, and ripped the top half of the wrapper off as he left the station.

Walther had agreed to meet Anne Cramer at the high school and, from there, she would accompany him to Ellis's for the second time that day. They'd decided not to call ahead for fear that he would leave and they'd miss him again. Walther was pretty sure Ellis would not easily agree to see them, anyway. It was going to take a little work on their part to convince him that they were willing to listen to anything he had to say and that they wouldn't assume he was crazy. They honestly wanted to help, but Ellis wasn't likely to believe that.

Chewing his Milky Way slowly, enjoying the taste, Walther thought about how easily he had been talked into involving himself with a case from which he had been officially dismissed. Normally, he probably would have listened to what Miss Cramer had to say, then politely backed away from it. But last night's call from Reggie had cast a different light on the whole matter. Something very unusual was happening, and Walther had not been particularly surprised by Miss Cramer's rather unusual story. Perhaps there was no connection at all. But then again . . .

Popping the last of the candy bar into his mouth, Walther wadded the rest of the wrapper up and stuffed it in his pocket. Still chewing, he said quietly to himself, "Who knows *how* weird things can get?"

Anne tidied up her office before going out to meet Walther; she stacked papers neatly on her desk, straightened some books on the three shelves that ran along the side wall, and put the cover on her typewriter. She had timed her afternoon well. She'd finished the work she'd allowed to pile up over the week just in time for Walther's arrival. Donning her coat and getting her purse and umbrella, she left her office, switching off the light and closing the door.

She hoped Donald was home—Donald and whoever was with him. Earlier, when Anne and Walther had gone to Donald's and received no answer at the door, Walther had started back down the front steps, saying, "Well, maybe they'll be back this evening."

"They?" Anne had turned to him suddenly.

He'd stopped on the bottom step, turned, and looked up at her. "Ellis and the girl."

"*What* girl?"

Walther's face had immediately assumed the look of someone who realized he'd probably said too much.

"There was a girl with him?" she'd asked, a little softer this time.

Walther nodded and started, once again, toward the car. Anne followed him.

"Well, who *was* she?"

"Ellis introduced her as a former pupil of his who cleaned house for him. Freddie Santos is her name."

"But you don't believe she's a house cleaner."

"I *know* she isn't. I saw her overnight bag. You don't know her?"

"No, I don't."

But she was very eager to meet her. A young girl—"about twenty," Walther had said—who was very pretty, staying with Donald, claiming to be a former student? Perhaps she was, but that was no explanation. It simply wasn't like Donald to take someone in that way, especially someone so young. She sighed heavily, thinking how strange Donald had suddenly become.

"You really should see a doctor, Don," Freddie said as she gently dabbed alcohol around the gash on Donald's jaw. "That might need some stitches."

"No." Donald winced. "I don't want to see a doctor. I'm not in the mood to make up a story, and that's just what I'd have to do. If I told him the truth, he'd have me committed." He reached up and moved her hand away from the wound. "Please, Fred, that hurts." They both saw how badly his hand trembled.

"Why don't you come lie down," Freddie suggested, putting a soft hand on his bare shoulder.

He was sitting on the toilet seat, wearing only his undershorts, slouching wearily. He nodded once and got shakily to his feet. Freddie walked with him to the bedroom, her arm around his waist. She looked over at his profile, seeing only the swollen patch of black and blue around his right eye, and clicked her tongue pityingly.

"Dammit, Don, why didn't you just get the hell out of there?"

"Oh, I don't know," he breathed, sitting down on the side

of the bed. "There was nothing I could've done for that guy, I realize that now. But I wanted to see it. I wanted to see what it was *doing*." He closed his eyes and licked his dry lips, swallowing hard against the memory that he knew would never fade. It would always be every bit as vivid as it was just then.

"So you saw and you got your face smashed. Was it worth it?" She sat on the edge of the bed, too, as Donald lay back.

"Yes, it was. We know they can change shape, become different people. That's what it did in that stall: it transformed itself. And, in the meantime, it ate that poor guy from the mall." He rested his forearm on his forehead and squinted with disgust. "*Ate* him, Fred. And, from the sound of him, the guy didn't even *feel* it!"

"But why did it go to all that trouble? Why didn't it just go off someplace by itself and change? Why did it . . . do *that* to him?"

"Oh, I don't know," he sighed, somewhat impatiently. "Maybe it *needs* that for its transformations. Food, or whatever. I don't know." He smacked his lips a few times, to show how dry his mouth was. "Could you get me a drink, Fred? Some Scotch?"

"Sure." Halfway to the door, she stopped and turned to him. "This is just because I think you need it now. You're not going on one of your drunks." She flashed that smile that Donald loved so much and left the room.

During the ride back, Donald had told Freddie everything he'd seen in that parking-lot rest room. She'd listened silently, but not with disbelief. Rather, with partially concealed fear. Donald knew she was more scared than she was letting on. He wished he could climb into her mind as easily as she could his; he would try to comfort her, reassure her. But she had closed herself off. Even if he could step into her head, he wasn't at all sure he'd be able to ease her mind. Suppose she managed to read beneath all of his confidence and see the uncertainty, the fear lurking there? He decided things were probably best as they were.

A couple of things were eating at Donald, nibbling away beneath the memory of what he'd seen that day. First of all, he wondered, was there any particular reason for the form that thing had taken in the stall, the large muscular figure that had socked Donald? Was it simply chosen at random, or was there some connection between that and the fat guy who had been the creature's victim? There was something else . . . a hand—the handprint on the wall, pressed into the blood. What had been wrong with it? Why had it struck Donald as being strange? He closed his eyes and tried to recall it with as much detail as possible.

"Here," Freddie said as she came into the room, tossing a pack of cigarettes and a matchbook onto his stomach. "I thought you might like a smoke."

"Thank you." Before lighting up, though, he took the glass of Scotch from her with a trembling hand and drank it, then rested it on his chest. "God, that's good."

Freddie knelt down beside the bed. "Want me to run a bath for you? A nice hot one?"

"Not just yet. I'd like to lie here and not move for a while." He closed his eyes, handing her the glass. She set it on the nightstand, then leaned her head forward, gently resting it on Donald's shoulder.

The only sound for several moments was that of Donald's slow breathing and the crinkling of the plastic wrapper on the cigarette pack as it rose and fell with his stomach. Then Freddie sniffed loudly and caught a sob in her throat as a single tear rolled from her eye and trickled over Donald's shoulder. She put a hand on his arm and clutched it tightly. He turned his head toward her and started to speak, but didn't.

I'm scared, Don. Real scared.

I am too, Freddie. We have every reason to be.

Another sob caught quietly in her throat as her shoulders convulsed once, then once again.

She continued: *I don't want that to happen to me. I don't want some thing to eat me while it's fucking me. Please don't let that happen to me.*

I won't.

Kill me first.

Donald blinked back his shock. "What?" he said aloud.

"Promise *you'll* kill me first, if they get me. Then it will be quick and not . . . not *that* way." She sniffed and gulped.

Donald propped himself up on one elbow and looked into her tear-filled eyes.

"Please promise me, Donald. Please."

"On one condition. You promise *me*, too. I don't want that to happen to me, either."

She nodded, slowly.

Donald leaned forward and kissed away her salty tears, and she kissed him back, careful not to touch the gash on his jaw. They kissed softly for a long time. And then Freddie stood, slipped out of her clothes, climbed onto the bed, and, slowly, savoring every sensation, they made love.

Freddie dozed with her still-sticky cheek on Donald's chest, her body resting in the hollow of his left arm. Donald had lit a cigarette and was smoking it silently with his head propped up by a couple of pillows. Right after they'd finished making love, it had begun to rain, and the patter of drops on the roof of the house sounded to Donald like applause for their performance. He smiled and chuckled a little at the thought. It had been pretty wonderful. Wonderful enough to cleanse his mind of all that had happened. That was quite a feat.

But the respite did not last long. By the time Freddie's

breathing had fallen into the slow, regular rhythm of sleep, Donald's mind had once again turned to the dark shadows that had infected his life. The scene in the rest room kept replaying itself over and over in his mind, as he was sure it would for some time to come.

He kept hearing the voice of that tall, lanky black woman (*"sweeeet sex, fucking, wet and hot"*), whose true appearance he did not even want to try to imagine. And he kept hearing that poor man's ecstatic moans and gasps mixed with that wretched smacking sound, that wet, slobbering *chewing!* Christ, where were the screams? Why hadn't the guy been crying for help? *Surely* what was done to him must have hurt! Unless that thing had somehow numbed him, anesthetized him. But for what purpose? To keep him from screaming? To make him a more willing victim? And how was it done?

Donald let a ribbon of smoke drift from between his slightly parted lips as he scowled with disgust for himself. He possessed some sort of ability—often called a gift, but, as far as he was concerned, a curse—to see things other people couldn't see, know things they couldn't know. Yet he was unable, in this instance, as in so many others, to use it to his advantage because it was not something that stayed with him all the time. He couldn't just sit down and *do* it, like someone might sit down at a piano and play. It was like an epileptic seizure: it came and went of its own accord, striking without warning. And even *then* this third eye of his might not see what he *wanted* to see at any given time.

He jerked his head back and forth a couple of times in frustration, as if to rearrange the thoughts that inhabited it. Closing his eyes and inhaling deeply on his cigarette, he tried to line his thoughts up in some sort of order. He pictured that rest room again, scanning it from one wall to the next, in the way a movie camera may slowly pan a room. And he saw it again. That handprint. It stood out on the bloody side of that stall like a neon light, bugging the hell out of him. But he didn't know why. With a sigh, he opened his eyes and looked down at Freddie.

Her mouth was open slightly, the side of her face resting on his chest. One arm lay over his stomach; the other was tucked beneath her, invisible except for the hand, which rested near her face, palm up. She was sleeping soundly, something she'd done very rarely, if ever, since they'd met. She was always taking care of him, "keeping the nightmares away," as she put it. That made him feel so . . . dependent. As if he were a child and she his mother. It wasn't a bad feeling, not at all. In fact, it was rather comforting.

Donald watched her as the ash on the tip of his cigarette grew longer and longer; he wanted to stroke her hair, touch her face, but he didn't want to wake her. She had such a graceful neck, such pretty hands, such a—

His eyes snapped back to her hand, the one with its palm up, facing him. It had a sheen of perspiration that glistened especially in the creases of her palm, like ever-so-tiny bits of dime-store glitter. Donald could not take his eyes from her palm; he stared at it intently. For an instant, he was staring once again at the lone handprint in the parking-lot rest room, then at Freddie's hand. The handprint. Freddie's hand. Handprint. Freddie's.

Quickly, but carefully, so as not to wake her, Donald slipped out from under Freddie, easing her down onto the mattress. She stirred quietly and he watched her, waiting to see if she would wake up. When she didn't, he took his robe from the closet and slipped it on, padding out to the kitchen, his forehead tight with creases. He stood by the table, staring at his palm for a few moments, then looked around him for something thick. What? What would work? He opened a cupboard door and brought down a bottle of ketchup. He quickly took the cap off and poured the ketchup onto the tabletop. It *glubbed* its way out of the bottle slowly, just as the commercial had promised, spreading over the smooth Formica. Setting the nearly empty bottle aside, Donald slapped his right hand down in the puddle of ketchup, shifted the pressure of his hand from one side of his palm to the other, then lifted it, dripping red, from the table. Bending forward, he looked at the print, squinting. With an impatient grunt, he bounded over to the light switch by the fridge and flipped it on. Then he returned to the table. And smiled.

His palm and five fingers were well-defined in the ketchup, just as the handprint in the blood had been. But there was a difference, so subtle that it had taken some time for Donald to pick up on it.

His handprint was streaked with the same creases that covered his palm—*everyone's* palm. The joints of his fingers were very obvious in the ketchup, just as anyone's would be. Except for that thing's. He could see it in his mind clearly: a smooth, whole handprint, with no creases or breaks.

Just in case his experiment had been a fluke, Donald reached down and swept his hand over the puddle a couple of times, clearing away the print. Then he plopped his hand into it again. Pulled it away. Looked.

Creases, breaks, lines, just like before. They were there. He smiled again around the cigarette he held between his lips. Chuckled. One victory. One little victory. He *knew* something. He had something on them, something that was visible and could be used to identify them, even in their human form, if what he suspected were true.

If their hands are anything like that print, he thought, then they're unusually smooth, no creases, no wrinkles, probably not even any fingerprints.

The ash fell from the end of his cigarette, landing in the puddle of ketchup. He took the cigarette from his mouth and tossed it into the kitchen sink as he exhaled the last of the smoke through his nostrils. He leaned forward with one hand on the edge of the now messy table and the other on his hip, staring at the handprint.

There was a knock at the front door. Donald ignored it at first. It came again, and with it, the sound of the door being opened.

"Donald?" It was Anne.

With an irritated sigh, Donald crossed the kitchen, wondering why he hadn't thought to lock that damned door, and stood in the doorway that led to the living room.

The front door was open a crack and Anne was poking her head in, looking around. When she saw him, she smiled at first.

"Hello, Don—" Her smile was suddenly knocked from her face by a sharp gasp. "Jesus Christ, Donald," she squeaked, stepping into the house, "your face!" She started toward him but stopped when she saw his hand, red with . . . *something*. Her eyes widened as she stared at it.

"Ketchup," Donald said simply. He turned and went back into the kitchen to wash it off. "Why don't you come in?" he asked with a sarcastic chuckle. "Bring a friend."

"Well, as a matter of fact," Anne said, a bit cautiously, as she looked over her shoulder to see Walther coming in the door behind her, "I did."

Donald reappeared in the doorway, drying his hand on a small brown towel, as Walther was closing the door.

The detective smiled and nodded. "Hi there, Donald," he said pleasantly.

Donald returned the nod, curling half his mouth up into a cold half-smile. "Siccing the police on me, Anne?" He walked back into the kitchen.

Anne tossed a glance at Walther that seemed to say, "This isn't going to be easy, but let me try first." Then she followed Donald into the kitchen. "Of course not," she said, leaning a shoulder on the doorjamb. "Detective Walther isn't here as a detective."

Donald hung the little towel up on its hook above the counter and turned to her. "Oh? What *is* he here as?"

"Just someone who's . . . interested." She saw the mess on the table and cast a puzzled look at Donald.

"Ketchup again. I was just . . ." His words faded as she walked over to it and looked at his handprint in the middle.

"You put your hand in it? What . . . Donald, what's going on? You've been beat up, you're"—she shrugged uncertainly—*playing* with ketchup . . ."

Donald took a blue sponge from the sink and started wiping up the mess as he said, "I was just doing a little . . . I don't know, a little experiment, I guess. And my face is fine. So. What did you say Detective Walther is here as this evening?"

"I've been taken off the case," Walther said, walking into the kitchen.

"The case?" Donald continued wiping.

"These disappearances. Too widespread. The FBI is coming in."

"Ah. Good. So what can I do for you?"

"Donald," Anne said, "I've been talking with Lewis about you."

"Why not? You've been talking to everyone *else* about me."

"No, Donald, not *that* way." She sighed, looked down at her feet, then back over at Donald, still busily cleaning the table. "Donald, will you please put down that goddamned sponge and come listen to us?"

He stopped, a little startled by the sharpness of her voice.

"Please?" she continued, softer. "Can we go sit down, or something?"

Donald looked from Anne to Walther. The detective raised his eyebrows. Resignedly, Donald tossed the sponge back into the sink with a *plop* and walked between Anne and Walther into the living room. "Come have a seat."

"Anne here seems to think you know something," Walther said, once they were all seated.

"I have to," Donald replied. "I'm a teacher."

"Oh, Jesus, Donald," Anne groaned, covering her eyes with one hand, "will you please cut the sarcasm. We're serious. I've been doing a lot of thinking about the things you've told me in the past week or so. Those nightmares, those feelings you have. And I . . ." She took in a deep breath, as if to brace herself. "I talked to Barry Sereno. About those crib notes."

"Oh really." Donald leaned forward in his chair, resting his elbows on his knees. "And?"

"And he did have them."

"I knew that."

"But you *shouldn't* have. He said *no one* knew but him."

"And this has led you to believe that I . . . 'know something'?"

"I'm afraid I haven't been taking you seriously, Donald. But I am now. Some pretty terrible things have been happening to people lately, like your brother and Leslie Newell. I think you might know something about them. I'm not *accusing* you of anything," she assured him quickly. "I just thought perhaps you knew something that you were afraid to share with me for fear I'd react the way I did . . . last time."

Donald nodded slowly, chewing his lip. He turned to Walther. "She told you all of this, and you believed her." It wasn't a question.

Walther shrugged. "I had no reason *not* to. And, I must admit, after questioning you yesterday, I was rather suspicious. I couldn't help thinking you knew *something* that you weren't telling."

"But you're off the case, as you said. Why pursue it?"

215

Walther answered. "I'm interested."

With a chuckle, Donald asked, "You writing for the *National Enquirer* on the side, or something?"

"Look, Donald. I've got a wife and two kids I love very much. I don't want to come home one evening to three puddles of blood and spit." Immediately, Walther's face registered the regret that he felt for having mentioned spit. He looked down at his lap.

"Spit?" Donald asked. "What do you mean, 'spit'?"

"It's not important. But, if you know something that could help clear these—"

"I'd like to know more about this spit."

Sighing, Walther said, "The lab found something that resembled saliva mixed with the blood of Leslie Newell and your brother. It wasn't *exactly* saliva, but . . . similar, I guess."

Donald began chewing his lip frantically, turning his gaze to the window, becoming distant. He was silent for a while. Walther and Anne exchanged a curious glance.

"Donald?" Walther said softly. "Does that mean anything to you? Saliva?"

Donald turned to him, to Anne, then to Walther again.

What good would it do to tell them? he thought. What *harm* would it do, though? They came here *expecting* a far-out, crazy story. So, even if they don't believe it, they *did* ask for it. But. What if . . . what if . . .?

"This is going to sound kind of crazy," Donald said to Walther, his voice quivering just a bit. He stood and stepped over to the detective. "But, uh . . . could I see your palm?"

Walther tilted his head curiously and looked over at Anne for some sort of explanation, but she only gave a slight shrug of one shoulder. Cautiously, Walther held out his hand, palm up. Donald took it in his own hand, held it up closer to his face, examined it. Then he lowered it back onto Walther's lap and turned to Anne.

"Yours, too, Anne."

"Donald, what *is* this? What are you—"

"Just humor me. Okay?"

She gave him her hand and he looked the palm over carefully.

"Okay," he sighed, sitting down again. He ran his fingers through his hair and leaned back in the chair. "You're going to think I'm nuts. But, here goes . . ."

Kyle watched, wide-eyed, as Cary Grant and Eva Marie Saint hung by their cuticles from Mt. Rushmore, trying to escape James Mason and his cronies. Kyle's chemistry book lay open on his lap and he held a can of Dr. Pepper in one hand as he sat before the television in his beanbag chair. Suddenly the picture was replaced by the "8 O'Clock Movie" logo, and an off-camera announcer said, "We'll return to *North by Northwest* after these messages."

Kyle let out a sigh and relaxed, taking a drink from the soda can. The Mt. Rushmore scene never failed to grab him every time he saw the movie. He looked back down at the chem book to continue the reading he'd been doing—well, *trying* to do—during each commercial break. It wasn't easy because, hard as he tried, he couldn't stop thinking of Betty: her face, her smile, and *especially* her touch, her unbelievably smooth, soft, cool touch. Sometimes, if he thought about it for a while, he could *feel* it again, and his hand and arm would tingle just as they had earlier that day. He leaned back in the beanbag, letting his head hang over it. The room appeared to be upside-down to him. He turned his head this way and that, looking from one end of the room to the other. Empty, except for him. He imagined what it would be like if Betty were with him. Would they just sit and watch television?

God, no. He'd offer her a drink, and they would talk. Maybe he'd turn on some music. He wondered what kind of music she liked, although it didn't really matter. Usually it did; it was rather important to him. But in *Betty's* case . . . well, Kyle didn't care if all she listened to were recordings of African tribal music, or the sounds of whales in heat. She could listen to *anything* as far as he was concerned. He just wished she were there with him.

Kyle glanced at his wristwatch and wondered if Mr. Ellis had gotten home yet. He'd called him earlier, but there'd been no answer. He got up, went to the phone, and dialed the number.

"Hello?"

"Hi, Mr. Ellis. This is Kyle."

"Oh, hi there, Kyle."

"I thought I'd call and see how you were this evening." Kyle tried to put a smile in his voice, because Mr. Ellis sounded rather glum, even a little shaken.

"Well, I'm okay, I guess. I'm a little busy at the moment, though."

"Oh. I called at a bad time. Well, I can call back later."

"Tonight wouldn't be good, Kyle. How about calling tomorrow, maybe?"

"Sure. Sure, that's fine. I'll talk to you later."

With a puzzled shake of his head, Kyle hung up the phone and went back to the beanbag. Mr. Ellis sure was acting strange these days. He wondered what Mr. Ellis would think of Betty. He'd hoped to tell him about her, and perhaps get his opinion of what to do next. If he should meet her again, of course. He didn't know how to get in touch with her, didn't even know her last name. So, his only hope was that he'd meet her again by chance. And he hoped very much that he would.

* * *

Donald returned to his chair after hanging up the phone, seated himself, and sniffed. He looked at Walther and Anne with what he thought was a look of finality. He'd told them everything, slowly, sometimes reluctantly, but he'd gotten through it rather smoothly, he thought. Kyle had called just as he'd finished his recital of the events of the past week or so, perhaps making his two guests think he wasn't yet finished, that there was more to his story. But there wasn't.

"That's it," he said, folding his hands in his lap.

"The girl," Anne said. "Freddie. Is she here?"

"She's sleeping. She's very tired."

Anne nodded silently in reply, but it looked like the nod was just a reflex, something to do while she digested what Donald had said.

Walther sat on the sofa, legs crossed, one hand in his lap, the other arm stretched along the sofa's back. He showed neither belief nor disbelief. He just looked sort of stunned.

"Now," Donald said pleasantly, softly clapping his hands together, "you've heard my story and you each have your own thoughts about it, which, I hope, you'll keep to yourselves. I think I can make a pretty accurate guess as to what they are. I've told you everything, so if you would like to go someplace and discuss my questionable mental state, feel free."

Anne looked at Walther, waiting for him to say something. Walther, however, did not take his eyes from Donald.

"What do you plan to do?" Walther asked.

Donald arched a brow. "Do?"

Walther nodded.

Now it was Donald's turn to look stunned. "What do *you* think I should do?"

"I think we should forget about it for tonight. But tomorrow, I think we should get together again. Freddie, too. And I think we should make some very specific plans."

"You mean . . . you mean you believe me?" Donald's voice neared a whisper.

"Well, I believe the urgency of your story. I believe you're onto something. But, uh . . . well, I'm not sure I believe your interpretation of all that you've seen."

"I see. Well, that's a step in the right direction."

Walther stood and Anne followed suit. "My morning is taken tomorrow," he said, pocketing the pad and pen with which he'd taken a few notes, "but I'm free in the afternoon. Sound good?"

"It's okay with me," Anne replied.

"Fine," Donald said as he, too, stood.

"Good. We'll see you then, Donald."

The two men shook hands, and then Donald walked Anne and Walther to the door and said good night. Feeling strangely relaxed and at ease, he went into the kitchen and made himself another drink.

"What do you think?" Anne asked him in the car. "What do you *really* think?"

"His story fits," Walther replied. "Despite detailed descriptions, we've not been able to find Leslie Newell's unidentified boyfriend. The kid just disappeared, it seems. And we haven't found *any* of the people who have vanished. And that bit about the saliva in the blood—that really seemed to startle Donald. That fact fit *his* story just as *his* story fit *our* facts. But . . ."

"But what?"

"Well, it's just so . . . goddamned . . . *fantastic!*"

"What are you going to do?"

"Talk to a few people. Look over these." He patted the pocket holding the notes he'd taken of Donald's story and of the Xerox copies Donald had showed him from books about demons, of all things. "See if I can fill in any of the gaps in this whole thing."

"I don't know what to do or think, myself."

"Mm. Go home and get a good night's sleep. And, uh, just in case . . . don't bed down with any good-looking strangers." He turned to her and smiled in the dark, but when she didn't return the gesture, he turned his gaze back to the road.

Donald was sitting in the chair, drink in hand, staring out the window, all the lights off except for a small one in the kitchen, when he heard Freddie's groggy voice.

"How many glasses of scotch does *that* make?" she asked good-naturedly.

Donald turned the chair around and saw her standing, naked, in the very dim light. He smiled and patted his thigh; she walked over and sat down on his lap.

"Just my second," he assured her.

"Good boy." She put one arm around his neck and he put one around her bare waist, sliding his hand slowly over her silky skin. "Who was here?" she asked.

"Someone who, I think, wants to help us." He told her about Anne and Walther's visit.

"You really trust him?"

He thought a moment, then nodded. "Yes, I do."

"What about her?"

"Mm." He shrugged. "Doesn't really matter. What can *she* do for us? She's not a cop."

Freddie leaned forward and kissed his forehead. "Sorry I fell asleep."

"Oh, you *needed* that. I'm glad you did. And while you were sleeping, I did a little experimenting." He told her about the handprint in the rest room, and his own in the ketchup. She seemed pleased with the conclusion he'd reached, as well as the method by which he'd reached it, "Messy," he said, "but clever, if I may say so myself."

"You may," she laughed, leaning forward and touching her nose to his. She kissed him again, on the mouth this time, long and deep. Then they sat silently for a while, their foreheads pressed together.

"Question," Donald said.

"Mm."

"On the way home today, all we talked about was what happened to *me*. I'd like to know what happened to *you* in that mall. You were pretty shaken. What exactly did you feel?"

She closed her eyes and pursed her lips for a few seconds. "I'm not sure I can put it into words. I felt . . . it was *deep*, like an instinct, something you're born with. But *I* wasn't born with this, because it was horrible, it was evil. It was a very clever feeling, a feeling of superiority, like I was better than all the people . . . no, no, all the *creatures* around me. Mixed with all that was the knowledge that I had killed. And the anticipation of killing again. I also felt uncomfortable, sort of. Vulnerable, almost. As if I'd left a protective shelter and was standing in plain sight, for everyone to see. I had *become* that thing, and yet there was enough of *me* left to know that what I was feeling was . . . wrong." She sighed heavily, shifting her position on his lap. "Hope I never have to feel that again."

"Not if I can help it. I only want you to feel good things, Fred."

She giggled and squirmed suggestively in his lap. "Like what I'm feeling now?"

For a moment, Donald was glad the light was poor, because he thought he was going to blush. Like a goddamned *kid*, he thought chidingly. "Yes," he said, smiling. "Like that."

In a smooth motion, Freddie brought her body around so that her legs were hanging over the armrests of the chair, her hands on Donald's shoulders. After a bit of maneuvering, Donald's robe was open.

"This feels pretty good," Freddie whispered through a smile as she began to move slowly, but with purpose. "Yeah, this'll do."

"*Please*, Daddy, can I stay up and watch MTV?" Sherry asked sweetly. "They're having a special with Michael Jackson! Can I, please?" She sat on the sofa next to him, one of her arms wrapped around his. Walther's notepad was in his lap and he'd been looking over the notes he'd taken at Donald's.

"You need your rest, hon," he told her. "You're a growing girl."

"But how'm I gonna grow musically if I miss out on things like *this*?"

Walther looked over at Nancy. She was sitting in the easy chair reading the paper. She looked back at him slyly, a smirk on her face that said, "Don't look at *me*."

"Well, since it's Friday, punkin," he said, giving the little girl a squeeze, "I guess it wouldn't hurt you to stay up and watch What's-his-name."

"Oh, thank you!" She bounced up and wrapped her arms around his neck, then scurried over to the television set, the tail of her frilly pink robe trailing behind her, changed the channel, and plopped down in front of it.

"Not so close, hon," Walther said. "All that radiation'll turn you into a giant squid or something."

Nancy laughed as she folded the paper, stood up, and walked over to the sofa. As she sat down, she put an arm around Walther. "Hey, big boy," she said. "You're awfully quiet tonight. Anything wrong?"

"No, not really. Just a lot on my mind."

She looked down at the notepad, but he closed it before she could read anything. "Top-secret?" she asked.

Walther never kept things from her, even police business. So he knew his present secretiveness must seem strange. "Not secret. Just . . . undeveloped. I may be onto something, but I'm not sure enough yet to talk about it."

"I see. Well, I'm going to tuck Shawn in, and then I'm going to bed. If you *really* want to get *onto* something, come join me." She winked, kissed his cheek, and left.

Nancy was forgotten as quickly as the music from the television was crowded from his consciousness. Something else was on his mind. Dates. He opened the pad again and looked at the dates he'd written down. They were taken from the information given Donald by Cornell Hamilton. According to Hamilton and his books, it had happened before—people disappearing with no traces other than blood—as far back as late 1583. The incidents were widespread back then, as they were now.

Walther took out his pen and made two columns, separating the dates he had on hand—he assumed there were more someplace, there *had* to be—according to centuries, putting them in order:

1583 (Dec)	1784 (Apr)
1584 (Feb)	1784 (June)
1584 (Mar)	1784 (July)
1584 (May)	1785 (Jan)
1585 (Jan)	1785 (Mar)
1586 (June)	1786 (Feb)
1588 (Oct)	1786 (Aug)
1591 (Apr)	1786 (Sep)
1593 (Feb)	1787 (Nov)
1594 (Jan)	1789 (Mar)
	1790 (Aug)

1792 (Feb)
1794 (Mar)
1794 (Oct)

A gap of two hundred years existed between them. Walther realized that he probably didn't have all the dates of all the incidents—not even close!—because they probably hadn't all been recorded. But a gap this conspicuous made him suspicious. Even more so when he thought of the fact that . . . that—

Walther's eyes opened wide and he felt a bone-deep chill.

It's 1984, he thought. Two hundred years since the last series of disappearances.

He scanned the columns again. About ten years each, two hundred years apart.

"Every two hundred years," he breathed softly. "Jesus H. Christ." He stared straight ahead at his daughter's back. She was bouncing to the music, tapping her hands at her sides on the carpet. An image formed in his mind, with no effort from him. It was a Technicolor image of Sherry's small bed, empty, blankets pulled back, the Garfield sheets saturated with his little girl's blood. His little boy's blood. His wife's blood.

Gulping down the lump of fear that had risen in his throat, he stood and walked over to the phone, picked up the receiver, dialed.

"Gene?" he said when a voice answered.

"Speaking."

"Hey, Gene, this is Lew Walther. I'm really sorry to call you so late."

"No harm done," Gene Bradley said. He was a reporter for the Napa *Register* with whom Walther frequently exchanged information. "I'm just lying in bed reading."

"Good. So how's the newspaper business?"

"I write the articles and people line their bird cages with them. But as long as I'm getting paid, I guess I don't care."

"Well, I've got a question for you."

"Sure."

"This epidemic of disappearances, when did it start? I mean, not around here. When was the first one?"

"Uh, the first one? Let's see, we got it over UPI, uh . . . late September, I think."

"None before that?"

"No, none. It was late September, uh, the twenty-first, I think. Yeah, September twenty-first. Same day we had that big fire here."

"Big fire?"

"Sure, you remember. Big one, over by the river. A fireman got killed. Remember?"

Walther ran the tip of his tongue back and forth over the edges of his front teeth, but said nothing for a few moments.

"Lew? Remember?"

"Yeah. Yeah, I remember. Thanks a lot, Gene. I appreciate it." Slowly, Walther lowered his hand, gently replacing the receiver in its cradle.

"I christen thee 'Hot Seat,' " Freddie said, raising her hand high above her head, then lowering it in a regal fashion onto the back of the easy chair in which she and Donald had made love.

Donald laughed in the kitchen, where he was rinsing out his glass. "If I knew where to take it to have it bronzed," he said as he came back into the living room, "I would!" He took her arm. "Let's go to bed. I'm tired, and I don't think more sleep would do you any harm, either."

But once in bed, sleep did not come to Donald. His mind was too busy. It was hard for him to believe that so much had happened in such a small space of time. It seemed years since his brother had called and asked him to lunch, but it had been only a week ago.

("Those teeth, those fuckin' *teeth!*")

Already Bill seemed like a part of the distant past, not like someone with whom he'd had pizza seven days ago. It was while Donald was passing back and forth over the period of chaos he'd experienced in his life that he began to drift into sleep. As he teetered on the edge, no longer aware of the sensation of the bed beneath him or of Freddie's sleeping presence beside him, aware only of his hazy thoughts, images and voices hovered around him playfully, coming in and out of focus:

—Bill saying, ". . . the big fire a couple of weeks ago . . . never found out just what started it, but it sure was a biggie . . . sure was a biggie . . . never found out just what started it . . ."

—Anne saying, "I think you should talk to someone, Donald."

—Bill: "There she was, behind this bush, holding some clothes around her . . . And her clothes, they were really dark. There was something funny about the way they clung to her."

—The hospital bed, for just a split second, soaked with Bill's blood.

—Bill: "Eddie and I were both at the station . . . he picks up a magazine . . . all of a sudden he smiles real big and says, 'Yeah, yeah, that's what I want. Right there.' . . . and shows me the ad, the cigarette ad."

—The creased cigarette ad Bill had shown him: the beautiful girl with the blond hair, the long legs . . . and Bill saying, "Eddie showed me that and he says, 'Billy, this is my idea of beauty. Eve: the perfect woman . . . Except she'd have black hair. Black hair, not blond.' "

—The snapshot Bill had taken of his lady friend. Black

hair, not blond. Same woman as in the ad. Eve. Eden cigarettes. Eve. Same.

—A line from one of Hamilton's books: "The legions of hell come to claim their own."

—"My idea of beauty," Eddie had said. "My idea . . . *my* idea . . . mine . . . *mine* . . ."

—Bill again: "We never found Eddie's body, of course. It was his blood, but damned if we could find his body. *Nowhere!* Turned those goddamned woods inside out."

—Bill: "And her clothes, they were really dark. There was something funny about the way they clung to her. They were really dark . . . really dark . . ."

—The hospital bed again, nearly blackened with blood.

—Bill: "Big fire . . . never found out just what started it, but it sure was a biggie."

—That picture again, both women the same. Blond hair, black hair; "MY idea of beauty, MY IDEA!"

Donald sat bolt upright in his bed. He wasn't trembling, he wasn't sweating, but he was suddenly very aware of his surroundings, wide awake.

What had made Eddie Monohan scream the night of that fire? And if he had not disappeared, would Bill have met that woman in those woods? Eve?

"No," Donald breathed to himself. "No, because *that's* what *got* him."

Eve had been Eddie's idea of beauty. One of those things got Eddie out in the woods, ate him, and the result had been an exact replica of what Eddie had wanted, complete with black hair. And the name Eve. Eden Cigarettes . . . Eve.

Did that always happen? Was it *always* like that? Donald's mind spun at the possibilities.

The fat guy in the mall . . . *he* didn't end up as a beautiful woman. Why not? Of course! That thing had come out of the stall as a muscleman, the kind you see in those weightlifting magazines! And Donald was willing to bet his life that somewhere, in some such magazine, there was a picture of a man who looked exactly like the one who had given him a black eye. The picture had probably been seen by that thing's fat victim, and it had stuck in his mind. What overweight armchair athlete *doesn't* want to look like Charles Atlas? Then, the creature had apparently used that image as the model for its next disguise.

Is that too crazy? Donald thought, staring into the room's darkness. Is it any crazier than anything else that's happened? He didn't think so.

What about me? he wondered with a slight chill. Whose image will they take from *my* mind when they get me? *If* they get me?

(The ragged stub of his arm spurting blood while those jaws chewed noisily on the half they'd bitten off bitten off bitten off . . .)

What had they taken from Bill? Or rather, what had *it* taken? There had only been Eve. That had been enough for Bill. How many others were there?

And what about the fire?

(". . . Never found out just what started it, but it sure was a biggie.")

What *had* started that fire? Had that been kept from the public just as the truth about Eddie Monohan's disappearance—no, no, his *death*, goddammit—had been for a while? Donald wasn't sure how he would do it, but he was going to find the answers to those questions.

He lay in bed thinking for what seemed a long time. Then he leaned over and gently kissed Freddie on the forehead. Silently slipping out of bed, he dressed, got his umbrella and car keys, and left the house.

* * *

229

The black patch of burned woods blended into the dark night. Rain fell lazily, plopping onto Donald's umbrella. A solid bar of light sprang from the end of the flashlight he'd brought from his car and splashed a bright circle on the ground and trees around him. He stopped and lifted his head out from under the umbrella, the soft, wet ground squishing and crunching under his feet as he turned slowly. The charred trees reached sharply bent claws upward to the sky, as if they were in pain. A soft breeze whispered through the darkness. He walked on, his car parked beside the road some distance behind him, the sound of the river far ahead at the other end of the woods.

There was something bad there in those woods. Donald could feel it.

He'd wanted to see the place Bill had told him about, the place where Eddie Monohan had lost his life, where Bill had first met his death. Now that he was there, he could *feel* that bad things had happened around him. Whispers of vibration started in the center of his bones and worked outward. The charred remains left over by the fire were not the only black things in those woods.

As Donald walked on, the ground sloped downward and he crossed a small gully. The opposite bank was even steeper; he collapsed his umbrella and used it as a walking stick to climb the incline, his flashlight beam lighting the ground before him. The ground was wet and slick and, just a few steps up, one foot slipped out from under him. He fell forward and his flashlight tumbled from his grip as he slid backward a bit. Swearing under his breath, he got to his hands and knees, then stood, using the umbrella for support.

"Damned flashlight," he muttered, looking around his feet. He spotted it ahead of him. He saw its light, anyway. He stepped over to the puddle of light and bent forward.

It had fallen into an oddly shaped hole. It was nearly four

feet long, rectangular, almost like a slot in the side of the gully. Weeds and roots hung down over the opening, silhouetted by the flashlight on the other side. Beyond that, though, was only blackness, as if the hole went deeper than the light could reach.

Probably just a shadow, Donald thought momentarily as he reached forward for the light.

There was movement. Shifting. Scuttling. Deep in the hole. Donald's hand snapped back away from the opening and a tiny, sharp gasp came from his chest. He leaned forward a bit to peer into the hole, was starting to reach for the flashlight one more time, his hand trembling just a little, when he caught the smell. It was just a trace of an odor, but enough for him to notice.

("There was a horrible smell there . . .")

Donald sniffed once. Again.

(". . . awful . . . really sweet . . . kind of stung your nostrils . . .")

The smell was gone, as quickly as it had come. Donald leaned back away from the hole and reached the hook-shaped handle of the umbrella over the hole's edge and pulled the flashlight toward him. He lost it once and it slipped back into the hole, so he tried again. Once the flashlight was at the lip of the hole, he took it in his hand and pointed it down into the ground.

The walls of the hole were rounded and slightly ridged, uneven, as if the earth had been crudely dug or scraped out. The inside seemed to be bigger than the hole itself, seemed to open up, giving more space.

And it was deep. Very deep. The darkness continued far beyond his beam of light.

Turning the umbrella around, he held the handle and stuck the other end down into the hole to see if he could reach the bottom of it. The metal tip of the umbrella scraped along the sides of the hole as he pushed it down, trying to reach it in as far as he could.

Something moved again.

Donald froze and swallowed, making a dry clicking sound in his throat.

It moved again. It was closer now.

Taking in a tremulous breath, Donald started to pull the umbrella from the hole, but he wasn't fast enough. Something very strong snapped onto the umbrella and jerked Donald forward. His shoulder hit the hole's edge hard and a sharp pain shot down his back. With a short cry, Donald immediately let go of the umbrella and threw himself away from the hole. The umbrella was swallowed up by the darkness.

Donald crawled backward frantically, face up, keeping his eye on the hole. In one smooth motion, he turned over on his hands and knees, then sprang to his feet and shined the light on the hole. The weeds and roots hanging down over the edges moved. They were suddenly whipped aside, and for a split second Donald saw the eyes. He turned and ran. Going up the other side of the incline, his feet began to slip and slide beneath him and, for a few moments, he went nowhere. He could hear it coming behind him, scurrying rapidly along the ground, making sharp squeaking and guttural clicking sounds. Snapping. Biting.

Donald clambered over the edge of the gully and raced through the woods, the flashlight beam bouncing up and down ahead of him. He realized he was grunting as he ran, partially from exertion, partially from fear. He dodged blackened trees and spindly bushes, picking up his pace once the car was in sight ahead, his imagination picturing the thing behind him closing in, its teeth nearly close enough to—

He crashed into the side of the car, throwing the door open, dropping the flashlight to the ground as he got in. Frantically he slammed the door, locked it, fumbled with the keys—

"C'mon, c'*mon,* goddammit!"—started the car, put it in gear, and banged his foot down on the accelerator, tires spinning as he sped away. He'd been driving on the road a few seconds before he thought to turn on the headlights.

Donald's chest heaved up and down as his lungs groped for air. His heart was beating so fast, he thought it would explode.

When he got home, he was exhausted. But he could not sleep.

9

Walther chewed his sausage without tasting it, gulped his coffee as if it were water. The scrambled eggs were just lumps in his mouth that went down easily. He was absently watching a moth flutter against the windowpane above the kitchen sink, but his mind was elsewhere.

Nancy walked in from the living room, where she had set the children up in front of the television. On Saturday mornings they were allowed to eat their breakfast there so they could watch cartoons. She was carrying a pitcher of orange juice, which she placed on the table.

"What *is* this?" she asked, watching him eat. "A shot at the Guinness Book? You're scarfing that down like there's no tomorrow. If I'd known you weren't going to bother *tasting* it, I wouldn't have bothered *cooking* it." She went over to the stove and dished up her own breakfast, poured herself a cup of coffee, and joined him at the table.

"Sorry. I didn't realize I was eating so fast." He sipped his coffee, then took a bite of sausage and chewed it slowly. "It's good, hon. Really."

Nancy looked out the window as she stirred some sweetener into her coffee. "What lousy weather," she said. The sky was thick with black clouds that threatened violence, and the bare branches of the trees in the neighborhood swayed at the mercy of a cold wind that seemed to be growing in strength. "And on a Saturday." She turned to Walther. "There's a movie at the Cine Dome the kids want to see. I thought we could catch a matinee today. Sound good?"

"Sorry, Nance," he replied. "I've got a lot to do. I'm going to be pretty busy."

"Oh. Well, maybe we can go tomorrow. You got plans tomorrow?"

"I don't know. Depends on what happens today."

She inhaled deeply and exhaled slowly through her teeth, which told Walther she wasn't at all pleased.

"I'm really sorry, hon, but I can't get around it."

"What are you going to be doing?"

"I . . . I've got work to do. Left over from the week."

"You're still following up on that Ellis guy, aren't you?"

"Yeah. Sort of."

She nibbled on a sausage. "Unofficially."

He nodded.

"Hmph. My husband the go-getter. Works when he doesn't have to." Her voice was quite chilly.

Walther stood, unconsciously wiping his greasy hands on the grubby old sweatshirt he was wearing, and walked behind Nancy. He put a hand on each of her shoulders, bent down, and kissed the top of her head. "My wife the softy. Acts like a bitch when she really doesn't mean it."

She stifled a giggle as she reached around and swatted him on the thigh. "Go to work."

He went to the bedroom to change his clothes, but sat down on the edge of the bed, resting his face in his hands and his elbows on his knees instead.

The previous night, when Gene had mentioned that damned fire, it had hit Walther like a brick. The first disappearance took place the day of the fire—the fire in which Eddie Monohan had disappeared. Or *died*, if what Donald Ellis had said was true, because Monohan's disappearance had been the same as all the others. The circumstances had been kept rather quiet at first, until everyone saw the same thing happening elsewhere.

Bill Ellis had met that strange woman there, too. Eve. She'd been alone and naked. After what Donald had told him about Bill's relationship with this Eve, about what Donald suspected she'd done—actually claimed to have *seen* her do—to Bill, Walther wondered if he would be able to find her should he try. He doubted it.

He picked up the phone and dialed the station. Mitch answered. After an exchange of amenities, Walter said, "Mitch, remember the big fire last month?"

"Sure."

"You ever hear anything about a cause? Did they ever find out what started it?"

"Nope. They chalked it up as arson, but as far as I know, they're *still* at a loss. Why?"

"Mm. Just curious." He thought a moment, and there was an uncomfortable silence over the line. "Mitch. Did anything strange happen that day? The day of the fire?"

"Strange? What do you mean?"

"Well, I'm . . . not sure, really. Just something out of the ordinary. Anything at all."

"I couldn't say, Lew. I'd have to look back over the—"

"No, no, no, that's okay, Mitch. No problem."

"Why all the questions, Lew?"

"Just curiosity. See you Monday, Mitch." He hung up the phone, hoping he hadn't stirred any suspicion. It wouldn't do for anyone down at the station to know what he was up to. If it weren't for that, he'd go down there now and look over the records himself.

He got up and was starting to change when the phone rang.
"Hello?"

"Lew, this is Mitch again. You know, it just occurred to me that something kinda funny *did* happen that evening. The evening of the fire. Seems several people called in to complain about a horrible smell in the air. They were all within a mile or so of the fire. I heard the firemen could hardly stand it, too. It was really awful, whatever caused it."

Walther sat down on the side of the bed, his brow knit. "Look, Mitch, I'd like you to do me a favor. Just between the two of us, though, okay?"

"Well, sure, Lew." He sounded concerned.

"I'd like you to get me the names and addresses of the people who called in that night, okay? Just the people who called in about that smell. And, uh, don't tell anybody what you're doing, okay?"

"Hell, it's Saturday, Lew. I'm just about the only one here so far. Hang on."

While he waited, Walther readied his pad and pen. He copied the information he needed, thanked Mitch, then hung up. He sat on the bed, staring at his small handwriting for a while, not impressed with the apparent unimportance of what he'd learned, but determined to pursue it, anyway. He looked at the bedside clock: 10:42. He decided to call Donald and tell him that he didn't know when he'd be able to make it. Walther picked up the phone and dialed his number, but the line was busy.

The line was busy. Kyle hung up. Well, at least Mr. Ellis was home. That was all Kyle had wanted to know. He put on his coat, got his umbrella, clicked off the kitchen light, and went out to his car.

The day was dark. A light drizzle had begun to fall, but not enough to warrent opening his umbrella between the front door and the car. He started the engine, let it warm up, and drove off.

Last night Kyle had gotten the idea to go down to the bakery, get a few donuts, and drop by Mr. Ellis's with them for a visit. He didn't want to lose touch with his teacher just because he wouldn't be seeing him at the school for a while. Kyle hoped Mr. Ellis wouldn't be busy or gone by the time he arrived. As he started down the hill toward town, he switched on the radio.

The creature had been waiting all night and most of the morning for the boy. It had parked its car on a sidestreet not far from the boy's home the evening before. It had rested for a while during the night, knowing that when the boy came down the hill the next morning, it would see him.

It had stolen the car—a clumsy, old white Mustang—in town. It had been quite easy. The car had been parked in a dark lot, and there had been no one around to see.

The creature straightened its posture behind the wheel when it heard a noise some distance off. After a few moments, the boy's car sped by, going toward town. Reaching underneath the steering wheel, the creature made a few adjustments, and the car started.

The wait had been long, but it would be worth it in the end. It stepped on the accelerator and turned onto the main road to follow the boy.

"Do you think that fire was started intentionally?" Freddie asked, taking a bite of her toast. "Maybe by those things?"

"I don't know," Donald replied, exhaling cigarette smoke. "Maybe it was just arson, some kids playing with matches. But I'd like to know, just in case. So, as soon as the library opens, we're going to go look at some back issues of the *Register*. Maybe we can learn something.'' He nervously tapped some ashes into an ashtray on the table. ''I wish I knew when it opens.'' He'd called a couple of times already, but had gotten no answer. He would try again later.

Donald had not slept the night before. When Freddie awoke, he was drinking coffee in the kitchen. He told her about his experience in the woods. Her reply had been a silent, fearful stare. They didn't speak for a while after that. Then she showered and dressed, and he told her about his plans to visit the library later that day. Her spirits had improved after her shower and she smiled warmly.

''Sounds good to me,'' she said. ''I wish you'd calm down, though. You're as nervous as a cat at a dog show, if you don't mind my saying.''

''Yeah, I know. I can't help it.'' He stood and began pacing beside the table, occasionally glancing at the kitchen clock. ''I've just been wondering if I did the right thing in telling Anne and Detective Walther. Maybe they *will* help us. Maybe with his pull we'll get something done. But . . . maybe not.''

Someone knocked at the door. Donald froze and locked his eyes onto the front door through the kitchen doorway. He thought, as he held his breath for a moment, that it might be someone from the FBI. He had been expecting one of them to come and ask him a bunch of questions; at the same time he'd been hoping they would somehow pass over him. He stubbed his cigarette out in the ashtray and went to the door.

''Kyle,'' he said with relief when he opened the door.

Kyle smiled broadly at him. ''Hi, Mr. Ellis. Hope I'm not disturbing you.''

''No, of course not. Come in, you're getting wet.'' He closed the door once Kyle was inside, then took his coat and hung it up.

"I brought some donuts from the Butter Cream Bakery," Kyle said, holding out a little pink and white bag.

"Terrific. I've got a pot of coffee in the kitchen. To what do I owe this visit?" Donald seemed uncomfortable as he stood before Kyle, shifting his weight from one foot to the other, slipping his hands in and out of his pockets, chewing on his lip when not speaking.

"Just wanted to come see you. Talk." He smiled again.

"Well, come into the kitchen and meet somebody."

Kyle followed him in a little hesitantly, holding the bag of donuts in front of him with both hands.

"Kyle, this is Freddie Santos. Freddie, meet Kyle Hubbley."

Freddie flashed her bright smile and nodded. "Hi, Kyle. Nice to meet you."

Kyle nodded in return, but a little less openly. "Hello."

"Freddie is a former student of mine," Donald said, pouring a cup of coffee for Kyle. "We keep in touch. Have a seat." He put the coffee on the table, along with the sugar and cream. "So," he said, leaning on the counter, folding his arms in front of him, "how's life treating you, Kyle?"

"I can't complain." He spooned some sugar into his coffee, then opened the paper bag. "Have some donuts."

Donald grabbed one and bit into it. "How's school?"

"Well, you're missed, I can tell you that."

"That's good to know."

Kyle took a donut, dipped it into the coffee, and took a bite, staring at the tabletop all the while. Freddie popped the last bite of toast into her mouth, while Donald chewed his donut silently. Thunder growled in the distance.

"We're going to be getting a downpour soon, I think," Donald offered, but it didn't ease the tension in the room. He caught Freddie's eye and gave a slight, but suggestive, nod toward the doorway.

"You guys'll have to excuse me while I pay a visit to the

241

little room in the back," she said, getting up and leaving the kitchen with a smile.

When she was gone, Kyle looked up at Donald. "Pretty."

"Very." Donald sat down at the table, glancing at the clock again. Ten minutes after eleven. "Excuse me a second, Kyle." He sprang up from his chair again and went to the phone.

"Napa County Library," said an efficient voice.

"You're open!"

"Until four."

"Thank you." He hung up and returned to the table, hurried and preoccupied. "So, Kyle. Anything on your mind?"

"Sort of." He sipped the coffee. "I met this girl yesterday. Older than me, maybe. She's pretty. *Really* pretty. She looks a lot like Leslie Newell, I mean a *whole* lot. I thought she *was* Leslie at first. She was really nice to me, but . . . well, I think I might have made a fool of myself."

"How do you mean?" Donald was drumming his fingers softly on the tabletop, next to his donut, chewing impatiently on his lip.

Kyle gave him a brief account of his experience with Betty.

"Oh, Kyle," Donald said, "you did just the right thing! I'm proud of you! That's really a step in the right direction. Now just think how much easier it'll be to ask her out the *next* time you meet her!"

"You think I should?"

"By all means, yes!"

Kyle grinned and relaxed a little. "Well, then." He laughed lightly. "Maybe I will. *If* I meet her again, that is."

"Good boy." Donald polished off his donut and made nervous small talk until Kyle finished his coffee. Then he stood and said, "Kyle, thanks for dropping by and bringing the goodies. I hate to chase you off, but I've got a pretty important appointment to go to.''

''Oh, sure, sure.'' Kyle stood quickly. ''Thank you for the coffee and the free advice.''

''Stop by again sometime,'' Donald said as he got Kyle's coat for him.

''It was good seeing you, Mr. Ellis. Take care.''

Once Kyle was on his way down the front steps, Donald closed the door. ''You ready to go, Freddie? The library's open.''

''Weren't you a little abrupt with him?'' Freddie asked as she came into the living room, shrugging her coat on.

''Well, I might have been. But I want to get over to the library. I've been waiting for this since late last night.'' He hurried into the bedroom and came out wearing a shirt and coat. Opening the front door, he said, ''Let's go.''

Kyle was disappointed by his visit with Mr. Ellis. He'd wanted to spend more time talking—not just about himself, but about Ellis, too. He wondered, as he drove home through the rain, what had been on Mr. Ellis's mind. He'd obviously been preoccupied. Maybe Freddie was on his mind, Kyle thought with a smirk. That would be quite understandable. Kyle wondered if there was anything to that relationship. She hadn't looked as though she were just visiting.

Remembering that the milk at home was almost gone, Kyle pulled into the parking lot of a little market. He went in and made his purchase. On his way out of the market, he passed her, spun around, saw her go in.

''Betty?''

She stopped, holding the door of the market open, turned and faced him. ''Yes? Oh, hello.''

Kyle stepped back inside, letting the glass door close and ring the little bell that hung above it.

243

"Kyle, if I remember correctly," she said, smiling slightly.

"That's right. How are you?"

"Well, a little wetter than when I saw you last." She gently passed her hand over her blond hair, which was sparkling with beads of rainwater. "I came to get some groceries and some candles."

"Candles?"

"Yes. The power went off at my place."

"Oh."

("Now just think how much easier it'll be to ask her out the *next* time you meet her!")

"Um, well . . ." Kyle moved the grocery bag containing the carton of milk he'd bought from his right arm to his left, hesitating.

Betty tilted her head and cocked a brow, waiting for him to continue.

"Well, uh, the power's still on at my place, as far as I know." He sniffed and cleared his throat. "Why don't you come over for lunch? We can have soup and sandwiches, maybe." Once it was out, he was able to smile comfortably. "How about it?"

"I think that's a capital idea, Kyle. Some soup would hit the spot. Do you live around here?"

Inside he leaped for joy; outside, he simply moved the bag back to his right arm. "Up on Lokoya."

"Why don't we both go in your car?"

"Sure," he said, thinking that the upper half of his skull would topple off if he smiled any wider. "Let's go."

Jerry Brewster was tall, thin, thirtyish, and miserable with a head cold. His four-year-old daughter was standing with him at their front door, hugging his leg, as he said hello to Walther.

"You're here about duh fire?" he asked nasally.

"Well, sort of. That evening, you reported an unusual smell, is that right?"

"Yeah," he nodded. His little girl fidgeted.

"When did you first notice it?"

"Oh, I guess it was about nide o'clock. We were watching telebision with by daughter."

Walther crouched down and smiled at the little girl. "What were you watching?" he asked her.

"We was watching *The Wizard of Oz*," she said bashfully, hiding behind her father's legs.

"You were? We watched that, too, my family. I have a little boy about your age who really likes that movie." When he got no reply from her, he stood up and said, "What would you say it smelled like, Mr. Brewster?"

"Flesh," he replied with no hesitation. "A lot like burding flesh." He sniffed and coughed.

"I don't mean to sound doubtful, Mr. Brewster, but have you ever smelled burning flesh?"

Brewster glanced at his feet, then looked back up at Walther. "A few years ago," he said slowly, "I worked at a mill in Redding. There was a horrible explosion and the place caught fire. A lot of people were burned to a crisp that day. I was almost one of 'em. I smelled plenty of burding flesh then. I know what it's like."

"I'm sorry," Walther said quietly.

"It wasn't exactly the sabe, though," Brewster added, shaking his head. "I never thought anything *could*, but this smelled *worse*. It was stronger. It was . . . I do' know, it was albost like this was *greasy*. Den, when I saw the glow frub duh fire"—he turned away and sneezed twice in rapid succession—"I figured people were burding over there. Really upset me."

"I'm very sorry, Mr. Brewster. That you were upset, I

mean. As far as we know, though, no one was injured directly by the fire.''

"Den how cub you're asking about it?''

Walther had no reply. At least not one that made any sense. "We just wanted to look into it, Mr. Brewster. Thank you for your help.'' He looked down at the little girl. "And you take care of yourself, okay?''

She nodded cautiously.

Back in his car, Walther drummed his fingers on the steering wheel. Brewster had been the last person on his list. His story was the same as all the others'. The smell had begun around nine. It was strong and clinging, and those who were familiar with the odor of burning flesh said it strongly resembled that, except it was worse. Walther had heard that the firemen who'd fought the fire over by the river had complained of a horrible smell, but he'd never given it a second thought. Now it seemed to be important.

But *why?*

"It had to be one of *them*,'' Donald said. They were driving back from the library. They'd looked through several *Napa Register*s, but found nothing definite concerning the fire's cause, only a suspicion of arson. They did, however, come across several references to a sickening odor that seemed to come from the fire and that spread out as far as two miles or so. "No *people* were burned in the fire that I know of,'' he continued, "so it *had* to be one of those things. Last night, there was a sweet, sickly smell coming from that hole, but it was very faint. Maybe when they burn, they smell much worse. Hell, they must reek.'' He thought silently for a while, chewing gently on his lip. "Maybe the fire really *was* the result of arson, and those things came out of the hole right in the middle of it. Walked right into the fire.''

"You think they all came out of that hole?" Freddie asked, doubtful.

"Well . . ." Donald shrugged, his voice trailing off.

"They're all over the country, though. Everywhere."

He nodded slowly, his hands twisting nervously on the steering wheel. "Yeah. And I'm willing to bet that there are more of those holes. Everywhere. In forests. Deserts. Where no one sees them. And those things keep crawling out of them." He paused and his throat bobbed as he swallowed. " 'The legions of hell come to claim their own.' "

Walther stood in a pay phone outside a small liquor store. He'd called Anne and told her everything he'd learned. The sound of the rain spattering onto the booth was amplified on the inside, so Walther had to raise his voice to be heard above it.

"Okay," Anne said, "every two hundred years for periods of ten years each. But *why?*" She sounded annoyed, impatient.

"Look, Miss Cramer," Walther snapped, a sudden sharp edge to his voice, "you got me into this and I'd appreciate it if—"

"Yes, yes," she interrupted quickly. "I know. I'm sorry. Where are you now?"

"I'm in front of Val's Liquors on Soscol."

"Well, my car won't start. It's been doing this for the last week or so. Think you can come get me before you head for Donald's?"

"Sure." He got the address from her, said he didn't know when he'd be there, and they exchanged goodbyes. After hanging up, he leaned on one wall of the booth and rubbed his face with both hands. Despite the weather, he was perspiring lightly from the tension he was feeling. "Jesus," he sighed, thinking that at some point in the future he would probably be thought of by his peers as either a hero or a fool for getting involved in this whole thing. He'd prefer the former. But better safe than sorry, fool or not.

Opening the clumsily bound telephone book that hung from a chain beneath the pay phone, Walther looked up the number of Todd Doyle, the local fire inspector. Once he got Doyle on the line, they engaged in some small talk, and then Walther asked him about the fire.

"We determined arson as the cause of the fire, Lew," Doyle replied. "It was in all the papers."

"Well, it was never stated very definitely." He paused a moment, piecing his next question together carefully before asking it. "What about the smell, Todd?"

"Smell?"

"The one the firemen complained about. And people living nearby. We got a lot of calls at the station. They said it smelled like burning flesh. Know anything about that?"

"Sure, I heard about it. But we never found out what it was."

"No one was burned in the fire?" Walther quickly added, "I mean, badly enough so it would smell like that?"

"Dammit, Lew, *you'd* know about it if someone was burned in that fire!" Doyle barked defensively. "What the hell do you think's going on here, some kind of cover-up? Why all the suspicion?"

"Oh, I'm not suspicious, Todd," Walther said soothingly. "I'm just working on something and I want to make sure I touch all the bases. Make sure I haven't missed anything. Thanks for your help, Todd. Sorry to bother you on a weekend." Walther replaced the receiver, left the booth, and got into his car with a weary sigh.

Donald and Freddie silently removed their wet clothes when they got in the house and tossed them on the back of the easy chair. Donald went into the kitchen for a glass of water to rid his mouth of its cottony feeling. He drained the glass, set it on the counter, and turned to see Freddie standing in the kitchen doorway staring at him.

"What's the matter?" he asked.

"I'm scared, dammit, *that's* what's the matter!" she retorted quickly.

He crossed the floor, took her in his arms, and said, "I know, Fred, so am I. But we're catching on, you know? Things are falling together. Slowly, maybe, but we're doing pretty damned well, if you ask me." He held her close, smelling her hair; it was a fresh, outdoorsy smell that made him smile. Pulling back, he looked into her dark brown eyes. "We're doing *very* well. It won't be long now before we're out of this mess." He smiled warmly, but inside he wasn't quite as certain as he sounded. He was, however, pleased with their progress and reasonably confident that, before too long, they would be able to put up a fairly good fight against whatever it was they were facing. Because they would *know* what they were facing.

The phone rang and Donald answered it promptly. It was Anne calling to say that she and Walther would indeed be coming later, although she didn't know when because Walther was busy gathering some information. She filled Donald in on what they had so far, repeating what Walther had told her in an unemotional, noncommittal tone. When she was finished, Donald muttered quietly, mostly to himself, "Every two hundred years. But why?"

"We don't know that yet. Just what I've told you."

"Anne, something happened to me last night . . ." And, in great detail, Donald told her of his experience in the woods the night before. "When Freddie bumped into that thing in the mall, she said later that it was almost as if she'd merged with it, entered its mind. She said that she suddenly felt vulnerable, as if she'd left a protective shelter and was out in the open, where she could be seen. That makes sense, doesn't it? They came out of that hole, out of holes in other places. They've come from underground.''

Anne was silent for a while. "I . . . I'll tell that to Lew when he gets here.''

"Anne. You still don't sound very convinced about what's going on. But whatever your thoughts and reasons are, thank you for bringing Lew to me and . . . well, for trying to help.''

"I thought my reasons were obvious, Donald. I care. *That's* why. I want to help you.''

"Well, thanks." He was about to end the conversation when Anne broke the momentary silence.

"Donald, I . . . I miss you, Donald.''

"I'll see you later this afternoon, Anne. Goodbye." He hung up. When Donald turned away from the phone nook, he saw Freddie hanging their coats up in the closet by the front door. When she was finished, she faced him and asked firmly, "Are you in love with her, Don?''

Donald's mouth twisted to the right and he nibbled thoughtfully on the corner. He slowly sat down in the chair by the phone.

"I love her," he finally answered. "But I'm not in love with her." He shook his head. "Not anymore.''

"Why not?" Freddie asked, approaching him.

Donald's eyebrows lifted and he repeated her question: "*Why not?* You're a mind reader, Fred. I wouldn't think you'd need to ask that question.''

She knelt down in front of him and folded her arms across his knees, smiling. "Why not?" she asked again.

"Because of you, Fred," Donald whispered. He bent forward and kissed her. "I'm in love with *you.*''

"I just wanted to hear you *say* it," she said softly, a grin stretching across her face as she reached up and put her arms around his neck. "That's all."

Anne lay on the sofa in the silence of her house, knowing she'd lost Donald. Whether it was because of her initial disbelief in him or because of the problems they'd had earlier, she didn't know. But he had cut himself off from her. She missed him and loved him, but perhaps this was best, she thought. Of course, she didn't like the idea of being replaced—however temporary the situation might be—by a *teenager!* She also had to deal with the fact that she had, for reasons that really didn't seem clear to her anymore, allowed herself to get caught up in this ridiculous mess. Not only herself, but Detective Walther, who had apparently adapted to the whole thing much better than she.

Did she believe Donald had the power of second sight? A sixth sense? Perhaps. And perhaps he *was* receiving things he didn't understand—signals, so to speak, that frightened and confused him. That wasn't too hard to believe, was it? No. But this business of monsters coming from out of the ground every two hundred years and taking the shape of human beings . . . *that* was a bit much.

Anne closed her eyes and dozed on the sofa for a while, thinking that perhaps she'd gotten herself a little too deeply involved in this whole thing.

"Any of those donuts left?" Donald asked as he poured himself a fresh cup of coffee.

Freddie peeked into the pink and white Butter Cream Bakery bag. "Yep."

"Good." He sat down and took one out, biting into it.

"So," Freddie sighed, sitting down with him, looking at the bag, "your friend's got himself a girl, huh?"

"Ah, you eavesdropped. Yes, there's someone Kyle's interested in, I guess.'' He sipped his coffee and stared thoughtfully at the donut in his hand. ''I forget what her name—ah, *Betty*, that's it. Somebody a little older . . . than . . . he . . .'' His brow slowly creased into a frown. The tip of his tongue lodged in the corner of his mouth as he ran over his conversation with Kyle. He'd been so preoccupied, so distant at the time.

He'd paid too much attention to his own thoughts (''. . . *pretty . . . really pretty . . . looks a lot like Leslie Newell*'') and not enough to what Kyle had been saying (''*I thought she was Leslie at first*'') about his new friend (''*a lot like Leslie Newell, I mean a* whole *lot*'').

Leslie Newell . . .

Self-centered, conceited Leslie Newell, who, if given the choice, would probably want to be no one other than—herself. *Herself!* Leslie Newell was probably her *own* idea of the perfect woman, the perfect *anyone!* The donut slipped from Donald's fingers and fell to the tabletop. His mouth hung open slightly. ''My god,'' he whispered.

''You think she's one of them,'' Freddie said knowingly.

''Why didn't I pay attention!'' Donald hissed at himself as he stood from the table. ''Goddammit, why didn't I *listen!*'' He rushed out of the kitchen, through the living room, and over to the phone, where he looked hurriedly through the directory for Kyle Hubbley's phone number.

''You have an interesting music collection, Kyle,'' Betty said as she browsed through the records by the stereo.

''Thank you,'' Kyle replied. He was squatting in front of the fireplace, trying to start a fire. ''Feel free to put something on, if you like.'' He was very relaxed in her presence now. They'd had an easy conversation on the way up the hill. She'd seemed very interested in what Kyle had to say, even his small talk, like weather and school stuff. He realized suddenly, as he stoked the fire, that he'd learned nothing of her yet. He didn't know where she lived, where she was from, what she did. But that would come, he was sure. It sort of seemed unimportant when he looked at her, noticing something even more beautiful each time: how perfect her fingernails were, how straight her teeth, the fine shape of her jaw. But mostly, that strange and yet exciting look that she gave him now and then. A look that seemed to be smiling, but wasn't, that seemed to know something . . . a secret, a *fun* secret.

Kyle stood and was about to ask her what kind of soup she wanted when the phone rang. "Excuse me," he said, leaving the living room and going to the kitchen. "Hello?"

"Hi, Kyle, this is Mr. Ellis. I have a few questions to ask you."

"Well, do you think it can wait? I've got company."

"Company?" He sounded shocked, almost afraid.

"Yeah, Betty's here. Remember her? We're going to have lunch in a—"

"Kyle, listen to me!" Mr. Ellis interrupted urgently. "Listen to me, Kyle, get *out* of there. Get out of your house *now*."

"But . . . what are you—"

"For Christ's sake, Kyle, get away from her! Don't let her know you're leaving, just get in your car and *leave*. Come here, *anywhere*, just get away from her!"

"Get away from *her?* From *Betty?*"

"Yes! Quickly!"

It seemed to Kyle that Mr. Ellis was worse off than he'd thought. His teacher's actions over the past week or so had been very strange, but this took the cake.

"What's wrong with you, Mr. Ellis?" Kyle asked with genuine concern. "You don't even *know* her."

"I know what she *is*, Kyle, believe me. You're in danger. She's going to—"

Kyle gently replaced the receiver.

* * *

The creature's sense of danger was pricked as it listened carefully to the boy, picking up most of what he said. Someone knew, someone was trying to warn him. Then it heard the name: Ellis. *Him!* News of Ellis and his young female friend had traveled among the creature's companions in the area ever since their meeting that day in the classroom, and it had thought that, by now, something would have been done about them. It had heard that action was being taken to eliminate those two and the threat they posed, but it had heard nothing specific.

How had Ellis heard about "Betty"? Perhaps Kyle had told him. Perhaps it was Ellis's house that Kyle had visited that morning while the creature had watched him from a distance.

All that was unimportant now, however. The important thing was to get on with the feeding.

"Goddammit!" Donald shouted as he slammed the receiver down. He opened the telephone book, ran his finger down the page until he found Kyle's number again, then looked at the address. "Lokoya Road," he muttered nervously.

"He won't believe you?" Freddie asked.

"No, and she's there with him. *Now.*" Donald stood, letting the book drop to the floor as he hurried into his bedroom. When he returned, he held his brother's pistol in his right hand. "You stay here and wait for Anne and Walther," he told her as he took his coat from the closet. He stuffed the gun in the pocket and put the coat on, all very clumsily.

"Oh, Jesus, Donald," Freddie breathed, covering her mouth with her hand, "please don't go."

"Don't worry, Fred, I'll be back. Hopefully with Kyle." They both knew how empty those words were. He kissed her quickly, started to turn, but thought better of it. He took her in his arms and gave her a long, deep kiss before he left. Just in case it was their last.

"Now," Kyle said as he came back into the living room, rubbing his palms together. "What kind of soup would you like, Betty?"

She smiled at him from the sofa and said, "I'm really not that hungry, Kyle." She licked her lips. It was a simple gesture, not in the least bit suggestive. "Not for soup."

"Oh. Is there something else you'd like?"

The fire in the fireplace cracked loudly before she spoke. "Yes. I'd like you to come sit down." She patted the space next to her on the sofa.

Kyle went over and sat down, leaving a comfortable space between them. Mr. Ellis was already forgotten.

"Kyle. Why did you ask me here?"

"To have lunch."

"And?"

"To talk, to get to know you better."

"Is that all, Kyle?"

"Well . . ." He began to fidget. "Yes. Sure."

"Oh, come now, Kyle." Smoothly, she moved closer, turned her body toward him, putting one elbow up on the back of the sofa. "There's more to it than that, isn't there?"

He didn't know what to do or say. Of *course* there's more, he thought. But dare he tell her that?

"Isn't there?" she asked again, placing her hand on his shoulder.

Kyle's skin tingled under her palm, and he had to repress a delighted shudder. "Well, I wanted to . . . I hoped . . ."

She leaned forward, almost touching her nose to his, so close that Kyle could feel her breath on his face. "Did you want us to make love, Kyle?"

He tried to speak, but couldn't.

"You did, didn't you? You wanted us to make love." Her voice became a thick, hot whisper. "You wanted to *fuck* me."

He swallowed, and his mouth smacked open. "No, I—"

"It's all right, Kyle. There's nothing wrong with that. Nothing at all."

Jesus God, he thought, this isn't really happening! It's too wonderful!

She pressed her lips softly to his, ran her tongue around the edges of his mouth playfully, then pushed it forward, probing, searching.

"You *do* want to fuck me, don't you, Kyle?" she whispered, moving back only a little, her hot breath hitting Kyle's lips. She took his hand in hers and placed it over her breast, pressing it down into the warm softness.

"Yes," he replied, barely audible.

"Say it, Kyle, tell me what you want to do."

"I want . . . to . . . make love to you."

"No." She lifted her hand from his, which was now gently kneading her breast. "There's more." She put her hand on the side of his head, just above his ear. Then the other hand on the other side. "What do you want to *do* to me?" When she began moving her fingers in small circles on his head, twirling them in his hair, Kyle closed his eyes, leaned his head back, and let out a long, deep groan of pure pleasure. He was in heaven.

"Can I use your phone?" Walther asked Anne as he walked into the house.

"Sure." She closed the front door.

Walther called his house and Nancy answered.

"Are you planning on going out with the kids?" he asked her.

"Mm-hm. To a movie."

"Look, hon, I can't explain now, but I'd rather you stay in."

"What's wrong, Lew?" She immediately sounded worried.

"I'll explain it all later, Nance. Just stay in the house with the kids. And, uh . . . lock the doors, too. I'll see you later. Love you." He hung up and turned to Anne. "Let's go to Donald's."

The heaviness of the gun in his coat pocket pressed against Donald's side as he drove through the now pouring rain as fast as he dared. The wipers were barely able to keep up with the rainfall. He was trembling all over and knew that if he didn't calm down and stop breathing so rapidly, he would hyperventilate. Then he'd be doing no one any good.

They came out of the ground, apparently every two hundred years, and slaughtered god knows how many people. Hundreds of years ago they were labeled incubi and succubi, and who knew what else? Vampires, maybe? Werewolves? Things were different now, though. It would be harder for them to remain undetected, although they'd done a pretty good job of it so far. They'll be found out this time, Donald thought, if I have to die to see to it. And he knew he very well might.

Lokoya was a winding road, narrow and steep in places, and Donald slowed each time he came to a mailbox, or a cluster of them, to check the numbers. He was looking for 710, but had not yet gotten beyond the 500s.

If only he'd *listened* to Kyle that morning, *heard* what the boy had been saying, realized the danger he was in, he could've stopped this before it happened! Why hadn't it hit him when Kyle said the girl looked so much like Leslie Newell? And the name—*Betty*. Only now, when it might be too late, did Donald realize that the owner of the house in which Leslie had been killed was named Betty. These creatures seemed to take everything they could get from their victims.

Donald felt that if he didn't get to Kyle's house in time, the boy's death would be just as much *his* fault as the fault of the thing that would kill him.

Kyle felt as if a floodgate had been opened and the most delicious feelings in the world were pouring through his body. It seemed to start with a fuzzy, cloudy sensation in his head, cover every inch of his body, then end between his legs where his penis was straining stiffly against his pants. He opened his mouth and tried to speak, but the words he wanted to say *("yes yes I want to fuck you Betty yes please I want to fuck you")* melted into senseless gibbering. He tried again, but with the same result. So, instead of speaking, he laughed. It was a lazy, drunken laugh that seemed to roll slowly up from his chest and tumble out of his mouth.

"Kyle."

He opened his eyes to see that, with one hand, she had unbuttoned the tight wool top she was wearing and her breasts were free. They were so round and inviting, the nipples so hard and dark. He lowered a hand onto one gently, reverently, squeezed it, caressed it. Just as he had imagined, just as he had hoped it would be.

"I'm yours now, Kyle," she breathed.

He leaned forward and put his mouth over the tip of one breast, rolling his tongue over her nipple, sucking on it, pulling it deeply into his mouth. His breath puffed frantically from his nose as his lips smacked again and again over the breast. She lay back on the sofa, holding his head in her hands, as he clumsily began to unbutton her pants.

Tree branches hung ominously over the road as Donald drove through the downpour. He squinted, craning his head forward, gently pressing the brake pedal each time he came to another mailbox. 705: he was getting closer. He drove a little farther, absently hitting one fist on the steering wheel, slowed, strained his eyes. 709.

"Shit!" he hissed.

At the next box, 710, Donald turned the car quickly into the driveway and stepped on the accelerator, rapidly nearing the house up ahead.

They were naked. The sensation of her skin against his drove Kyle insane. He wanted it to last forever, he didn't want to press on, move it toward its conclusion; but the pounding feeling of wetness between his legs told him he *had* to, told him it couldn't possibly last much longer. With the help of her hand, he slid into her with an uncontainable moan. It was wonderful, this feeling he'd wanted so badly, for so long.

"Fuck me, Kyle," she whispered to him, clutching his head between her constantly moving, caressing palms, her fluttering fingers, making the inside of his head buzz pleasantly. "Yessss, *fuck* meeeee." The voice seemed to deepen, become guttural.

Kyle, however, did not care, because now it was happening, it was actually happening to *him*, and soon the volcano inside him would be released, finally. He groped for her breasts, the soft, round . . . They felt different. Smaller? Harder? Flatter? The skin seemed not quite as smooth as it had been. Kyle slowed his movements, began to push himself away from her, but her hands squeezed together on his head and his body weakened, his muscles relaxed, and a long sigh passed his lips as she pulled him toward her once again with a demanding grunt. He continued moving, thrusting, in and out of her. But something was wrong, something about her was different.

She felt rough, coarse, like old leather. He opened his eyes and choked on the scream that caught in his throat.

Her face was gone.

"KYLE!"

Kyle felt a hand on his shoulder and he was suddenly being pulled away, thrown back, off the sofa, onto the floor, just as the glistening space between the creature's legs opened up to reveal gaping jaws, razor-sharp fangs that extended, snapped, snapped again, then pulled back and seemed to swallow themselves.

Holding the gun in an unsteady hand, Donald pointed it at the thing on the sofa. Its shape was now vaguely human, gray, creased, and shifting. What had once been an attractive human head was now nothing more than a pulsing lump; what had been arms and legs were now elongating, narrowing, and the torso was flattening out.

Donald squeezed the trigger and the gun fired. The bullet made a small hole in the thing's tough flesh, but seemed to do no real damage. He fired again. Another hole appeared. The area around the two small wounds began to swell. The holes seemed to turn themselves inside out and, slowly, the bullets were rebirthed; they eased out of the holes and rolled lazily over the creature's body to the floor.

Without warning, the creases that lined the gray skin smoothed out. The dull gray was replaced by a healthy skin-pink, then a soft, creamy color. The breasts rose and were peaked with chocolate-colored nipples. The limbs puffed up, shortened, and delicate hands and feet appeared. The deadly orifice below was covered with a honey-colored, triangular patch of hair. The lump on top took shape, eyes opened, a mouth smiled to reveal straight, white teeth. And the woman-creature stood . . .

*   *   *

Kyle stared in disbelief at the thing on the sofa, feeling much the same way he had the one time he'd tried pot: distant, uninvolved, as if what he was seeing wasn't happening to him. But it *was!* And he hadn't the faintest idea of what to do other than remain on the floor, sprawled naked by the fireplace, the wonderful feelings he'd been experiencing moments before now buried in fear and horror as the thing, beautiful once again, murmured, "Donald Ellis," in a low, sultry voice. It stepped around the sofa, which lay between it and Donald, nearing him slowly. "Such a brave man."

Donald was gasping for breath, trying to will his eyes not to tear up and blur his vision. He could not believe what he had seen. In a matter of seconds, that thing had become this beautiful, only slightly altered version of Leslie Newell. It smiled alluringly at him, thrusting its perfect breasts forward. Donald aimed the gun and fired again, lodging a bullet in the creature's flat, firm belly, and, once again, the bullet was spit out like an olive pit. A fear-filled, sickened whimper escaped Donald. He began to back up as the creature continued to advance toward him. Realizing its uselessness, Donald lowered the pistol.

"What are you?" he croaked.

"I am what you've been searching for, Donald," it replied with great promise.

"Stay away from me." He continued to walk backward.

The creature's hand reached down and began massaging the golden patch of hair. Its smile trembled and its eyelids lowered passionately. "Mmm, don't you want me, Donald?" it whispered.

Donald staggered backward at the sound of that horribly familiar voice; he caught his balance before he fell, dropping the gun as he did so. "Stay . . . away."

"Let's do it together," the creature offered, still slowly

coming forward, its hand rubbing between its legs. "Sweeeet sex . . . touching and licking . . ."

"N-no, please," Donald pleaded, his voice high and thin.

". . . sucking and fucking . . . please, let's do it . . . let's do it together." It chuckled with pleasure, the sound coming from deep inside it. "Rubbing and sweating . . . fuck me . . . fuck me, Donald Ellis."

Donald's leg struck something—a hassock—and he tumbled backward. His shoulder hit the chair that was behind him and a sharp pain shot down his back as he rolled to the side, landing with a grunt on the floor. He felt helpless; his muscles seemed to have turned to jelly, making his attempts to stand up again futile. Partially propped up by one elbow, Donald stared at the creature as it took another step forward . . . another . . . and another. The same horrible feeling that had held him in an iron grip during his nightmare now kept him down on the floor, as helpless as a newborn child. This is what he'd been hearing and feeling in his sleep.

"We can suck and lick each other," the thing continued, "and I'll eat you if you like . . . I'll eat you if you like."

"Dear god," Donald muttered tremulously, "dear god, de—" He spotted Kyle in the narrow space between the creature's legs; he lay a few feet away, naked, frozen, his face as white as flour, his mouth open with shock, his chest rising and falling frantically with each terrified breath. "Kyle!" Donald gasped. "Kyle, help me . . . for Christ's sake, *help me!*"

The creature stood at Donald's feet now, towering over him victoriously. It spread its legs and straddled him, moving its hand away from its vagina, revealing the delicate, inviting lips. "I'll eat you if you like, I'll eeeeat you . . ."

Desperate, Donald used one arm to pull himself backward, away from the creature, at the same time raising the other arm to hold the thing off. "No, no—"

The lips yawned open, the deadly jaws extended with lightning suddenness and snapped shut on Donald's arm, then immediately pulled back and disappeared once again.

For a flash, Donald was back in bed with Freddie, feeling her naked body under his, as he stared, screaming, at the bleeding stub of his right arm, but the vision lasted no longer than the blink of an eye. He began jerking his arm from right to left as it shot blood from its jagged end, which protruded from his now-tattered coat sleeve. He screamed so hard— again and again and again—that the tendons in his neck stood out distinctly, his face turned beet red, and blue veins appeared on his forehead and temples. Donald's blood dripped from the mock vagina that hovered above him, and strings of blood shot from his arm, through the air, slapping onto the skin of the smiling creature that, Donald was sure, would be the last thing he'd ever see.

Kyle felt his gorge rising, but fought desperately to hold it down. He looked away from the bloodshed that was taking place just a few feet away from him, knowing he had to do something! He turned to the brick hearth, pressed his palms onto the cold, hard surface, lifted himself shakily to his knees, then to his feet. His stomach churned, his heart pounded, and his head felt light as he staggered away from the fireplace, out of the living room, down the hall, and into the den, where he stopped in front of the gun cabinet. He grabbed the latch and pulled. The door wouldn't open. He rattled it, angry and frustrated. His father had locked it! Bending his arm, pulling it back, and bracing himself for the impact, Kyle crashed his elbow through the front of the cabinet. The glass shattered and pieces fell to the floor around his bare feet, clinking sharply against each other as they landed. Kyle reached through the new opening, his elbow bleeding, and, with both hands, grabbed the Marlin 30.06.

As he turned to rush back into the living room, Kyle thought of how upset his father would be about the cabinet. How very upset . . .

The creature dropped to its knees, still straddling Donald, still smiling, reached down, and pressed a hand to each side of Donald's head. All of his surroundings immediately disappeared and his vision exploded with rapid, disjointed, flashing scenes, his mind was filled with foreign, but real and vivid, feelings, and, most importantly, he knew that he had, if only for a moment and if only in a limited way, *become* the creature that had him in its grip at that moment:

—The cool darkness of the passageways that twisted and turned, climbing upward to the outside, tunnels splitting in separate directions, then splitting again, full of activity now at the height of the rush for the outside before the cover of night lifted, hurrying, pushing past one another, scraping and digging until the holes opened up and they were able to dash out into the open.

—Heat! Fire! The secretive silence was shattered by painful sounds of others, the clicking and squeaking sounds, warning of danger, but those behind continued to push their way out of the hole until it was too late to notice the bright, dancing flames all around them, the thick smoke and the rushing, angry heat, the others who had run into the fire and were staggering, aflame, over the burning ground, screeching in pain, rapidly wasting away, the smell of their burning bodies alarming those who were just coming out, some of them running for safety away from the flames, others who were burning retreating into the already crowded holes, seeking the safety of the vast, cool underground passageways.

—Safe! Hidden beside the running water, waiting for the danger to pass, feeling the hunger, an almost unbearable pain

now, the hunger that had brought them out, roused them from their foggy state of semisleep to feed on the creatures that lived on the surface; the ravenous feed, the scan—searching for the next disguise that would be used to blend in with the humans and bait the next one—and the excitement of extracting it from the mind of the human during the feed, of going through the invigorating transformation.

—The two humans, the male and his young female companion, who were able to see through the disguises . . . must be stopped; action is being taken, rest at ease, don't worry; he *will be taken now with pleasure, with great pleasure pleasure pleasure, and* she *will be found and killed found and killed foundandkilled—*

FREDDIE!

And then, with a sudden, skull-splitting blast, it all returned: the living room, the blood that continued to spurt from his arm and rain down on him, his own screams . . . But the creature was not on top of him as it had been.

A few feet away, Kyle stood holding a smoking rifle, still aimed at the creature, which was now lying beside Donald, part of its shoulder gone. Instead of red blood, a yellow, milky fluid flowed from the gaping wound. The creature convulsed on the floor, its human façade rapidly decaying, revealing the thing that lay beneath.

The creature's body was round, roughly three feet in diameter, with a thin, bony ridge running down the center of its back. The ridge started at the top of its vicious mouth, which was positioned vertically between two bulging yellow eyes. Its four wiry legs were spiderlike; each limb had a strong, knobby knee that bent to a point high above the flat body. At the end of each leg was a three-toed talon with razor-sharp claws. On the right side, between the creature's two right legs, a large chunk of its tough, gray flesh had been removed by Kyle, and the creature was grunting in pain, jerking spastically, its vital fluids pulsing from the wound. But only for a few seconds. Until the flesh began to grow back. Until the wound closed. Its thin, ragged lips pulled back tremulously over its bloodied fangs which still sported pieces of Donald's flesh, and it bolted toward Donald for another blow.

A second shot tore from Kyle's gun and the left eye burst, sending its yellow fluid in all directions as the creature staggered back a couple of feet. It turned to face Kyle as the eye regenerated. It began to make clicking, snorting sounds and, when the eye was once again whole, it raced toward Kyle, tumbling over Donald's legs, its jaws snapping loudly.

With a weak moan and trembling hands, Kyle snapped the bolt back, sending the discarded bullet through the air, and fired another shot. It blew a hole just above the creature's mouth, and the thing slid backward on the floor. With a sob catching wetly in his throat, Kyle jerked the bolt again, fired again. The creature's wound was suddenly larger and one leg began jerking uncontrollably. But it began moving toward Kyle once more, determined.

"You fucker!" Kyle breathed, and he fired again.

The creature's leg was now flopping up and down on the floor as its body spun around and around in a pained circle.

Kyle pulled the bolt. Fired.

The creature squealed and scurried backward, rammed into the corner of the sofa once, twice, its bloody jaws snapping, extending, snapping, its legs trembling uselessly now.

Kyle kept firing.

The creature's claws were slapping down into the puddle of yellow slime that was gushing from its wound. The wound that was no longer healing.

The rifle clicked. Empty.

The creature was still.

Donald allowed all his muscles to collapse; he let his head drop back to the floor, let his bleeding arm fall to his side, and closed his eyes, trying to speak, but failing. There was a dreadful sticky odor in the room, but it couldn't penetrate the dark red blanket of pain that covered Donald. Donald tried to fight the thick darkness that was filling his head, but succeeded only enough to feel Kyle tugging at his belt buckle, removing the belt, using it as a tourniquet on the remaining half of his right arm. Kyle hurried to the sofa and quickly put on his clothes.

"Freddie," Donald gasped. "We have to get Freddie."

"I'm taking you to the hospital," Kyle replied firmly.

"No! Freddie needs . . . help . . . They're going to . . . kill her."

I didn't believe him the last time, Kyle thought, and look what happened. "Okay. We'll get Freddie."

The rain fell with a loud roar on Walther's car as he drove slowly through the blinding storm. Anne had been telling him about Donald's experience in the woods the night before, and he was having a difficult time listening to her and driving at the same time.

"God*damn!*" he snapped. "I've *never* seen it rain this hard in Napa."

"Can you see at all?" Anne asked nervously.

"Well, sort of. I guess."

"Maybe we should pull over and let it die down," she suggested. "Donald isn't expecting us right away. I told him I didn't know how late we'd be." She glanced at Walther hopefully.

"Yeah. I suppose we should. It can't keep up like this for long." He pulled into a gas station, parked, and, looking out the watery windows, they waited.

*   *   *

Freddie sat stiffly on the edge of the sofa, her hands folded before her, elbows on her knees, and listened to the rumbling downpour outside. She'd tried to watch television, listen to the radio, even read. But she couldn't. She was too scared.

Hopefully, Walther and Anne would arrive soon. Freddie wanted the company. Being alone, not knowing what was happening . . . it was too much. Like Donald, Freddie often became very frustrated that she could not simply *use* her mental abilities at will. But it wasn't that easy.

She stood and crossed the living room, going into the kitchen. Perhaps, she thought, a glass of Scotch would ease the tension. It always seemed to help Donald. Maybe it helped him *too* much, sometimes, she thought with a smile. The tip of the bottle was just clinking onto the rim of the glass when there was a knock at the door. Walther and Anne! Freddie put the bottle down and rushed to the door. As she reached for the doorknob, she looked out the little peephole in the door. And froze.

The knock came again.

Two hooded, shadowy faces stared back at her through the tiny lens, the heads distorted by the shape of the little glass. Freddie held her breath. They knocked yet again. Hard.

"Who is it?" she asked, trying desperately to keep her voice from cracking.

No reply at first. "Your neighbor," answered a deep male voice.

Staring at the doorknob, Freddie touched her fingertips fearfully to her lips. Gently, silently, she locked the door.

The knock again. "Can we come in? We're getting pretty wet."

They wouldn't let the door stop them. They wanted her too badly.

She slowly backed away from the door, searching her mind

for what to do next. A weapon . . . what could she use? She started to go back into the kitchen, but there was movement out on the porch. Then she saw them.

They came to the front window. Two men—no, no, they weren't *really* men, she could feel it—one in a long, green rain slicker, the other in a puffy jacket, both with hoods which hid their faces in shadow. They stood there, soaking wet, and stared at her through the window for a few moments. She stared back tearfully.

Then one stepped forward and crashed through the glass.

Kyle had not been able to find his car keys back at the house, so he drove Mr. Ellis's Toyota wagon. They'd almost wrecked twice because of the rain, but Kyle was more concerned with speed than safety. His trembling hands clutched the steering wheel and he leaned forward, trying to see as clearly as possible through the rain that cascaded over the windshield. Still unable to comprehend what had happened to him and to Mr. Ellis, Kyle concentrated only on what he was doing, what he was *going* to do: get to Freddie, see if she needs help, then take Mr. Ellis to the hospital. Kyle glanced over at his teacher-friend, who had suddenly become so dependent upon him.

Mr. Ellis was rocking back and forth rhythmically, holding his right arm—what was left of it—tightly to his side. It was wrapped in a dark brown towel that Kyle had gotten from the downstairs bathroom just before leaving. The towel was now wet with Mr. Ellis's blood. He was sobbing and babbling senselessly.

"Two hundred years," he blurted. "Maybe longer. They've been living in the ground . . . maybe as old as time . . . hidden for so long . . . feeding on us . . . demons!" He laughed, a short, staccato laugh that held no joy. "People thought they were demons. Jesus God . . . they're *real* . . . horrible *things* . . . living in the ground . . ."

He rambled on and on, and Kyle tried not to listen. It made him sick to hear Mr. Ellis raving like a madman, saying things that he, Kyle, didn't understand. Didn't want to. The rain seemed to let up a little; it was no longer coming down with such a vengeance. Kyle took advantage of the respite and pressed down on the accelerator.

The pounding of the rain relented slowly. Walther, who was slumped behind the wheel, sat up and smiled. "That's more like it," he said as he started to drive the remaining blocks to Donald's house.

"We've got to help Freddie," Donald moaned, his voice becoming weaker by the minute, as Kyle turned the car onto Donald's street.

"We're almost there, Mr. Ellis," Kyle said, but he sounded distant, far away.

Donald tried to sit up; he was so weak, so tired. He looked out the windows to watch the houses of his neighborhood pass by as they neared his own little yellow house. Dear god, he thought, let Freddie be all right, let her be—

There she was! Running into the street! Donald blinked, squinted, tried to clear his blurred vision, hoping that, when he did, he would see that it was not Freddie at all, that she wasn't being chased by someone—

But it was. They had her, two of them, one on each side. They grabbed her despite her struggling.

"Mr. Ellis?" Kyle squeaked, slowing the car and turning to Donald. He was scared, terrified, and he didn't know what to do.

Freddie stopped struggling and looked at them. Looked at him, at Donald. She froze between her two assailants.

"Mr. Ellis, what do I *do?*" Kyle asked urgently, slowing to a complete stop.

Don! Our promise, Don—remember our promise!

The two figures jerked roughly on her arms, pulling her toward a large, dark car parked across the street.

You promised, Don!

"Mr. Ellis!"

"Drive on," Donald gasped suddenly, realizing he'd been holding his breath.

Kyle passed them slowly, passed Donald's house, two more houses, three more—

"Now . . . nuh-now, Kyle," Donald panted, "make a U-turn."

"Why?"

"Do what I say."

Jerkily, Kyle turned the car around in the street until they were once again facing Freddie and the two strangers. *Monsters.*

"Now," Donald said, turning his pasty-white face to Kyle, his chest heaving, his breath scratching in and out of his wide-open mouth, "run them down."

"Mr. Ellis—"

"Run them down!"

"Ah-ah-I can't d-do that, Mr. Ellis, I can't do that, I can't!" Kyle stammered, his voice crumbling as tears began to roll down his cheeks.

"God—DAMMIT!" Donald roared as he reached over and slapped his hand around the wheel, kicked his left leg underneath it and stomped on the accelerator, "RUN THEM DOWN!" The car jerked forward suddenly, and everything, as if in a dream, slowed down.

Freddie's back was to Donald as the car neared her. Donald clenched his teeth together so hard that his jaws ached as his mind screamed:

I'm sorry, Freddie, I'm so sorry! I love you so much! So very much!

I love you too, Donald. I did from the start.

The three figures came closer and closer, got larger and larger, framed perfectly in the windshield, blurred only slightly by the very light sprinkle of rain that was falling on the glass.

"Jesus, no, Mr. Ellis, *no!*" Kyle screamed shrilly, struggling for the wheel, swerving the car once to the right and once to the left, but unable to wrest control from Donald's violently determined grip.

I do love you, Donald, I—

The instant before impact, Freddie turned her head, jerked her arms from the grip of her captors, and spun around to face Donald. Her lips—her perfect, lovely lips—smiled as she screamed "—LOVE YOOOUUU!" When the car hit her, Donald's mouth opened and let out a long, painful scream.

"Jesus Christ!" Walther blurted as he rounded the corner just in time to see Donald's car plow into Freddie and two faceless, hooded strangers. To avoid crashing into Donald's oncoming car, Walther jammed on his brakes, throwing them into a skid on the wet pavement. They slid past Donald's car and came to an abrupt stop when the tires hit the curb and bumped up onto the sidewalk. Walther immediately turned the ignition off and got out of the car, turning to see the man in the rain slicker roll wildly away from the car that had hit him. Walther stuck his head back into his own car and snapped at Anne: "Call an ambulance, right away!" Then he rushed to the side of the fallen stranger, who had come to a halt in the middle of the road.

Freddie's body was thrown upward slightly with the car's impact, then fell back down, face first. Her face crashed into the windshield, shattering it into a webbing of fine, glittery cracks. Her arms were sprawled out to each side of her. She died instantly.

The figure on the right was merely grazed and rolled away The one on the left, however, was lifted up onto the hood next to Freddie and rolled agilely upward, over the shattered, but intact, windshield, and onto the roof of the car, out of sight.

Kyle was screaming like a child, nearly choking on his own tattered cries. He pulled his right arm to his chest, then swung it outward at Donald, hitting him in the face with his forearm. Donald was slammed back against the door, bumping his head on the side window, which suddenly burst inward, shattered by the powerful fist of the creature on top of the car. Its gray, leathery hand—now looking only half-human—slapped onto Donald's forehead and the thumb and fingers, which were beginning to splice together to form thick talons and sprout sharp, curved claws, dug hard into Donald's temples. Donald fought to avoid the creature's grip, reaching over with his left hand for the door handle so he could open the door and throw the thing off. But just as he pulled the handle down, he suddenly relaxed.

The throbbing, relentless pain in his arm stopped; his fear and the horror of what he had done to Freddie all left him; his body felt warm and loose; he felt the familiar rippling pressure begin behind his groin, preparing his whole body for a wonderful, powerful orgasm. And he knew that this was what they did with those strange, smooth hands: they sucked the will out of their victims.

Donald closed his eyes as the thing slowly began to crush his skull.

Kyle didn't even notice the arm that had broken through the window. Crying hysterically, he was trying to regain control of himself and the car. His visibility was distorted by the shattered glass and Freddie's blood, which was seeping into the weblike cracks, but he could see well enough through the windshield and his tears to avoid hitting large objects, like the telephone pole with which he almost collided when the car swerved up onto the sidewalk, jarring Freddie's body off the hood. He took out someone's front fence before getting back onto the road. It was almost too late, however, when Kyle saw the large sedan that was going through the upcoming intersection. He pounced on the brake pedal and the car went into a swerving slide, then a roll, throwing Kyle suddenly into merciful unconsciousness.

Walther dropped down on one knee beside the stranger in the green rain slicker. He put his hand on the man's shoulder.

"Are you—" Walther began. But all breath was knocked from his lungs when the stranger sent his fist slamming into the middle of Walther's chest, knocking him flat on his back. Gulping air, Walther watched dazedly as the man leaped to his feet, dashed to a car, got in, and sped away. He heard brakes squeal and turned his head in time to see Donald's car, with someone—some*thing!*—clinging to the top, roll three times over the street and sidewalk, then ignite with a rushing *whump*, coming to rest on its side in someone's front yard.

Walther looked around him, stunned by what had happened, his legs spread straight out in front of him, his arms holding him up in a sitting position. Halfway between him and the wrecked car lay Freddie's twisted, bloody body. He looked back over his shoulder and saw Anne hurrying toward him, followed by a small crowd of people.

Then they *all* began to come. Front doors opened and people hurried out; children peeked out of windows and from behind mothers who stood, shocked, on their porches. Walther heard a woman scream, then heard a man over by the wrecked car shout, "Quick! Get an ambulance!"

"Are you hurt?" Anne asked the detective.

"No. No, I'm fine," he assured her as he stood up.

"An ambulance is coming."

He looked toward the wrecked Toyota, began walking, then broke into a jog, saying quietly to himself, "I hope it's not too late for that."

The creature was first seen by Mrs. Joyce Burnett, who looked out her front door to see a battered Toyota lying on its side on her lawn. When she saw the hideous thing that was pinned beneath it, in flames, jerking and quivering, its teeth snapping blindly at its pain, she screamed. Her husband, Charlie, pulled her away and stepped outside the door, chewing on a cigar. He held a newspaper in one hand and was wearing jeans and a long-sleeved, plaid wool shirt. He glanced at the two passengers who were lying a safe distance from the burning car, being tended to by neighbors until an ambulance arrived, and scratched the little bald spot on top of his head. He turned with a puzzled look to the man who had just run over to the wreck.

"What in the hell *is* that?" Burnett asked, wrinkling his nose.

Walther looked down at the dying thing that was burning to a crisp, spilling a thick yellow fluid onto the green grass. He winced at the wretched odor that was rising with the flames. "I don't know," he replied. "But I'm going to find out." He looked back down at the thing, which had stopped moving. "We're *all* going to find out."

Donald returned to consciousness slowly. His eyes felt as though they'd been glued shut. When they were finally open and his vision had cleared, he saw Anne standing next to his hospital bed.

"How long . . .?" he asked, his voice jagged.

"You've been unconscious for nearly three days," she said tearfully.

"Kyle?"

"He's going to be fine, Donald. You shouldn't talk. You're—"

"Fr-Freddie . . .?"

Anne looked down at her feet and sniffed a couple of times. "She's dead." She looked at him again. "Why, Donald? Why did you do that to her?"

He closed his eyes and shook his head, dismissing the question.

The door opened and Walther came into the room quietly and cautiously.

"Hello, Donald," he said with a weak smile.

"Hi." Donald smacked his dry mouth open and shut a few times. "You gonna . . . lock me up now?"

Walther and Anne glanced at one another.

"For being crazy or . . . for murder?"

"Certainly not for being crazy, Donald." Walther shook his head. Putting his hands on the railing of the bed, Walther leaned forward as he said, "The thing on your car . . . it was killed in the wreck. Its remains have been examined. Your story has been passed on. My information has, too. We've found them out, Donald. Now all that has to be done is to put a stop to them. And that's in the works."

Donald closed his eyes again, moved his head back and forth. "But"—he gulped—"what *are* they?"

Walther sucked his cheeks in thoughtfully. "Well," he sighed, "the TV preachers are saying they're the devil's servants. Sort of like that line from the Xerox you gave me, about the legions of hell coming to get their own. Kind of like Satan's rapture, or something. But the more scientific minds are saying they're a cunning, highly intelligent race of creatures that have been living beneath us for centuries. Possibly even longer than *we've* been here. I hope they're right. I'm not ready for the devil's rapture yet." He chuckled, but it was forced. "We don't know exactly *what* they are yet, Donald. But what matters is that they're being stopped."

Anne stepped forward, her tears flowing freely now. "You should sleep, or something, Donald. We want you to get better so you can leave here, okay?" She tried to smile. "You can come stay with me for a while. If you like. I'll take care of you, Donald. I *will*."

Donald "hmphed" with weak sarcasm, giving her a look that approached anger, bitterness.

"Can you . . . can *you* keep the nightmares away, Anne?" he asked. "*Can* you?"

She tilted her head curiously, puzzled.

"No," Donald breathed, closing his eyes and relaxing. "No, you can't. Nobody can."

He wept quietly, privately, until he slept. And when he slept, he dreamed about hell, the devil, and Freddie.

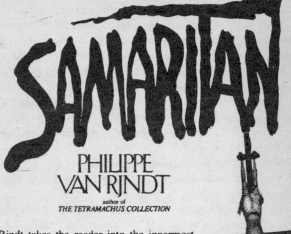